BERTIE
&
THE KINKY POLITICIAN

BERTIE
&
THE KINKY POLITICIAN

Mike A. Vickers

Published by Accent Press Ltd 2014

ISBN 9781783752782

To Jan
Wife, best friend, soul mate, giggler.

Anodorhynchus hyacinthinus

The Hyacinth Macaw. The largest of all macaws and widely regarded as the most majestic, with fully grown specimens reaching almost forty inches in length and possessing a wingspan of up to five feet. The species is noted for the brilliantly rich violet-blue plumage which covers almost the entire body, the only contrasting colour being bright yellow spectacle rings around the eyes and similar small patches bordering each side of the lower mandible. Now critically endangered, those small populations still found in the wild are concentrated in the open savannahs of Eastern Paraguay and the Matto Grosso region of South-west Brazil. Hyacinths are friendly, sociable and unusually long-lived, with authenticated cases of specimens reaching the age of sixty. In nature these beautiful macaws are normally shy and gentle while hand-reared birds tend to be inquisitive and outgoing. However, its sheer size, powerful bill and large claws make the hyacinth an intimidating and formidable creature when roused.

You've been warned …

Chapter One

There is a sound, of all the sounds in the world, which has long tantalised and fascinated men. Some sounds evoke delicious memories, such as the comforting hubbub of conversation in a friendly pub or the soft breath of a sleeping lover. Other sounds are entirely natural in origin; storm waves thundering up a shingle beach, for instance, or the exquisite call of a nightingale. We live on a surprisingly noisy planet and as a consequence are thoughtfully endowed by nature with the means by which to detect these sounds. The provision of ears, in addition to simplifying the design of spectacles, has also proved especially beneficial for those who need to keep a pencil handy.

Sounds permeate our existence. Language has led us to a position of complete planetary domination. With language came argument, and argument, when combined with that other early discovery of mankind, alcohol, naturally evolved into philosophy. Which in turn busied itself with the nature of sound. Sadly, all philosophy appears to have come up with – bearing in mind we've been labouring away since the Ancient Greeks – all philosophy has provided us with on the subject of sound can be distilled down to the single conundrum of the branch in the forest. Does it make a sound if there's no one about to hear it fall?

It would be fair to say this has been the subject of much debate over the years. Assuming the observer is close enough to the action to witness the event then the answer is yes – unless, of course, the spectator is deaf, at which point matters get really complicated.

In short, the ancient and exceedingly lively history of Earth has been peppered with examples of colossal noise; the planetary collision which produced the moon, titanic volcanic explosions, the walloping great asteroid impact that finished off the dinosaurs, terrifying storms of catastrophic magnitude, but frankly, since no one was around to hear these momentous events, who cares? After all, a sound is merely a noise that can be heard.

But there are some sounds that are entirely human in origin, owe no debt to nature, are not unduly associated with prickly matters of philosophy, and it is one of these sounds with which we are concerned at this particular time.

It is the rap of steel-tipped stiletto heels on a bare wooden floor.

A man detected the approaching tip-tap-tip and quivered in anticipation. He reached out blindly, wrapped in a comforting darkness, warm and safe. The sound stopped directly in front of him and he searched until his questing touch settled on a towering instep, gloved fingers tracing the curvaceous foot and spiked heel. He took his time, savouring the moment before finally reaching his destination.

Somehow, the straps seemed more awkward to tighten than usual.

Celeste – whose shapely feet filled the boots – watched with a fond smile. She stood in the centre of her salon looking down at the bizarre figure crouching in front of her, his knees cracking ominously on the highly polished parquet. His touch on the loosened buckles beside her ankles was gently respectful.

'I would've thought you were accustomed to this task by now, James, so why the fumbling?' She shook her head with mock disapproval, bright copper hair sliding across the back of her shoulders. James replied, but his muffled snort was not really identifiable as speech. She felt his diffident caress again until at last he was able to finish tightening the straps of her leather boots.

Celeste examined herself in a nearby dressing mirror. A haughty, powerfully feminine reflection stared back, her body laced and boned into a sensuously erect severity. Leather gleamed softly as she turned this way and that, checking the symmetry of her elaborate costume. She was generously gifted with that obsessive fastidiousness found in every true fetishist. Flowing scarlet enclosed her from high collar to mid-calf. An old-fashioned Victorian hourglass corset imparted a significant reduction to her waist, making her pant slightly. She did so suffer for her hobby! Long sleeves overlapped evening gloves made from the finest kid. With her burnished copper hair drawn back and bound into a pony-tail with a studded thong, she projected an image of implacable female superiority. There was no doubt she was in charge, which, of course, was exactly what James wanted.

Celeste turned to face him again, teetering on the outrageous stilettos. These were bedroom boots, their polished tan soles unsullied by London's gum-spotted pavements. The heels imposed a dramatic arch to her feet, lengthening her leg line to create a shapely silhouette and forcing her to walk on tip-toe with an exaggerated swing of the hips. Their steel tips rapped sharply on the wooden floor whenever she moved and James's head turned blindly to follow the noise, his response was classic Pavlovian. She had him well trained. Maybe he was even drooling under his hood, but it was difficult to tell. She slowly flexed her hunting-crop between gloved hands and stared imperiously at the figure squatting before her toes.

Completely covered in black leather, the vaguely human shape was bound with chains and swinging padlocks. Lifting his chin with the tip of her crop, Celeste gazed with heavy-lidded anticipation into the blank ebony oval of his hide-covered face. 'Time for a little punishment,' she purred.

James trembled at her words, struggling within a world of constricting warmth. He tried to ease his weight from one aching knee to the other, conscious of Celeste's presence on the other side of his self-imposed darkness. She wouldn't spank him if he complained – and he so wanted to be spanked – but her parquet was just too damned painful. A lazy but very pleasant stiffness stabbed at the tough leather of his punishment briefs; he gasped for breath through tiny eyelets piercing the helmet covering his entire face. A runnel of sweat trickled down his spine, the collar was too tight, a muscle quivered ominously in his thigh, his back was cramping and both calves burned like hell.

God, wasn't life great!

He revelled in these timeless moments of erotic bliss with Celeste.

Before they'd met, James had been forced to tread a wary path among the professional dominatrices of Pimlico, constantly fearful of recognition. It said much for his compulsion that he was willing to take those risks despite the devastating effect discovery would have on his career. Oh well, you can't fight nature. On top of all these inherent problems, which always had a debilitating effect on his libido, to actually have to pay for his arcane pleasures really galled him; after all, it wasn't as if he wanted to sleep with any of them. No, indeed, his sole pleasure in life was to be tied up by a beautiful woman and spanked – but not too hard – until he achieved satisfaction! Now where was the harm in that?

Only after meeting Celeste had he finally been able to fulfil his complex fantasies. Unburdened by guilt and in complete confidence, James had grown to adore this exceptional woman as his Mistress. He heard the crop whistle through the air followed by a spectacularly loud crack. A keen cut lanced across his middle-aged bottom. Sweet pain exploded and he twisted from side to side against the binding chains, breath panting, a moan escaping gagged lips. His leather costume was no protection from her vicious sting – and without bidding a sudden memory of their first fateful meeting came flooding back...

'Ah, James, hiding again, are you? Anyone would think you didn't enjoy my company. Now, stop guzzling my food like a starving refugee and pay attention. I'd like you to meet Celeste Gordon. She's recently returned from Brazil and the poor girl simply does not know a soul in London, so do be a good boy and entertain her for me.' Patti Duke-Warrender's gushing introduction annoyed James.

As did Patti herself.

4

James had only accepted the invitation to her party because the unpalatable alternative was the Institute of Chartered Accountants' annual dinner and liver-pickling booze-up – and that was definitely to be avoided. Besides, he had a life – and quite a good one as well – despite the insurmountable social handicap of being an accountant. Consequently, in comparison, Patti's party actually looked like a promising affair, especially as her catering was, to his bachelor stomach, much more of a lure than the ICA's traditionally unimaginative cuisine.

However, one had to balance the siren call of the canapés with the dubious attention of the hostess and so, employing that aura of bland camouflage all in his profession possessed, he'd melted quietly into the background, flitting from room to room, nodding here, passing a few murmured words there, while all the time navigating his way through the house like a grey-suited phantom, homing in with quiet determination on the comestibles. Once there, he'd worked his way manfully along the buffet table until spotted.

James felt irritation at her intrusion into what was undeniably the most agreeable part of the evening. The table was brimming with all manner of juicy morsels laid out on Patti's best porcelain. Exotic dainties invited him to sniff, sample, and scoff. He remained uncommunicative and concentrated on his choice of nibbles, so Patti propelled Celeste forward and took her leave, no doubt to seek out and introduce more totally incompatible people to each other. Despite his natural West Country amiability, James found it difficult to show enthusiasm and did not even bother to turn around as he spoke.

'So what brings you here, Celeste?' he asked around a mouthful of delicious honeyed ham. Not very original but it would have to do for the moment.

'The same as you, my dear James – utter desperation!' He noted absently that her voice was a lovely contralto. There was an awkward pause. James fervently hoped this Celeste woman was sufficiently bright enough to take the hint and move on to pastures new. No, he decided, he really wasn't in the mood. Ten more minutes at the table and then he could slide off home, having satisfied his rumbling stomach and discharged his minimal duties as a guest. His pockets were already stuffed with a few tasty snacks purloined for consumption off the premises. BBC Two was screening a classic Bogart film later on and he felt sure he could successfully combine both to round off a satisfying evening.

He leaned across the table and ladled something yoghurty onto his plate, but a few wayward dollops succumbed to the call of gravity and plopped onto the knee of his trousers. They looked uncommonly like bird droppings. James tutted irritably and, hoping his questionable manners would further discourage the silent woman behind him, scooped up the goo with a bread stick and popped it into his mouth.

'A man who turns a crisis into a dip! You have a rare talent.' Despite his grey mood, James had to chuckle at the witticism, delivered in a dry tone that tickled his funny bone. He turned and found himself instantly seized by a pair of penetrating malachite eyes dancing and sparkling with girlish mischief. Celeste Gordon stood only a few inches shorter than him, a trim woman with amazing copper hair tumbling down in glorious waves over her shoulders. Her flawless complexion, although not exactly tanned in the traditional way, seemed to glow from years of exposure to the sun. Of course, she would have had to cover up for most of the Brazilian day; redheads burned terribly. That was a tough genetic predisposition in a society where a bronzed skin was still equated with healthiness rather than incipient melanoma.

A pair of generous lips twitched in amusement. Her open face displayed a striking bone structure, with high cheeks and fine, arched brows. She wore a green and blue patterned waistcoat over a cream silk blouse and a plain black knee-length leather skirt. Dark nylons sheathed shapely calves, but it was her shoes that caught his eye.

James had always been a sucker for killer heels and, to his great delight, found himself confronted with the shiniest black Oxford pumps he'd ever seen, the vamps laced snugly over precipitously inclined insteps. Towering heels transformed her stance, gracefully elongating her legs and boosting her height.

The shoes were obviously new, the soles unblemished, the steel-tipped heels unscuffed, and she stood in complete comfort. Now that took practice! James found himself staring. He was a man who could easily become mesmerised by a decent pair of stilettos!

He dragged his gaze upward from her feet and, for a second, the cool stare of those incredible green eyes reached right into the deepest recesses of his soul and lay him bare, stripping away those onion layers to touch the real man beneath. His heart thumped hard, his internal organs jostling like pensioners on the first day of a Co-op sale. He gaped, struggling to maintain his equilibrium, and knew instinctively he was in the presence of a supremely powerful and utterly intoxicating personality.

Talk about love at first sight!

'Please, James, I would appreciate it very much if you could shut your mouth. I can see the remains of some half-chewed dainty lurking in there and I have to tell you it's not a very pleasant sight at all.'

James coloured badly and swallowed behind his napkin. 'I do apologise,' he mumbled, wiping his lips. 'How inexcusably rude of me.' Bogey would have to wait. She was absolutely stunning – without doubt the most attractive woman he'd ever seen at one of Patti's soirees, and let's face it, he'd been to a fair few over the years! 'I have to say I don't normally behave like this, it's just that Patti can be so exasperating sometimes. Did you notice how she homed in from behind so I stood no chance of fleeing?'

'You're thinking of escape? Am I that ugly?'

James went very hot and gooey inside. 'No, no, of course not.' His cheeks burned even brighter. She made him feel like a schoolboy on his first date, and he knew quite clearly that was her intent. 'But Patti never ceases in her misguided attempts to marry me off. It's been going on for quite a while now and sometimes gets a little trying. I can only say I'm truly sorry.'

'No matter,' she said lightly. There was another of those dreadfully difficult pauses. James couldn't think of anything to say and stood awkwardly, almost hopping from foot to foot, suddenly terrified she would dismiss him and walk away. Celeste found the child-like expression of agony on his face rather appealing. He obviously found social niceties difficult to handle, which demonstrated an intriguing paradox. She knew he was a very influential person, as confided breathlessly by Patti, yet his reticence contradicted his public image and indicated an honesty of character rarely admitted in a man, especially a man in his line of work. His blue eyes were warm and curiously sharp. There was, without doubt, a first-class mind lurking in there beneath the yoghurt stains. She guessed he had hidden depths.

Potential.

He was quite handsome in a vaguely shambolic sort of way, with a good head of dark hair just greying at the temples, but scruffy enough around the edges to indicate no wife was there to advise on the daily use of a comb. Crow's feet at the eyes betrayed a love of laughter – always to be desired – but his mouth was, to her mind, easily his best feature. Very kissable indeed. She guessed plenty of women would have no objection at all to find his lips on theirs, so just exactly why was he still single? He was obviously not gay and his response to her was one of a strongly heterosexual man. He clearly possessed manners, held down a tremendous job, suffered from no obvious defects, neither in body nor character, possessed a lovely soft West Country burr which, in London, was music to the ears, and was plainly affluent, yet he still remained firmly unmarried. Intriguing.

She spotted a few tell-tale crumbs on his jacket pocket and guessed he'd stowed away a selection of Patti's morsels for a late supper. It was so typical of a bachelor. Here was a man of considerable standing who was prepared to steal food from one of the most famous socialites in the capital and not even bat an eyelid at the preposterousness of it all. The crumbs swung it for Celeste. 'Listen, James, shall we escort our annoying hostess upstairs, tie her hand and foot and suspend her by the ankles from her own bedroom balcony? I have my handcuffs with me. That rain drumming on the window should dampen her matchmaking ardour! What do you say?'

'Tempting, but only if we can gag her with some of those awful blue pastries.'

'They are particularly inedible, aren't they?'

'Blue is not a good colour for anything sitting on a pastry.'

Celeste leaned close. 'I do hope you have none in your pocket,' she whispered conspiratorially.

James smelt her delicious fragrance. The perfume she used was faint and subtle, enhancing rather than swamping. How on earth did she know? 'Only the best make it out of here. I may be a thief, but I'm not a stupid thief.'

'I'm sure you're not. Don't worry, your secret is safe with me.'

James finally managed to recover most of his composure. Across the room, Patti introduced an internationally recognized Nobel Prize-winning professor to a stunning young woman less than half his age. The two new acquaintances seemed to be getting along famously. 'There goes Patti again. I had the dubious pleasure of meeting the pneumatically spectacular Tawny a few months ago. Now what sort of a name is that?'

'A professional one, no doubt.' Celeste had Tawny's measure already.

'Much more appealing than Mildred.'

They watched Tawny at work, coaxing, flattering, simpering and pouting. She was good. Oh yes, she was very good. The professor began to dribble as only a long-married grandfather can dribble. She leaned in close to whisper something breathy in his ear, pressing top-quality silicone puppies against his arm, her shimmering low-cut dress barely able to corral the trembling hooters.

'Surely they're not natural,' whispered James.

'My father used to call an oversized bosom "Cabman's Rests", which always caused us great hilarity,' mused Celeste.

'I seem to recall "Bumpy Jumper" was my brother's favoured euphemism.'

'Well, however you care to name them, she's certainly skilled in their deployment. Have you ever seen a man so goggle-eyed?'

'I'm prepared to wager one of the Queen's bright shiny

shillings they leave together within the next fifteen minutes,' said James.

'As you were about to do yourself.'

'Not any longer,' he replied gallantly, sticking out his chin and straightening his tie with an exaggerated air.

'I'm very relieved to hear it. So, back to my original question – what about Patti? You want to liven up this party in a way even Tawny would struggle to match?'

James gave a measured sidelong glance at their hostess and smiled. 'Suspended, you say. Bound and gagged! What a splendid idea, although such an action would lead to blackballing by the more outraged elements of London society. One wonders how the incident would be reported in the gossip columns. Dear Patti is almost a minor royal, you know.'

Celeste already liked his dry and articulate wit. 'Then again, word would get around and perhaps new and more interesting avenues of entertainment might open up for us.'

'Lovely. What do you have in mind?'

'You tell me; I'm new here. I can assure you this is a hell of a change from sunny Brazil.'

'I imagine it is. Still, despite the lousy weather, London always has one thing strongly in its favour.'

'And what's that?'

'You can get anything here. It's what defines London as the leading city on the planet. Believe me, if you can't get it in London, you can't get it anywhere in the world.'

'It?'

'Whatever you want. Anything. Anything you like – animal, vegetable, or mineral. Anything at all.'

'So that's anything, then?'

'Nothing gets past you, does it.'

'Legal or illegal?'

'Certainly.'

'Unusual?'

'Indubitably.'

'Perverted?'

'Ah, forever the preserve of the clergy.'

'Even, perhaps, fetishistic?'

'Dear me, especially that, if you know where to look.'

'Excellent. That makes a pleasant change. Brazil is a tremendous country and I will always love it dearly, but despite the population's zest for carnival there are still some disappointing inhibitions.' Celeste had already begun to register James. She realised she was in the company of an exceptional man. It was so good to be back home. There was something wonderfully eccentric about English society, a society which would always provide fertile pickings for a woman of her unique predilections. This was the real reason for her return home – she knew she would never be able to find true love in Brazil. The Latins she'd met had been so unresponsive in that respect.

She'd found herself at the centre of much amorous attention once her interesting bits started to ripen, primarily because of her pale skin and unique hair, a combination which proved a beguiling lure to the local boys. However, an endless string of persistent suitors displayed little interest in anything other than their own gratification. Perhaps it was in their blood, but no sooner had she managed to lure a young man into her room – always the easy bit – she discovered her own participation in the proceedings was expected to be limited to lying back passively and moaning in appreciation at the appropriate moment. All Brazilian men wanted to do, without exception, was screw her brains out. How odd! They showed absolutely no enthusiasm at all for submissive role-playing, bondage, or its traditional companion, flagellation, by then three subjects very close to her heart. Without exception they dissolved into screaming fits of panic the moment she produced the handcuffs and started cracking her whip! It really was most frustrating and despite naturally healthy urges she was, technically, sort of, more or less, just about, still a virgin!

Not that it bothered her much. Busy fingers keep a girl happy.

'How distressing for you. It's widely acknowledged the British plutocracy has embraced the more recondite side of life with great enthusiasm,' offered James with the exaggerated air of a pompous university lecturer addressing his bored students.

'You sound like the good professor over there,' observed Celeste, nodding at the couple across the room. There was now a smudge of very red lipstick on his cheek, a pair of tan-sprayed arms wrapped around his neck, and a slender, sinuously voluptuous body pressed against his chest.

'I don't think our Tawny understands many words with more than one syllable. "Money" and "condom" probably top the list.'

'Her tongue is skilled in other areas. No doubt she's a native of Cockermouth!'

'Now, Celeste, that's a very naughty thing to say. It's a lovely town.' James chided gently. There was a pause. 'But I do wish I'd said it,' he added with a chortle.

'Let's get back to the interesting side of life. Are your opinions based on first-hand experience?' she enquired.

'Well that's a long story. I wouldn't want to bore you.'

'My boredom disappeared the moment Patti introduced us.'

'Now that was good fortune, wasn't it? You could have ended up with the professor.'

'And you could have had another shot at Tawny. She seems to like distinguished men.'

'Heaven forbid. Even though I haven't exactly been active recently, I wouldn't risk involvement with such a woman. Her body may be soft but her business acumen most certainly isn't. Allegedly!' he added hurriedly, in response to a raised eyebrow from Celeste. 'Anyway, I don't want to talk about her any more. Why would I with you here?'

'James, that was the correct answer I was looking for. I like a man with manners. Come now, you were about to enlighten me on the pleasures London can provide. You've left me intrigued so spill the beans. Don't hold back.'

'And risk the chance of being overheard? Such tales are not for the sensitive.' He scanned the immediate area furtively and Celeste smiled at his sly expression. 'Do you really have a pair of handcuffs?' he wheedled, hoping his flush of excitement wasn't too obvious. He was on home territory and determined to test her reactions. The small leather handbag hanging from her shoulder certainly looked large enough to conceal such an item.

'A lady must keep the contents of her bag a strict secret.' She tilted her head to one side and smiled roguishly. 'Why? Does the employment of such equipment interest you?'

James started loading fancies onto a plate for her, avoiding the blue ones. 'I couldn't possibly comment.' It was a politician's answer, neutral and bland, yet said with just enough emphasis to intimate he was interested. Very! His good friend, Mr John Thomas, who normally had no difficulty slumbering through Patti's little gatherings, found himself stirring into a delightful perkiness and began to nose outwards against the sturdy constriction of his M&S trousers.

'Because if it does, we'd best lay out the ground rules.'

'Intriguing. Do go on.' He poured two generous glasses of Patti's most expensive champagne and passed one to Celeste. Her nails were almond-shaped and scarlet red. A covert examination of her ring finger revealed no wedding band shadow. Excellent. Now suitably provisioned, they gravitated away from the table to a quiet corner where they could observe the dynamics of the room whilst maintaining their own little bubble of privacy.

'I merely point out that in this situation it might be wise to determine who would be the prisoner and who the jailer.' Celeste nibbled on a pastry and regarded James with a calm and unwavering stare. For a second, he stood quite still. She could feel the decision coming. What a stroke of absolute good fortune – chance meetings like this were so unlikely they only ever exist as convenient plot developments employed by first-time authors.

'Do you know the stories of Alexandre Dumas?'

'I take it you're referring to The Man in the Iron Mask.'

'I've, er, always felt a certain affinity towards the poor chap. Wondered what it would be like to experience such a situation. I guess most people would consider it unfortunate to find themselves in that sort of pickle, but I'm not so sure, especially if his jailer was someone like you.' There, he'd said it – whatever happened now was up to her.

'James, believe me, I'd not disappoint you in that respect.

13

A fresh flight of skateboarding butterflies launched themselves into James's belly, bouncing around in a most delicious way. Vital organs nearby joined in with the general merriment, somersaulting with excitement, adding to his most agreeable feeling of well-being. He struggled to return to his narrative but Mr Thomas's wayward swelling was now threatening to burst through his fly. Little wonder he found himself momentarily distracted 'I, ah. Um. Sorry, where was I?'

'In a French prison, if I recall.' Celeste's gaze dropped to his groin and her lips twitched in amusement at the burgeoning bulge. She seemed extremely pleased at his reaction to her presence. 'James, all this talk of incarceration is promising indeed. I assume your previous relationships were disappointing in that respect. Had one been in any way remotely successful then you would certainly not be here and I would be talking to myself, no doubt to the concern of our hostess.'

'Quite. My instinct has always been to conceal the more exotic side of my life.'

'A wise move, but, and this is important for you to understand, I like exotic. I really like exotic, as you are now most certainly going to find out.' Celeste stared intently at James, her green eyes gleaming with what could only be described as eager expectation. 'And so, with that thought in mind, let's begin!' she deliberately let a drop of creamy mayonnaise fall onto the pointed toe of her shoe and fixed James with a steady gaze. He hesitated for a moment, then setting aside his plate, knelt to wipe the sticky blob from the shiny black patent leather with a napkin. His touch lingered just long enough over her neatly laced instep to confirm his profound interest, his fingers still gently caressing the warm surfaces and towering heel long after the mess had gone. When he stood, flushed and alert, she slipped her arm through his and very gently kissed his cheek. Across the room, Patti Duke-Warrender witnessed this obvious display of affection and hugged herself with glee. Success at last.

She might not have been so self-congratulatory had she known the utterly devastating results of her efforts ...

Two years had passed since that fateful first meeting and yet James could still clearly remember their evening at Patti's; how they'd talked and talked, flirting outrageously. James had recounted some of his more disastrous moments at the hands of financially astute but stunningly uninterested consorts, amusing Celeste with his dry, oddball sense of humour. She teased details from him with little effort, charmed by his immediate faith and trust in her. They had freely consumed Patti's champagne, then sneaked upstairs to find a quiet bedroom where, with hands strapped behind back with his own belt and mouth stuffed with his tie, Celeste had spanked his bottom with expert aplomb using a fish slice he'd been ordered to steal from the kitchen. She had been most gratifyingly enthusiastic!

His descent into sexual servitude followed with blissfully indecent haste!

'Kiss my hem!'

Suddenly jolted from his wonderful reverie, James heard the sharp order through the leather helmet pulled over his ears. Celeste's voice carried all the compulsion and force of a born dominant. There was no thought of disobeying. James was now hopelessly bonded to his beloved Mistress. He crawled forward, nose rubbing the parquet as he searched for her boots.

The floor smelt of old-fashioned wax polish. He inhaled deeply and vacuumed up a wispy ball of fluff. Damn that cat! He tried to concentrate on maintaining his subservience, but the nasal tickle wouldn't go away. The chains prevented him from rubbing his nose, psychologically enhancing the itch. He quivered for a moment in respiratory agony, then the inevitable happened and he sneezed with surprising violence.

The explosive force was simply too much for the tiny breathing holes to accommodate and the helmet inflated like an air bag, lifting from his face before slowly contracting back into its original shape. A long, drawn out flatulent rattle of escaping sneeze issued from somewhere beneath his collar.

Celeste giggled behind one hand. Such a comical thing could only happen to James. He was so endearingly sweet. However, it was still vitally important to maintain The Ambience. She recovered her composure and held herself still, allowing him to press gagged kisses all over her boots. He worked his way slowly upwards to her shins, finally reaching the supple hem of her dress, then lovingly buried his blank face into the aromatic leather.

James sighed in joy. He continued to pay homage, lost in a timeless moment of supremely erotic delight. He absolutely worshipped Celeste. She was the perfect woman for him, the ideal sexual partner, which appeared odd considering much of her body remained firmly off-limits. Even after two years he had never kissed her on the lips nor seen her in any state of undress, let alone naked,

Two years! Two years – and in all that time he'd just about made it up to her knees! Theirs was a unique relationship thriving on an amalgam of domination in all its forms, psychological role-playing, unusual clothing and very little physical contact – and both found it divinely satisfying.

Eventually, after a long silence broken only by his snuffling respiration, Celeste decided he'd enjoyed himself enough and released the web of chains. 'Stand! Do not move!' He rose unsteadily, rubbing his knees, but she wrenched his unresisting arms behind his back and shackled his wrists with her favourite pair of handcuffs, the chrome plating worn thin from much use over the years.

'Enough play.' Her voice assumed a steely edge. She knew he liked that. Celeste was a consummate Mistress, and all Mistresses were inventive and skilled actresses. 'It's time for you to retire. Downstairs, I think.'

James grunted alarmingly into the gag and wrestled against his bonds.

'No protests, James Timbrill,' she said in a businesslike tone. 'You knew this was going to happen.' He continued his futile, albeit pleasurable, resistance. 'You'll be hooded, gagged and strapped in the bondage wardrobe.' She clipped a dog leash to his collar and jerked hard. James staggered blindly, breath hissing, and knew they were heading for the cellar. Mmmm, total enclosure! He felt another tug at his neck and stumbled toward an ecstatic night of warm and cosy restraint.

With a firm grip on his leash, Celeste led the Right

Honourable James Alan George Timbrill, BA, FCA, and Member of Parliament for Gloucester North, through the salon door and away for an appointment with his own personal padded wardrobe, where he would be spending the night indisposed.

Very indisposed indeed.

The salon fell silent, but it was certainly not empty. Their departure had been noted by a creature of surprising intelligence. He sat on a perch behind the sofa and watched the conclusion of this entertaining ritual with great interest. The Kneeling Man was by far the most frequent of the few friends who visited his mummy's home and the only one who always brought him some small tidbit to eat. He enjoyed these visits very much, even if only to see Celeste at her happiest and most relaxed. His mum exercised domination over her guest in the same way he did over Sebastian, the household Persian and source of the fluff that had caused James's earlier respiratory problems. She always wore her most spectacular and colourful plumage when The Kneeling Man visited. Of course, despite her best efforts, she really could not hope to match him. He preened complacently for a few minutes, adjusting immaculately clean azure feathers, then stared at the closed door with a strange intensity, his large brown eyes unblinking.

'James Timbrill, hooded, gagged and strapped in the bondage wardrobe,' he announced with the clarity of a BBC newsreader.

Bertie didn't know what the words meant but had long associated them with The Kneeling Man. He liked the musical cadence of the sounds and repeated the oft-used phrase several times in his best authoritative voice before tucking it away in his jumbled mind to delight Celeste at a later date.

Chapter Two

Celeste Gordon had always delighted in the domination of men. Well, more than delighted, if truth be known. Hers was a strange and powerful addiction, evidence of which first manifested itself in her inventive childhood games. Even then she showed natural talents in manipulation and control, talents that first appeared for no apparent reason thirty years earlier.

An angular young girl with a pale face and spectacularly bright orange hair, she lived with her parents on the outskirts of Oakham in the tiny county of Rutland. Ray, her father, was a tall and athletic man, wiry and energetic, but constantly away co-ordinating the shipping department of Pringle and Padley, purveyors of fine timbers for the joinery trade. He had an infectious grin and loved his young daughter without reserve. His own mother, both his aunts, his sister, and several female cousins were all blessed with hair in varying shades of copper, so when he fell hopelessly in love with and married Barbara Phillips, herself a striking redhead, it came as little surprise to anyone in the Gordon family that their daughter was born with a mop of truly incandescent ginger curls.

The family home was a large Victorian red-brick country house full of passageways and interesting corners, where imaginary creatures lurked in darkened alcoves waiting to pounce. Celeste loved its outdated architecture and the smell of old woolly carpets. Its Gothic decorations were a delight and the house had a powerful and defining influence on her early childhood, allowing her vivid imagination to blossom.

Outside, the grounds ran to several unattended acres with the house encircled by mossy lawns. Gravel paths lined with low hedges intersected the abandoned vegetable gardens, all leading to the centre where an ancient corkscrew walnut dominated the formal plots. The convoluted limbs simply begged to be climbed and she was able to spy out the whole of her magical kingdom hidden amongst the foliage.

As an only child in a rural house, the potential for boredom had been of concern to her parents, but Celeste did not seem to mind the isolation and compensated by populating her world with imaginary characters who stood at her shoulder while she fought dragons and poked sticks into rustling anthills. Fortunately, the garden provided endless opportunities for healthy play and so her parents made the fatal assumption all was fine and under control. As it turned out, Ray and Barbara couldn't have been more wrong. They had no idea, no idea at all, that the tranquillity of home life was not exactly mirrored at Celeste's school. Matters were moving to a head ...

Miss Rose Jelf, the most kindly of junior school teachers, shivered uncontrollably. Playground duty in February really sucked. She stamped her feet on the icy concrete and watched over her flock. At least the children shrugged off the biting cold. Young blood ran hot.

'Skip-py! Skip-py!'

A chant floated down the breeze and caught her attention. Children began to drift around the corner of the library. The shouting swelled ominously. Rose recognised the signs of trouble and scampered off to restore the peace.

'Skippy! Skippy!' screamed a ring of nylon anoraks. Rose, seriously height-challenged as she was, couldn't exactly see what was going on in the centre of the swirling crowd so caught Bobby Dukes as he ran past.

'What's going on, Robert?'

'It's Skippy, Miss Jelf!'

'Skippy?'

'Celeste Gordon, Miss.'

Confusion. The only Skippy Rose knew of was the jolly antipodean marsupial who used to appear on television.

'But that's not very nice, calling Celeste a kangaroo.'

'Not that Skippy.' Robert sighed patiently, as if explaining to an idiot. 'We call her that because she likes to catch the boys with her skipping rope. Now it's Marty's turn.'

Startled, Rose experienced a splendid example of middle-aged lady bewilderment as the chanting reached a crescendo. A whiff of hysteria made her skin crawl. She had to act immediately.

'Stop!' she squeaked at the top of her voice, but her cry was swamped. She wrestled her way forward, heaving shoulders apart, but was badly jostled. 'Stop! Stop!' She struggled to a point mid-way towards the gladiatorial ring before becoming stuck in the tightly packed throng like a wanderer caught in quicksand, but now she was able to witness the proceedings – and what she saw instantly arrested her attention.

Celeste stood calmly, her manner supremely confident, and faced Martin Shufflebottom, the school bully. Both were surrounded by the circle of baying children. Slowly, the chanting faded to leave a silence which Rose found even more unnerving than the screams. Her spine crawled but she shared the paralysis of her fellow spectators. She could have easily leapt in to break up the incident. Well, not exactly leapt, perhaps, but a sudden need to see what would happen next stayed her hand. Instinctively, she realised she was witnessing something extraordinary.

There appeared to be a stand-off. Marty glowered at Celeste but seemed disinclined to attack, as if things were not entirely going to plan. Normally he would simply wade in with smashing blows to batter his opponents into sobbing submission, but now he just stood there staring with piggy eyes at the willowy Celeste. She showed no fear at facing what could only be described as an apprentice psychopath who enjoyed spitting into the bleeding faces of his defeated victims.

He lunged, and Celeste evaded his grasp with the twisting grace of a gymnast. Again, Marty leapt, again she nimbly avoided him – and each time it happened the audience cooed in admiration. Marty shook with fury but could not catch her. Celeste merely smiled at his clumsy charges. Rose was mesmerised. He was being humiliated by an expert. Only good

21

could come of this – his reputation was being shredded before the entire school. What happened next left her speechless.

Celeste pointed down at her feet. 'You know what to do, Martin. Don't make me embarrass you any more.' For a seven-year-old girl, this was an impressive example of masterful psychology.

'Knob off!' replied Marty, employing language he'd learnt from his father in his dealings with the local constabulary.

'Then I'll have to use the rope, Marty.' She was in total command. The finger pointed again and to Rose's disbelief, Martin howled, shook his fists violently and slowly sank to his knees. There was a gasp of astonishment from the audience. Celeste stepped forward and flipped the skipping rope over his shoulders, lassoing him neatly. With that action, the spell was broken and Rose sprang into action.

'Stop this at once!' she yelled.

Celeste turned to see Miss Jelf wriggling forward. That was lucky. The rope had gone over Marty just in time. She'd caught all the boys in school but saved the toughest for last. Martin was damned difficult to pin down, but she'd picked her moment to perfection. Had he known he was the subject of such cunning he might have thought twice before popping behind the library for a quick leak.

As planned, Celeste caught him at his most vulnerable. My, had he cursed and sworn at the gathering crowds who pointed and laughed at his diminutive embarrassment. Celeste had waited for a very cold day! Unable to control a full bladder, he'd been compelled to endure the tinkling disgrace before zipping up and leaping into action. 'Hope you like hospital food, you ginger bitch!' he'd spat. Subtlety was a concept entirely alien to Marty's intellect. There then followed the cat and mouse dance of survival for Celeste, so necessary to undermine his morale until …

Rose made a valiant final lunge and burst through at last, hot and agitated, several buttons missing from her coat. A lock of hair escaped from her schoolmarm bun and hung in disarray over one ear. 'I will have silence!' she barked, recovering her confidence. 'Celeste Gordon, what are you doing?'

'Catching Martin.'

'Why?'

'Because I like it.' There was genuine puzzlement in Celeste's voice. Perplexed, Rose stared at the kneeling bully. This was no casual playground game – Celeste's strategy for emasculating his reputation had been faultless.

'I don't understand,' she said.

'It's not the rope, Miss. The rope doesn't really matter. It's symbolic. Making him submit, that's important. That's what I'm after.' Rose found the depth of perception in Celeste's answer simply staggering.

Martin's eyes, so often filled with malignancy, suddenly brimmed with tears at his colossal humiliation. To the lasting astonishment of all present, he suddenly started sniffling. 'Leave us alone, Miss Jelf, I – I want her to finish...'

Celeste's sunny smile of triumph completely unnerved Rose.

The consequences of this regrettable incident proved to have a much more profound impact on her life than she could have ever imagined. Raymond Gordon, having pondered for several weeks on an exciting new career offer from P&P, had an uneasy feeling Oakham's friendly rustic welcome was about to become as frosty as the weather – and promptly moved the entire family to Brazil!

Shortly afterwards, due to a bureaucracy gone mad, the delightfully minuscule county of Rutland ceased to exist altogether.

Brazil!

Even now, the very mention of the country still created a surging excitement in Celeste. For a young girl from a sleepy English shire, the world instantly became a spectacular and mesmerising riot of sight and smell and sound. Ray was based in Manaus in the heart of the rainforest, a bustling, colourful and noisy city on the banks of the Amazon. It was a hell of a change from Oakham! She often rode the company tugs with her father for hundreds of miles up the Madeira, chugging past vast uncharted tracts of tropical rain forest, entertaining the crew with her endless chatter and extravagant fantasies. Each passing day provided a kaleidoscope of never-ending fascination. She had many memories and they were all still very precious to her, but above everything else, she remembered the Amazon for one thing.

Bertie.

The love of her life!

Early one evening, just at the sodden end of the daily tropical storm, when the very ground steamed and smoked in the failing light, her father strode out of the rising mists carrying a tatty wire cage. Inside, shy and startled and very frightened, was a baby parrot. She ran out of the villa to meet him in a transport of joy.

'Daddy, he's so pretty!' Celeste thought it was the most beautiful thing she had ever seen. In truth, the parrot was not exactly endearing, with a comically outsized head connected to the oddly shaped body by a scrawny neck. Gawky, pop-out eyes protruded on either side of a viciously hooked bill and both stumpy wings were naked and angular. Its pinky-slate skin was only partially covered in immature plumage sprouting in threadbare tufts. The poor creature looked like it had fallen into a tub of depilation cream, and sat awkwardly on folded grey legs equipped with barbarous-looking claws, but Celeste saw it with different eyes to her father. Without hesitation, she opened the cage.

'Careful, sweetheart, he's a wild parrot and might try to get away.' This was unlikely – even Celeste could see that the chick was about as aerodynamically svelte as a breeze block – so she ignored the warning and cradled the gangly fledgling to her chest, stroking at the spiky, half-formed feathers. To Ray's surprise, the bird instinctively snuggled down into her protective embrace and showed no signs of distress.

'He's so – so blue,' was all she could manage to say. This was an accurate observation. The infant's immature feathers were, well, blue! An incredible, wonderful, dazzling, beautiful deep blue. All over. 'What is he?'

'He's a hyacinth macaw.'

'I thought you said he was a parrot.'

'Macaws are a type of big parrot. In fact, hyacinths are the largest macaws in all the world.' Celeste's face was a picture of wonder. She stroked the bird under its stringy chin, ignoring the wickedly hooked bill. Ray winced. That beak looked vicious enough to remove a fingertip. 'Be gentle – they're very rare.'

Celeste thought about this. 'But if he's so rare, hadn't we better put him back with his mummy and daddy?'

'That's the trouble, angel. We don't know where he came from. Captain Carlos at the police station has arrested some poachers down by the docks and discovered this lonely baby. He's a real long way from home. Carlos says these birds are only found down south, near to Paraguay, where the forest opens out a bit, so this one's been well and truly kidnapped.' Ray knelt and wrapped a comforting arm around Celeste. The macaw absorbed her attention totally. Ray saw wonder and love in her eyes. 'Well, do you like him?' he asked.

She nodded vigorously, her plaited copper pigtails dancing.

'Good, I'm glad, because he's all yours, Celeste.'

Little did Ray know when he uttered those words he had put into motion a chain of events that would lead, with unshakable inevitability, to the spectacular and humiliating downfall of the British Government thirty years later.

However, on that particular day, his only motivation was the simple desire to see a smile on his daughter's face.

Celeste squealed with joy. 'Is he? Really?'

'Sure.'

'Oh, thank you, Daddy. I love you so much!' Ray felt a lump in his throat. She was growing up so quickly. 'Does he have a name?'

'Not as far as I know, but you'll have to be careful with a name. Macaws are frightfully clever and soon learn to talk, so he'll want his name to be grown up and sensible. Also, they live for a very, very long time; years and years, as long as you and I, so you must pick a good name.'

Celeste looked serious and tried to imagine an old parrot leaning on a walking stick, but the scruffy bundle of violet fluff just looked so endearingly sweet. It was at that moment inspiration passed her way and dropped a suggestion into her mind.

'Bertie! I'll call him Bertie.'

Ray groaned and rolled his eyes, but then saw the gleam of stubborn determination in his daughter's eyes and knew better than to argue.

'OK, Honey, Bertie it is …'

Chapter Three

There was no question that Bertie loved Celeste. His was a true love which had developed steadily over the years, maturing and deepening, growing into an almost human emotion which would endure for the rest of his life. It was not the helpless affection dogs expressed, nor the aloof, calculating condescension exhibited by Sebastian, or even the vague, friendly, uncomplicated inquisitiveness of Barnstaple, the household hamster, but a strong and permanent bond underpinning the cornerstone of his life.

Sebastian was Celeste's Persian. Thoroughly pedigree and a real joy to torment, the cat had arrived in spring and immediately laid claim to the territory with that supercilious air of nonchalant arrogance exclusive to felines. Bertie was taken aback at Sebastian's total lack of respect, not only for him but also for his beloved Celeste, and quickly concluded that the Persian was a lowly beast whose loyalty extended only as far as his next meal. Why on earth she found him appealing was anybody's guess. Bertie let him settle for a couple of weeks, lulling him into a false sense of security, then showed him who was the real boss. Sebastian barely survived the encounter, both physically and psychologically, and now fled in mortal fear of the macaw because, in the intervening years since his days as a lonely and frightened chick in Brazil, Bertie had indeed grown to become a handsome chap.

Now a hefty and muscular adult, he measured forty inches from beak to tip of tail and generated a formidable physical presence – even with everything tucked in neatly. When flying, he could justly be described as magnificent, the combination of a full five-foot wingspan and consummate aerial skills drawing gasps of admiration from all. His vivid plumage had deepened to a stunning cobalt, a deep, rich blue almost violet in its intensity, which set off the dazzling sunshine yellow patches edging his lower mandible and matching spectacle rings around his dark brown eyes. With lethally powerful claws and a razor-sharp bill capable of nipping through metal and reducing the hardest Brazil nut to powder, it was either a brave or monumentally stupid cat who stood up to him.

Sebastian undoubtedly fell into the latter category.

The fracas had started one evening with a bit of needling over who received the lion's share of Celeste's affection. Sebastian employed the usual underhand trick of insinuating himself onto her lap and once lodged across her thighs, began to purr in that smug, self-satisfied way Bertie found so infuriating. He endured this intolerable situation for the best part of an hour, watching with haughty contempt from his perch until Celeste left the room for a few moments. Once alone together, the cat foolishly decided to follow up its tactical advantage by actually having the gall to stalk Bertie.

Sebastian sneaked around the sofa and crept to within a yard of the perch, his haunches swaying threateningly, belly pressed to the floor. He tried to project an air of terrifying menace, that of a predator at the very pinnacle of the food chain, but the Persian was simply too coiffured to convey any serious threat. To Bertie, who'd retained a little more of his instinctive Brazilian aggression than Celeste realised, the cat was merely a joke. He stared down and refused to panic. This was no crouching jaguar below him, no sleek and sinewy panther, just a soft barrel of ivory fluff that honked up soggy fur balls with disgusting regularity. There was a tense moment, but Bertie's long tail proved too much of a temptation for Sebastian and he suddenly leapt forward and took a nifty swipe at the trailing feathers.

It really was an astonishing tactical error. Bertie flicked himself clear of the lunging paw and flew across the room to land on top of the tall dresser, where layers of old carpet were tacked to stop him skidding. This display of power should have been warning enough, but, as Bertie had already surmised, even by the modest intellectual standards of his species, the cat was thicker than a tub of treacle on a frosty Yorkshire morning.

The attack came from over the back of the sofa in a blur of blue. Bertie launched himself silently, needle-tipped claws thrust forward. His huge wings swept around the petrified cat, enveloping him on all sides, buffeting powerfully. Sebastian froze under the overwhelming assault, then let out a truly spectacular screech of absolute terror and bolted, colliding unceremoniously with a table leg in his blind panic to escape. Bertie twisted in mid-air and raked along the cat's flank before soaring back up to his perch with majestic fluidity. It was all over in less than three seconds.

He shook himself to settle his feathers again. On the whole, that had been a most enjoyable interlude. When Celeste returned a few minutes later, the salon was quiet and tranquil.

'Bertie, where is Sebastian?' she asked, peering behind the chairs.

'Gone,' he said indifferently, discreetly cleaning his claw to remove an incriminating scrap of blood-speckled fur. He didn't think Celeste would appreciate his use of jungle law to readjust the household's animal hierarchy back to its rightful order. No pallid, flaccid-brained, four-footed, honk-happy, wingless, moronic fuzz-ball was going to get the better of him. 'Bertie loves Celeste.'

'I love you too, Bertie.' Celeste gave up her search and sat back with a magazine. 'Come here, darling.' He hopped onto the sofa and settled on its arm. Celeste stroked him affectionately and he nuzzled against her, rubbing her shoulder with his head and leaning forward to comb the hairs behind her ear with meticulous care, using his bill to lay each long copper thread perfectly flat.

'That's nice, Bertie. Do you want some nuts?' she asked. Bertie continued to preen her hair but didn't answer. Celeste persisted. 'Well? Do you?'

'Oh, yes, I do.' he answered promptly, and was rewarded with a big fat oval walnut. The tough shell crumpled under the application of pressure at just the right point. Bertie consumed the brain-like nut fastidiously. All was well in his world and presently, as if to emphasise his victory and show the cat was indeed superfluous, he began an impeccable imitation of feline purring. Celeste laughed and tickled under his chin. 'Bertie, you are incorrigible.' The purring waxed in amplitude. Oh, yes, there was no doubt who she loved the most.

James entered the stern MoD building in Whitehall and took a lift up to the ministerial floor. The place was huge, with eight floors above ground and five below. All the ministers, for some reason no one could quite figure out, were shepherded by the staff on to the fifth floor, probably because this was the floor most likely to receive the maximum amount of damage in a nuclear attack. Should such a distressing incident arise, those civil servants of importance planned to sneak off to the subterranean wine cellars of Henry VIII, still preserved in their arched glory several floors down in the basement, where they intended to spend an agreeable few days while London gently cooked.

Recently refurbished for the cost of fifty Challenger main battle tanks, two squadrons of Tornado fighter bombers, and four and a half frigates, the interior had been converted into a sumptuous palace of extraordinary luxury, with original artwork, fine oak doors, carpets that pampered the feet, the most comfortable office chairs on the planet, and designer glass roofs enclosing the internal courtyards. The MoD didn't mess about when it came to spending public money! The original labyrinthine layout had now given way to a series of endless open-plan offices, perhaps to minimise the chance of someone sneaking in a quick war without their fellow workers noticing. Nevertheless, there still remained over three miles of corridors, ample to confuse those with even the most accomplished navigational skills.

So it was that James strode purposefully into his modest suite of rooms, nodding at the one or two people who greeted him on the way. He used his politician's stride for the benefit of the staff; firm, quick and decisive. He liked to think they appreciated it but was pragmatic enough to realise that they probably thought him a total tosspot. Why should he be any different to any other politician? So much for respect.

'Good morning, Angela. A pleasant weekend, I trust?'

His solitary Personal Assistant glared at him from over a red folder marked *Top Secret*. James was actually entitled to any number of official secretaries and assistants, but his needs were modest and he was happy with just one, the one who sat in the outer office and organised his official life with supreme competence. Angela Lucy Hutchinson was a pure-blood English rose, possessing a peachy complexion, blushing cheeks, cornflower blue eyes, and honey-blonde wavy hair, qualities that had easily won her the coveted title of 'Miss Most Shaggable' by the departmental porters. But she was no bimbo. No, sir. Bandage up her breasts, cut her hair, squeeze her into a suit, and give her a mascara moustache and she could certainly run the MoD on her own, and, what's more, she'd still find enough time to lay her crop-haired Teutonic stud in a series of demanding positions gleaned from the advanced gymnasts' section of the Kama Sutra.

The frigid glare from those lovely blue eyes should have warned him, but he was still reliving his heavenly Saturday night locked inside Celeste's padded wardrobe. 'How's Helmut? Still rehearsing with the band?' James still felt youthful enough to think he knew all about the younger generation.

The younger generation felt otherwise.

'I'd rather not discuss it,' she snapped.

Foolishly, James inquired further. 'But wasn't he supposed to be playing a gig at some new Norwegian death metal club in Walthamstow?' God only knows what Norwegian death metal was, but it sounded like it might, just possibly, be noisy.

'It's next Friday.'

'Ah.'

'At Wanstead.'

Oh.'

'And no, I won't be going.'

There was a truly glacial silence. A sense not all was well finally dawned on James. Too late, he realised this was possibly not a good time to be discussing Angela's love life. Her face, normally so refreshing to behold, was set like stone. She threw the file across the room in sudden disgust, spilling its sensitive contents all over the floor. The discreet placement of a new military attaché at the British Embassy in Paris would have to wait.

Military attaché was the industry standard euphemism for "spy". The British had been cheerfully spying on their Gallic neighbours since the Middle Ages, but events in 1789 seriously upgraded the intensity of their operations. The Revolution changed for ever the relationship between the French and their rulers, all of whom, without any signs of remorse, were carted off for an appointment with Madame Guillotine. Subsequent French governments have always borne this in mind and although decapitation is no longer on the menu, the masses remain perfectly prepared to take to the streets in unassailable numbers if their leaders overstep the mark.

Since the absolute number one priority of any government has always been to maintain the continuation of government, suspicions remained in London that, along with their runny cheeses and exasperating non-committal shrugs, the French might still decide to export their revolutionary zeal to good old Blighty in a pique of garlic-scented malice. Consequently, France has always been regarded with deep suspicion as a country barely under control and that's why, once the post-revolutionary dust had settled, all the other European powers quietly clubbed together and for the last two hundred years have been working hard to keep the French firmly corralled inside the borders of France.

Nowadays, this club is known as the EU.

Further relations were not exactly improved by the Iron Duke, who dented French grand plans for global domination at Waterloo, and more recently, a sudden realisation that wines from, *quelle horreur*, Australia and, *sacré bleu*, even California, were now regarded worldwide as being far better than their own, resulting in much pompous indignation and furious waving of the tricolour.

The French have always been, and will always remain,

absolutely superb at pomposity! The best on the planet, bar none. No other nation even makes it to the starting blocks.

'The retard dumped me for some chlamydia-riddled sow with plastic tits and a face full of rat poison.' There was a coldly reptilian sibilance to her voice that was quite unnerving.

'Um, well, I'm very sad to hear that.'

'Yeah, like sodding bloody hell you are,' she ground out. 'Three years down the frigging tubes and that's all you can bastard well say?'

James winced at her seething vitriol.

'Jesus, I hate men and their, their ...' She clenched her fists and shook with brittle fury, obviously not entirely enamoured of the trousered half of the species. Thankfully, specifics eluded her. 'I just hate them all,' she fumed eventually. It was odd – but not that odd – how women lumped every man into this one particular basket. She picked up a pencil, rammed it into the sharpener clamped to the corner of her desk, and turned the handle with what could only be described as malicious deliberation. 'I wish this was his –'

'Thank you, Angela,' interrupted James hurriedly. 'I think I get the message.' He knew exactly to which part of the errant Helmut's anatomy she was alluding. Now that was a truly uncomfortable thought. A silence stretched out between them as James pondered on the image. He sighed sadly and, gathering up his despatch box and the morning papers, departed towards the sanctuary of his office. Displaying characteristic timidity, he decided it would be wise to avoid contact with her for as long as possible and began planning how far he could get through the morning without the need for a memorandum or letter. This interesting intellectual exercise had barely begun when the phone trilled. James stared at it warily and lifted the receiver.

'What is it, Angela?' he asked in as neutral a tone as possible.

'Downing Street.' That was all she said. No warning. None at all. Usually she delayed the call long enough to allow him to gather his thoughts – but not this time. It seemed she *really* was racked off with Helmut's amorous indiscretion!

'Timbrill speaking.' He strove to sound efficient. Crisp.

33

Smart. Very much the professional politician's tone. God knows, he'd spent long enough honing it to perfection.

'James? Hello.'

James froze. Calls from the Prime Minister were extremely rare. Almost non-existent, in fact. Usually, the protective ring of advisors and spin doctors did all the donkey work, basking in the reflected power of their master, delivering their messages in arrogant tones designed to spread nervousness. The main man himself was renowned in the party for being aloof and uncommunicative – except, of course, when there was a television camera around. James knew for a fact he'd never before received such an august call, yet the clipped nasal tones, so loved by satirists and impressionists, were unmistakable. Something moved unpleasantly in his bowel. This was almost certainly not good news.

'Good morning, Prime Minister.'

'Just in? I'm a little late myself.' The PM used that irritating insult so often nobody bothered to take notice any more. Not even the cleaners over at No. 10. It was intended to be a ploy to ensure James knew exactly who was in charge, but it didn't work. 'Had a cracking weekend. You?'

'Yes, indeed.' James considered the PM's idea of cracking and his own were two entirely different matters. He squirmed in his chair and felt the residual glow of Celeste's enthusiastic crop still warming the seat of his pants.

'Good. Now, to business.' Here it comes, thought James. The first stages of panic knocked on the door. 'I want you to drop everything and pop over to see me as soon as possible. Say, ten? Tea and biscuits provided.'

'Certainly.' James paused. 'Can I ask what's going on?' This jovial camaraderie was a distinctly unsettling, especially from a member of his own party, despite the ritual offering of comestibles. These were not normally forthcoming if the interview was going to be difficult.

'Don't worry, you're not in the doghouse. Ten sharp – I'll be waiting.'

The phone went dead. James sat back and pursed his lips. What on earth was happening? The PM felt far more

34

comfortable with the other two senior ministers at the MoD, Austerly and Sharples. These two colleagues of James's had subtly emasculated his own sphere of influence to their advantage until at times it hardly seemed worth turning up for work. As Parliamentary Under-Secretary of State for Defence with responsibility for home bases, James's primary duty was to achieve the efficient financial operation of all UK military establishments. Boring, perhaps, but well within his abilities as an experienced accountant. To his best knowledge, Bermuda wasn't about to launch a pre-emptive, no-holds-barred airborne strike on Stoke Poges, so what the hell was going on?

Quentin Austerly was Minister of State for the Armed Forces and Wallace Sharples Minister of State for Defence Equipment and Support. With James, they made up the second rank in the MoD under the watchful eye of Alan Denmark, who occupied the prestigious office of Secretary of State for Defence. Now that was serious power. Alan was a patrician figure much respected for his charm, manners and ability. It was generally agreed he would have made it to No. 10 had he been fifteen years younger, where, no doubt, he would have done a considerably better job than the present lacklustre incumbent.

All senior ministers sat on the Defence Council, together with the Chief of Defence Staff, the heads of the three armed services, and a small number of specialist civilian advisors. James was also nominally entitled to sit on the Council but had been told by Austerly some time ago that his duties had declined to the point where it was not really necessary for him to attend regularly. Most politicians would have considered this a deadly insult, but these were people who were addicted to the accumulation of power. James's addictions lay in a quite different direction. He was addicted, for instance, to accumulating red stripes on his bottom! However, it was made perfectly clear he would be called in should one of the others be incapacitated. James didn't like the sound of that. It implied a national emergency and he was keen to avoid one of those at all costs.

James liked Alan Denmark. They worked well together. It

was on Denmark's personal insistence that he'd been offered his ministerial post, but James had soon found himself outmanoeuvred by the supremely devious pair of Austerly and Sharples. Both would have jumped at the chance of another visit to Downing Street, striding along the pavement and smiling smugly at the cameras now camped permanently outside the famous front door before stepping up to the PM's study for some cosy brown-nosing.

They loved riding around in tanks and knocking seven bells out of anything that moved. On one famous occasion just after the last election, Austerly had been invited up to Coningsby for a jolly in a Typhoon, but unfortunately for him it had been announced only the week before that the RAF was to be trimmed by one fighter squadron. The pilot's brother-in-law was about to lose the job he adored so, with Austerly firmly strapped in and unable to reach the eject lever, they spent an entertaining hour exploring the absolute limits of the aircraft's handling envelope. Whiplashed into jelly by wickedly vicious high-Gee barrel rolls, he came back with legs that refused to function and a face covered in dried puke! James, despite his current apprehension, smiled at the pleasant memory. What was even more amusing was the RAF had then sent the poor sod a stiff bill for cleaning the inside of the cockpit. James even remembered the amount. Plus VAT. His accountant's mind worked like that sometimes.

Abandoning his embryonic plan of avoidance, he buzzed for Angela. She came in, took a chair and waited.

'As you are no doubt aware, that was the PM. In all my years as a loyal party lackey I don't think I've ever received a truly personal summons before. He's only spoken to me on a handful of occasions, and then in passing at the House when my vote was needed. I suspect I'm not very good for his public image. It's all a question of perception, and I'm perceived as –'

'Indifferent?' offered Angela brutally. She was obviously still in no mood for delicacy.

James nodded sadly. It was going to be a long day. 'Even when I was offered this job it was Alan who approached me on the PM's behalf.' James paused, wondering exactly why he'd been offered an invitation to join the Government above others he considered infinitely more talented. Still, never look a gift horse in the mouth. 'I don't know what's going on and that worries me. Have you heard anything on the grapevine?' It was not uncommon for the resident staff to know much more than their political masters and James was pragmatic enough to accept this disconcerting state of affairs.

Angela's bristling fury subsided. Pencil sharpening apparently proved to be excellent catharsis. She looked thoughtful. It was obvious from her manner that the subject was potentially delicate. 'I've heard nothing which can be corroborated ...'

'Meaning you can bet your Aunt Fanny's mahogany dentures it's true.'

'... But there's a persistent rumour someone's been caught with sticky fingers in appropriations. Actually, quite a few people. Strictly unconfirmed reports, of course.'

'Oh, strictly,' he agreed genially. 'So I wonder what that has to do with me.' James was carefully manoeuvred clear of appropriations by his two fellow ministers. Considerable influence lay there. Money was power. On the whole, he was glad. He was far better at discovering ingenious ways to save revenue than to spend it on bullets and grenades and the fussy internals of H-bombs. Being invisible had its advantages. With greater responsibility came the unwelcome stress of a high political profile, and it was already difficult enough to tread a delicate path between the demands of his career and the desire to maintain a private association with Celeste. He would become alarmingly visible if he was moved up into appropriations. The press might start digging, and boy, let's face it, did James have front page potential!

'What time do you have to go over, Mr Timbrill?'

'Ten. I'll leave now and take the scenic route, I think.' A walk of several hundred yards would bring him into No. 10 via the famously well-known top secret tunnel, a journey of a few minutes at most, but James decided the subterranean route was far too unsettling. 'This could get messy and I want time to think.'

Outside, he turned his back on the frowning windows and strolled down to the Thames. Lost in thought, he gazed across the turbid waters with elbows resting on the parapet. He hadn't the faintest idea what was in the wind and no politician ever liked that, even one as inept as himself. The art of surviving depended entirely on recognising what form of poo was about to hit your own personal fan! Finally, he was forced to the distressing conclusion the secrets of his sexual preferences had been discovered at last and that he would be encouraged to slink off into political obscurity. His only hope was that the press would leave Celeste alone. He sighed unhappily. Things looked pretty bleak.

A woman stood at his elbow.

James started in surprise at her sudden and utterly silent approach, but the woman just stared out across the river with narrowed eyes. She was close enough to make it obvious she wanted to speak to him, yet had that distant, vague, look normally associated with those who were not entirely in touch with the real world. She was cadaverously tall, a lean and gaunt figure with a disproportionately long neck jutting up from the collar of a black gabardine raincoat. The sunken-cheeked head was crowned by a fringe of very bright ginger hair, shot through with grey and frizzed by neglect beneath a wide-brimmed hat protected by a transparent plastic covering. Celeste's hair was ginger, but whereas her unique tint was a glossy, rich and beautifully burnished copper, this woman's was pale by comparison, like an overcooked carrot. The hat didn't help. It seemed incongruous apparel for such a sunny morning. The stranger ignored James's stare and continued to study the Thames. How could such a gangly character be so stealthy?

Perhaps she was a ginger ninja.

'It's going to rain,' she said suddenly, as if letting him in on a big secret. A prominent Adam's apple bobbed up and down her scrawny throat like an epileptic elevator.

His politician's reluctance to engage the woman in conversation was overcome by a powerfully inbred sense of West Country courtesy. 'Are you sure?' he ventured, looking upwards. There wasn't a cloud in sight. His knowledge of meteorology was rudimentary, but he felt reasonably confident in his assessment. Rain had to come from somewhere and as far as he could recall, the traditional source was a cloud, but this sky was a glorious deep blue in all directions.

The old woman noticed James's perfunctory examination. 'Not here, idiot – on Mount Wai-'ale-'ale!' James looked blank. 'Hawaii!' she barked impatiently, snorting at his ignorance. 'Rains there every day.'

'Er, I believe that's some distance away,' he replied carefully, confident there were probably a couple of continents and at least a dozen time zones separating them from a place that sounded like a terminal hacking cough.

'The rain will spread, you know. It's coming. Very soon. Better prepare yourself. The Government won't lift a finger to help. It's all a conspiracy, you see, this global warming.'

'Quite.'

'It's true, I tell you,' she snapped. There was an intense fervour in her pale eyes. 'They know all about it. Forget greenhouse gases – that's just a cover-up to raise fuel prices and taxes. No, climate change is really caused by something much more insidious.' Again, the look of total incomprehension on James's face elicited a further reluctant release of information. The old woman reminded him of his school physics master patiently trying to explain Fleming's Left-Hand Rule to a class of foundering pupils.

'Mobile phones. They use microwaves. Ever heard of microwave ovens, moron? We're cooking the atmosphere. Warm air holds more moisture. The hotter it gets, the more clouds are formed, the more rain we get. Take my advice and head for the high ground. Government knows all about it. Still, at least *I'm* protected.'

She touched the brim of her hat and seemed to regard James's lack of preparation against the oncoming tempest as a personal insult. 'I know you work in that faceless office yonder.' She jerked her head back at Whitehall, an action that threatened to snap her emaciated neck and send her head rolling across the pavement. 'I did once myself – until I found out what was going on and got booted out for my troubles. Dig deep, sonny, and you'll soon find out that I'm right. I must hurry home now before the heavens open. Come along, Agnes.'

She strode away with some urgency, one hand shaking out an umbrella, and James noticed for the first time a big fat pigeon sitting in the pocket of her gabardine, its head jerking this way and that. She was a dozen paces away when she turned back, pointing a bony, accusing finger. 'There's a lot more going on than you can ever hope to discover, but one day you will find yourself in a position where you can do something about it. You'll do well to remember me then, James Timbrill!' She turned on her heel and was gone.

James stared in slightly shell-shocked disbelief. She *knew* him. That had never happened before. His accountant camouflage offered no protection this time. James watched woman and bird scuttle off to prepare for the Biblical deluge and couldn't help but feel a certain foreboding. Mobile phones? Surely the old girl was cracked.

Wasn't she?

The traffic along Whitehall was heavy. Fumes smarted in his nose and he knew London was in for another Black Snot Day. James showed his pass at Thatcher's Gates and strode up the crooked length of Downing Street. None of the reporters gathered opposite No. 10 even bothered to peer in his direction. He looked like a minor functionary. A clerk. Perhaps someone delivering pizzas. As he approached the famous old house, several men hurried out of the front door and clambered into a Jaguar to the staccato supernovae of flash guns. Cameras swung in choreographed unison as the car accelerated away and swept past. James stopped in his tracks and stared, goggle-eyed. Inside, partially hidden by raised arms, were Quentin Austerly and Wallace Sharples, their faces frozen masks of anguish. A sudden fear gripped him and he had to force himself forward again on legs distinctly wobbly.

'Oi! Who are you?' The stolid policeman on duty gazed suspiciously at James. His voice was as friendly as a nail-spiked cudgel. No wonder, really. To stand there all day and look like you're actually enjoying your job would have tried the patience of a saint.

'Timbrill. MoD.' James stared straight ahead at the middle of the man's chest. He was as big and solid as the polished black door behind him.

'Tringbowl to come in,' said the bobby into his lapel mic. James couldn't be bothered to correct him. He wasn't planning on being a regular visitor. The policeman knocked once and the gleaming door opened. Constructed from armoured steel but painted to look like wood, it was without doubt the most recognised door on earth. He stepped over the threshold, glad to be out of sight, but once inside immediately detected a definite atmosphere in the place. People scurried past in silence with handfuls of buff folders and lowered heads. Nobody even looked at him.

A sage advisor beckoned, elderly but still well-built. The man was from Scotland, decided James. The kilt was a big giveaway. Legs emerged from below the swaying hem like the mighty towers of the Forth Bridge. The proper bridge, not that spindly upstart next door. There was something about a Scotsman's knees James found faintly intimidating. They always seemed unnaturally muscular, possessing huge sinews and corded tendons bunching and flowing across gnarled, hirsute surfaces, implying resolute strength, fortitude, and brutal Pictish virility. These were the sort of knees you wanted on your side in times of crisis. These knees were the real reason why James VI was asked if he wouldn't mind warming his chuff on the English throne. The Union came into existence through fear of Scottish knees. Let's face it, when you're close up and personal with your enemy and things are looking tough, there's nothing more stirring for you – or terrifying for your opponents – than the sounds of approaching bagpipes skirling down the breeze accompanied by hordes of heavily armed, pumped-up, glassy-eyed and hairy-arsed Scotsmen wearing skirts and waving their woad-tinted testicles at you!

James followed the taciturn man up the stairs, the portraits of former prime ministers staring down at him in frosty silence. He wondered how many of them ever had their backsides striped like a stick of Blackpool rock once the bedroom curtains were pulled.

Probably quite a few.

His guide knocked and gravely ushered him into the prime minister's spacious study.

James took a deep breath to steady his nerves and stepped through the door. This was it …

Chapter Four

'James, have a seat, I won't be a minute.' The PM sat alone at his leather-tooled desk surrounded by a clutter of files, laptops, and open despatch boxes. James waited in silence, glancing around at the choice of art on the walls. Each premier who lived in the grand old house could decorate to their own personal taste. None of the paintings were permanent fixtures but were selected by the current PM from the Government Art Collection, a stately and dignified body which cared for thousands of paintings, sculptures, and other sundry works of art, all for use in official buildings and embassies across the globe. Getting to hang a few genuine masterpieces on your walls instead of cheap prints from John Lewis like the rest of the country was a real perk of the job, even though it was widely suspected the finest paintings were quietly put to one side whenever a prime minister came shopping. James discovered the PM had a diverse taste; there were classical portraits of Walpole, Nelson, Gladstone, and Sir Isaac Newton, a very fine bust of Charles Darwin, several dreamy Turner landscapes, a surprisingly racy Russell Flint, and a bright, cheerful Hockney. Not bad at all.

The PM ignored James for a full minute. He waited patiently, watching his leader scribble. Having already experienced one of the premier's pathetic psychological tricks that morning, the second proved merely tiresome. Eventually, the files were shuffled into order and dropped onto the floor beside his chair.

'You wanted to see me.' Cool and collected. James was a good actor when occasion called.

'Yes.' The two stared at each other for a moment, then the PM stood and walked slowly around the desk, hands in pockets and looking down at the floor. He was a very tall, solid man about ten years older than James, heavy in the shoulders and arms, who'd once played in the pack for Wasps. The famous broken nose was easily the most prominent feature of his face. Dramatic white eyebrows underpinned a broad forehead, their exaggerated bushiness compensating for the very few silver hairs still stubbornly refusing to decamp from his lofty crown. His lips were thin and firm. Decisive. A massive intellect lurked behind those guarded grey eyes, precise, sharp, and formidably penetrating, yet despite these advantages the PM was widely perceived as grey and monodimensional. 'This is a delicate matter, James. As you know, we've suffered from a run of extremely bad luck over the last few months and can ill afford to be subject to media scrutiny again.'

James thought it unwise to correct the PM. For *months* read *years*. Actually, things had started to go spectacularly pear-shaped with the last election, which had reduced the PM's previously comfortable majority of fifty-eight to a worryingly tiny nine. He'd soldiered on, however, as politicians addicted to power always do, but it was hard going. Several unexpected and frankly disappointing by-elections had eaten into that disastrously inadequate number.

Then came a massive financial scandal in the Department for Business, Innovation and Skills, resulting in a dozen arrests when the money was finally traced back to organised criminal gangs. This was followed in short order by the exposure of several MPs who had invested in a dubious Russian casino and its associated brothel. In an effort to re-establish moral authority and improve its popularity with the electorate, the Government then introduced a series of inflation-busting tax hikes and a natty selection of ill-advised schemes for raising extra capital, capital desperately needed by an administration hopelessly addicted to spending more than its income, just like any frivolous, credit-hungry teenager.

Some of these methods were described as 'inventive' by the Government and 'unfair' by the populace, such as the

44

introduction of an MoT test and mandatory fully comprehensive insurance for bicycles, skateboards, roller blades and even children's scooters, but what really angered every voter in the land was the unexpected arrival of a new and universally loathed levy on property – in an attempt to alleviate the chronic housing shortage by encouraging more people to move, the Government introduced a hefty annual charge to penalise householders for *not* putting their properties on the market!

That one hadn't survived for long. There'd been a short but lively campaign of civil dissent described by the populace as "inventive" and by the Government as "unfair" involving bombarding every politician – whether minister, MP or local councillor – with a barrage of eggs whenever they summoned up the courage to appear in public. The British Egg Industry Council, themselves subject to swingeing cuts to their grant, were so delighted their products had found new use as a medium of political change that they proudly printed "Democracy in Action" on each egg beneath the famous Lion Quality mark.

The Government had not yet been forgiven and there remained a great deal of good old British simmering over that little debacle. Even James, as innocuous and pleasant a politician as ever lived, had not escaped and got pelted on several occasions. 'I'm sure things will pick up. The public has a notoriously short memory span.' James's confidence was merely for the benefit of his companion. In his own experience the electorate had an elephantine memory, especially in Gloucester. There was no fault to be found in their powers of recall, none at all, particularly if they felt they'd been abused, but then all governments were guilty of arrogantly underestimating the intelligence of the people who voted them into power. It always came as a profound shock when those same masses voted them out again with wonderfully cheerful indifference.

'Thanks for the encouragement.' The PM seemed to be struggling with words. Not a good sign for a man noted for his concise oratorical skills. He tried a new tack. 'James, you've been an MP for –?'

'Fourteen years.' Fourteen bloody years! Thanks for remembering.

'And got an excellent first at Cambridge.'

'Actually, it was Durham.' James thought it best not to reveal he'd become an MP simply because, after leaving the City, he couldn't find anything else useful to do; accountancy degrees did that to you sometimes.

'Er, quite. Anyway, I know you've worked quite happily at the MoD these past few years under Alan. You've done an excellent job and although it seems to the contrary, I've kept my eye on you.'

Now James knew he was being thrown a yarn. Sharples, and particularly Austerly, were being groomed for greater things. It was generally acknowledged Austerly would replace Alan when he finally retired and departed for the glorious upland pastures of the House of Lords. James didn't like being patronised and showed his irritation sufficiently for even the PM to notice, but it would be an outrage to call him a liar, and because the PM knew James knew this, and because James knew that the PM knew he knew this, neither men wished to expose the lie. Thankfully, by wary mutual consent, the ethical conundrum passed and the conversation moved on into smoother waters.

'It's a pleasant duty to give praise where it's due. Unfortunately, as head of the government, I'm also called upon to occasionally chastise my ministers.'

James stared stony-faced. Celeste! How the hell did the bastards find out? He looked ruin in the face and felt his insides gradually drain away. It was a horrible feeling. Media interest was now guaranteed; hounding of disgraced officials was a national sport. He only hoped that Celeste would be spared and was consoled by the fleeting thought that Bertie would sort them out.

'… And that's why I had to make the decision,' concluded the PM. He waited for James to respond.

'I'm sorry, what did you say?' Shock at the discovery of his idiosyncratic peccadilloes had deafened him to the last few sentences. The PM misunderstood his confusion.

'Yes, stunning news, isn't it, but I'd no choice – Sharples

and Austerly had to walk! No two ways about it. Alan's resigned as well as a matter of principle, but that's merely cleared the path for him to take up his peerage.'

'A – Austerly? Sharples? W-what? Who? Did you –? Do you mean? You did what?' James dithered magnificently. It was truly of an Olympic standard. He was a man who could easily represent his country at international level.

'MI5 unearthed evidence of minor financial irregularities in MoD appropriations for equipment supplied by companies who have tenuous but definite connections with our two colleagues. The press got wind of it and there's a special Panorama next Monday. I've been forced to distance them from the Government.'

'You've sacked them! You've actually sacked them!' exclaimed James with incredulity. Ministers didn't lose their jobs if the financial irregularities were 'minor' or if the links were 'tenuous'. No way. They stuck to their careers like iron-hard dingleberries cemented to a Welsh sheep's bushy bum! This was *major*. As in indictable.

'Can't get much more distant than that,' said the PM with a cheery smile. 'Damned bad luck though, especially for Austerly. However, their misfortune is to your advantage.'

'How do you mean?' James recovered enough from his shock to sense the imminent arrival of the Crap Express on Platform Three.

'Well, the Ministry of Defence has had no Secretary of State since half past nine this morning. In fact, it has no minister of any significance – apart from you. That's an intolerable situation which needs to be rectified immediately. Your steady work within the department has made you the natural choice of successor. If you want it, James, it's yours!'

There was a faint roaring in James's ears. Something unusual was happening to his breathing. He suddenly envisaged hordes of desperate refugees stumbling in panic from the battlefields of Kent before invading European Union armies – inevitably led by the grinning French, happy at last to be back revisiting the fields they'd first trod in 1066 – then had a fleeting vision of his own face covered in blobs of desiccated orange vomit as he struggled out of a Typhoon on legs no longer connected to the rest of his body. He went a ghastly shade of grey. His mouth worked but nothing immediately recognisable as English slipped from paralysed lips. 'Uuuhh. I '

The PM slapped him on the shoulder in a comradely fashion. 'Good, I knew you'd be up to it.' He gave James no choice. 'Take the rest of the day to settle in and meet the top brass – I'm sure they'll remember who you are – then come to Cabinet tomorrow. We'll start making the necessary adjustments lower down the pecking order and bring in a few new names off the back-benches to fill the other posts. If I may make a suggestion, why not begin by concentrating on something you're familiar with and have a stab at maximising financial efficiency? I'm sure you'll be a dab hand at achieving all sorts of savings. Go as far as you like, burrow into the department, I'm sure there's all sorts of obscure administrative positions in there we don't need any more, so squeeze out some of the excess and I promise anything saved will be spent on lots of shiny new equipment. You have my full support in whatever you do, so there's an easy task you can get your teeth into straight away.'

'But –'

'Now don't you worry about a thing, old boy. We'll take care of the details and press release. I'll get my team to run up something for your first speech in the House. I want you to think of this as a great opportunity. Congratulations, James. You're on the front bench!'

It was a shell-shocked and totally overwhelmed James who staggered out of the front door and on to the pavement again, ejected like a disorientated reveller from a closing nightclub. Mercifully, none of the media noticed his glazed expression and stumbling footsteps.

'Goodbye, sir – and well done.' The policeman's deferential attitude couldn't have been more contrary to his earlier indifference. James was stunned. Holy Mother of God – news travelled fast in that place!

Meanwhile, back inside No. 10, the PM sat at his desk again with chin cupped in one palm and a pained look on his face. That had gone as well as could be expected. Timbrill was obviously totally unsuitable for the job, but the speed with which the changes had been forced on him required prompt action. Never be seen to hesitate; that was interpreted as a sign of weakness, even if the decision was wrong. No matter. He'd let loose the terminally confused James on the Chiefs of Staff with a remit to cut costs. The two forces should neatly cancel each other out and so produce a period of satisfactory inaction, then Timbrill would be quietly dropped from the Cabinet after the next election. Assuming it was won, of course. The PM stirred uncomfortably at the possibility of defeat. That was the only bad point about his job – its continuation depended entirely on the most fickle of electorates. The egg campaign was still fresh in his memory.

The biggest difficulty was going to be grooming a suitable long-term replacement from the back-benches. Timbrill was obviously honest, amiable, and pleasant, but far too much of a lightweight for such an important post. He lacked the killer instinct, a rather important qualification when one considered the job, but no matter. He was just about capable enough to run the ministry on a day-to-day basis and that was all the PM was after. Besides, any crisis would entail the immediate involvement of the entire Cabinet and their collective decisions would determine policy: decisions Timbrill would no doubt be relieved to follow without question.

Nonetheless, a successor-in-waiting needed to be found, and fast. Sure, there were several eminently capable MPs who had wide-ranging experience, good contacts and plenty of drive and intelligence. Unfortunately, they all belonged to the Opposition. The premier sighed. His own ranks were woefully devoid of talent nowadays, which in a way was partly his own fault. In true dictatorial style, he had kept the rest weak to make himself look strong, but occasionally this led to recruiting problems. If only Austerly hadn't mucked up, but the man had committed *the* cardinal sin in politics – he'd been caught!

There was a subdued knock and a portly man glided into the room like a silent, impassive hovercraft, his corpulent figure dressed in a top-class Savile Row three-piece.

'Everything satisfactory, sir?'

'I suppose so.' There was a note of hopeless resignation in the PM's voice.

'Come now, it was all you could have hoped for. We are now fully involved in a damage limitation exercise that will stretch us to the limit. Messrs Austerly and Sharples really were most indiscreet, but I shall do my best to protect them from prosecution.'

'Thanks, Hugo.'

'I suppose we can be grateful for one thing.'

The PM looked up. 'Yes?'

'I doubt if you'll have to call on my services regarding the ingenuous Mr Timbrill. I've the results of a preliminary appraisal. Do you wish a summary?'

'So long as it's quick.'

'Oh, it is. Painfully so.' Both men grinned. Hugo Chaplain chose his words with precision. He knew the PM liked that – his boss was a man weaned on sound bites. 'In addition to your own personal knowledge of the man and also what is on public record, I can add the following few snippets. The newest member of your Cabinet has recently discharged his mortgage on a surprisingly modest London flat and continues to maintain a family country cottage in his North Gloucester constituency. He owns two cars, one an old Sunbeam sportster. It also appears he still occasionally motorcycles, an activity which I find extraordinarily surprising for a man of his age.'

The PM sat back with fingers laced behind his head and regarded that last statement with sour antipathy. Hugo was a man who, as a result of an almost spherical rotundity, eschewed all forms of activity with the condescending distaste of one entirely incapable of any physical exertion. It was the very worst form of inverted snobbery and the premier didn't appreciate Chaplain's witty little comment at all. He often wished he himself was still sprightly enough to play rugby again, to bite the odd ear or twist a few inadvisably exposed testicles in the ruck. Those were the days, when a man's prowess was measured by the quantity of beer he could sink or the way he could skilfully evacuate the post-match showers with a truly noxious fart! Consequently, he thought rather well

50

of James and the fact he could still do something as youthfully foolish as motorcycling.

Chaplain droned on. 'He inquired about becoming a name at Lloyd's, but fortunately could not raise the capital and so escaped certain financial disaster by the skin of his teeth. Despite that, as you would expect from a man of reasonable financial competence, he has a useful portfolio of shares, exclusively British, that make a small but significant contribution to his income, and the sum total of liquid cash held or invested in national institutions stands at a trifle under three hundred thousand.'

'Is that all?' The Prime Minister was genuinely surprised.

'Not all your ministers are acolytes of creative accounting.'

'That was uncalled for.'

'I apologise,' replied Chaplain suavely. He liked planting barbs that hurt. 'We're checking to see if there are any foreign interests, but our initial searches suggest Timbrill's financial tastes are entirely patriotic.'

'What about the Members' Interests Register?'

'Squeaky clean and in rude health.'

'His constituency?'

'You already know he's one of your more popular MPs. The local party chairman has nothing but praise. Politically, Gloucester is a good, loyal city, or at least our half of it is, but a place to avoid if possible.'

'How so?'

'Apart from its very fine cathedral, certainly one of the best ever built but now no doubt surrounded by a car park, I hear it has no redeeming qualities whatsoever. Generations of myopically poor town planners appear to have effectively removed whatever charm it once had through a combination of stunted imagination and a misplaced enthusiasm for concrete.'

'Have you been there?'

'I don't have to,' replied Hugo with a dismissive sniff.

'Then you don't know what you're talking about, do you,' snapped the PM testily. He really wasn't in the mood for Chaplain's conceited pomposity.

'Not so, sir,' observed Hugo at his most pontifical. 'My

observation is merely an intellectual deduction. Degeneration through poor planning is a story common to almost all the shire towns nowadays, and if that wasn't enough of a burden, the city is unfortunate enough to suffer from annual flooding. The Severn is a dreadfully mucky river down there. Quite filthy.'

'Yes, I seem to recall they're always pestering us to spend more money on flood defences, but it's not exactly the Home Counties, is it. Not the stockbroker belt, or an area of industrial or commercial importance. I mean, they don't contribute much to the economy so we can afford to ignore them without it tarnishing our image unduly. It is an unfashionable part of the country, after all.'

'Quite so. The county itself is notably delightful, as several members of the Royal Family have known for years, but as for Gloucester, well, let's just say Cheltenham is infinitely more agreeable. You really must go. Most pleasant architecture and beautiful parks.'

'I shall endeavour to remember that when next planning a visit.' The PM made a mental note to arrange an immediate trip to Gloucester, just to annoy Chaplain. 'Anything else? Don't tell me he's a sheep-shagging, cross-dressing, alcoholic dope fiend!'

Chaplain smiled indulgently. The PM only spoke like that to a select number of trusted advisors. Very select. He flicked through his notes as if to confirm the PM's interesting thumbnail sketch. 'Nothing here to suggest anything so flamboyant, although it would indeed be unfortunate to have a second such colourful character in your Cabinet. No, on the contrary, our boy's never been as wild as that, more's the pity.'

The significance of Chaplain's last aside was not lost on either man. What would have been taken by others as simply a casual observation was of vital importance to them both. Indeed, the entire conversation hinged on the remark.

'Damn,' was all the PM said. Chaplain nodded, pursing his generous lips, and the most critical point of their discussion passed by without any further comment.

'Although still suspiciously a bachelor, Timbrill is most certainly heterosexual, and despite the debilitating misfortune of being an accountant, enjoys an active social life both here in London and in his constituency. He is apparently well liked by women and has had an acceptable number of liaisons over the years, enough to prove his sexual inclinations are mainstream but not enough for him to be considered in any way promiscuous. There is no evidence of an impending marriage at the moment, but he's a regular visitor to a spinster by the name of Celeste Gordon who currently lives in Greenwich.'

Pages turned slowly. The premier watched Chaplain's restless gaze flick over the salient points. The man fascinated him. His head was entirely out of proportion with the rest of his body, like an apple resting on a watermelon. Chaplain's hair had long abandoned the lofty reaches of his scalp and now resided in a furtive tonsure around the back of his head like a swath of spumed driftwood washed up on an inhospitable beach. He had a fine nose that barely separated close-set black eyes, eyes as cold as a January walk on the Northumberland coast. Despite his bulk, his hands were slender and delicate, the nails perfectly manicured; Chaplain had never done a day's manual labour in his life and clearly had no intention of doing so in the future.

'Miss Gordon returned from Brazil two years ago after the death of her father. Her mother died eight years ago. She is an only child and appears to be lucky enough not to have to work since her estate provides sufficient income for her to live in reasonable comfort. It seems her father was a capable man who invested wisely in several sound South American companies. Enquiries concerning her former connections abroad have revealed nothing unusual and it appears she has never fallen foul of the authorities either here or in Brazil.' He glanced at a note granting a certificate of importation for an endangered species of macaw but decided not to bother the PM with such trivial detail.

'Their relationship appears reasonably intimate – he stays overnight on most weekends. Nothing unusual or scandalous there, I'm sure. Miss Gordon appears to be of good character but we'll take a peek anyway. In short, I think you've picked a good one. Unlike his predecessors, I would say young James woefully lacks the ability to conceal any indiscretions.' Chaplain's avuncular condescension made the Prime Minister smile grimly.

'And as you well know, my dear Hugo, therein lies both our salvation and our problem.'

Chapter Five

Hugo Chaplain felt a smug pride in the achievements of the last two weeks. He returned to his scruffy office in the MoD building immediately after the short conversation at Downing Street and sat in solitude, surrounded by a comforting blanket of clutter. He liked being tucked away. Out of sight. It suited him, and while his sniggering fellow executives poured scorn on his modest empire, to all intent and purposes he ran the country.

Very few officials were actually aware of his true role or that of the tiny agency he so ably ran. The Joint Services Operations, Non-Military comprised merely a half dozen or so personnel, but its importance to the survival of the Government was entirely out of proportion to its scanty resources.

Bluntly, JSON was the covert operations wing of No. 10, specialising in clandestine political manipulation and control. It was a black organisation embedded deep within the Ministry of Defence, shrouded by a screen of absolute secrecy.

Established by necessity, JSON massaged statistics, collected interesting snippets of information, was well versed in the subtle mechanics of blackmail, exerted pressure on those troublesome to Downing Street, cleared up the detritus of ministerial blunderings and, when required, used every method, legal or otherwise, to ensure No. 10 rose above the embarrassment of its mistakes. Hugo offered an absolutely vital service to an accident-prone executive, ensured nothing unpleasantly noxious came to the attention of the press and public. JSON possessed intimate details of every minister, employed its knowledge to ensure their compliant behaviour, held those of lesser importance in an iron grip of fear and was a personal and very private do all, hear all, see all and report all

55

service for the Prime Minister.

Since its formation neither the media, the police, nor the Cabinet had any idea of its existence, and Chaplain was utterly determined to keep it that way. The very uppermost echelon of MI5 knew and occasionally seconded one or two of their more astute political officers to JSON, but then as MI5 never, absolutely never, told Parliament anything of importance anyway, it was unlikely JSON's secrecy would be compromised from that direction. It was perfectly concealed within the most shadowy of government institutions, a tiny group who reached out to intimidate and control through a tentacular web of influence. If MI5 were occasionally a law unto themselves, JSON was even more so and infinitely less accountable.

Paradoxically for the Prime Minister, the more he relied on JSON to make him look good, the more he became susceptible to their influence. This was the essential bedrock of Hugo's stratagem, underpinning his position, making him increasingly invulnerable to even the PM.

Chaplain *was* JSON. In no other agency was the essence of its leader more pervasive. He manipulated on an astonishing scale, had become so entwined in policy decisions and involved in concealing so many unsavoury episodes that he could exert political pressure in a way MI5 could only dream of, and as a result there were times when, effectively, he controlled the Government – and Hugo enjoyed wielding this power very much. Consequently, when he received rumour of storm clouds gathering to darken his unique position, he exerted all his considerable intellect to deflect the threat.

Ruthlessly.

As Quentin Austerly and Wallace Sharples had just discovered.

Having already rumbled a number of their lesser scams, Hugo rightly guessed they were disposed to more significant levels of corruption. A little routine sifting had produced all the evidence he needed. He knew it would be there if he dug deep enough. Austerly, in particular, seemed to be profiting almost uncannily each time a generous defence contract was awarded by Sharples' department. The route the dirty money took was certainly devious, involved several offshore accounts, a Central American bank of dubious honesty and more laundering than a pair of favourite Y-fronts, but Chaplain was skilled and tenacious and the link was forged.

All because of a chance remark by Austerly, overheard in passing, that plans were in the process of being prepared to convert the part of the building containing JSON's very modest offices into an entertainment and fitness suite for the exclusive use of senior ministers. The prospect of losing his comfortable lodgings to make way for Austerly's own private cinema and hot tub proved too much for Hugo. To be bundled out of his secluded corner and dumped who-knows-where would inevitably raise JSON's profile. The danger was immediately apparent. Awkward questions would inevitably result. Who were these people and what was their function? The protective veil of secrecy surrounding JSON would be breached, a consequence to be avoided at all costs. In Chaplain's experience, it would then only be a question of time before the media picked up on the story, and that would be the end of JSON. Fortunately, Chaplain was a consummate master of manipulation and knew that although his chief dangers lay in the direction of the press, he could also use them to his advantage.

Mysteriously, within the week, reports of serious financial irregularities within the MoD began to surface in the papers. Reliable but unidentified 'sources' leaked like a rusty bucket used for shotgun practice, pointing the press in the right direction. Their tenacity was admirable, once they had been teased with a few tasty morsels. Chaplain smiled. It had all been so easy and now the pair had fallen from grace, never to return. Austerly knew he'd been shafted by JSON but could not prove a thing, and that made Hugo's victory even sweeter.

And all because Hugo really rather liked his shabby office.

His pleasant reverie was interrupted by a knock on the door. He adjusted his tie to carefully conceal a tea stain garnered earlier at No. 10. 'Come!'

'You look pleased.' A wiry but powerful man in his early forties slipped his head around the door. Chaplain waved him in and the two sat at their ease on either side of the plain deal desk. The newcomer was strongly built, easily filling his shirt with an excess of well-developed musculature no normal person could possibly possess. His face resembled that of a clothing catalogue model, handsome in a nondescript way, with a long nose, blue eyes, and short dark hair. He lit a cigarette with an old-fashioned Zippo, then slid packet and lighter across the table. Chaplain helped himself. For some strange reason the smoke detector above the desk was always faulty. Chaplain didn't give a damn about anti-smoking legislation, political correctness or the injured sensibilities of his fellow non-smokers. 'My boy, there are times when I think I was born in the wrong century.' He leaned back and blew a thick blue cloud directly up into the detector overhead.

'Machiavelli? De' Medici? Edmund Blackadder?'

'All unfairly persecuted because of their extraordinary skills in the art of diplomacy.'

Bob Pritchard, his Number One, exhaled a fresh assault on the smoke detector. 'Hogwash! What's the colour of the sky in your world, Hugo?'

Chaplain chuckled softly. 'Look at the motto,' he said, nodding at the desk. A small plaque carried the inscription, *Sowing The Dragon's Teeth*, a reference to the ancient Greek mythological tale of Jason and his quest for the Golden Fleece with the Argonauts. Their enemies cast dragon's teeth on the ground to create a troop of armed men who Jason cunningly hoodwinked into fighting each other instead of himself. Chaplain liked the multi-layered inferences, not only to the abbreviated title of his agency, but also to the aims and methods of JSON. 'Is Greg in?'

'He's still checking on that dodgy timber deal between the forestry people and the Japs. This one's going to run and run.'

'I can imagine the outrage when our oriental cousins clear cut the New Forest and ship the whole lot back to Yokohama.'

'What happened up at the bunker?'

'We've got our new Secretary of State for Defence.'

'Squeaky Clean Timbrill?'

'The very same, and don't sound so surprised. He was the

only option for the PM.'

'You mean he was the man *you* wanted for the job.'

'I can't deny friend James will make our lives tolerably pleasant in the short term. At least we can now cancel the removal men. Timbrill is the sort of chap who would never dream of wasting money on such an extravagance as a personal cinema.'

'Good. I like it here. We're well buried.'

'Exactly so, and I'm not moving anywhere just so Questionable Quentin can put his feet up and catch a flick after lunch.'

'Will Timbrill be able to cope?'

'Doubt it, but our need to remain invisible takes precedent over the security of the country. I suspect the poor man will struggle to understand even the basics of his job, which will keep his mind nicely occupied. The PM intends him to be a temporary appointment at best and I'm sure his successor, when eventually found, will be prone to the kind of weaknesses that fill our files with such salacious reading, providing us with the usual leverage.'

'Dangerous.'

'What is?'

'Having a top line minister with no vices. Very difficult to control.'

'Possibly, but Timbrill will be far too busy struggling to comprehend the significance of first strike capabilities, CINCNAVHOME and collateral damage. The poor man is only an accountant, when all's said and done, and not even a particularly accomplished one at that, judging by the parlous state of his personal fortune.'

'Is it a good idea having a total dunce in control?'

'Nothing new about that,' snorted Chaplain, his beatific smile wreathed in cigarette smoke.

'I thought Denmark quite competent.'

'He was. Disappointingly righteous as well. We didn't really have anything to use against him and I wasn't at all happy about that, but I suspected he'd resign so we've killed many birds with just one accurately aimed stone. This new guy's equally virginal, but at least he's spectacularly lacking in experience so I confidently predict he'll be far too busy to notice us. However, just for my own satisfaction, I want you and Greg to keep an eye on our Mr Timbrill. Do the usual digging.'

'How deep?'

Chaplain leaned back in his chair again, unconsciously exposing his soiled tie. The stain fascinated Pritchard. It was a mystery to him how a man possessing so magnificent an intellect could manage to miss his lips with such astonishing regularity.

'Just have a nose around. Use the van, but I'm confident Captain Dull is incapable of harbouring anything damaging and since there are other more pressing demands on our services, I don't want to waste too much energy in that direction.' He nodded at a tiny data stick on his desk. 'That's the official record. I've added a few notes of my own at the back.'

'Sure.' Pritchard was halfway through the door when Hugo called him back. 'You might like to start in Greenwich.'

'Oh?'

'It's all in the file.'

James staggered into Angela's office on gelatine legs. There was no doubt his overall state of mind could best be described as confused. She stared at him with a concerned expression on her face. 'You OK?'

'Do I look OK?'

'No, can't say as you do.'

'Then I'm not. Want to know what happened?'

'You got the sack.'

'Your frankness is refreshing, but entirely inaccurate. Try again.'

'Well, with the others gone, you must now be the Secretary of State.'

James collapsed in a chair and smiled wryly. You had to get up early to beat Angela. Her analytical skills were faultless. 'I note you're using the exact same tone of disbelief as I did.'

'Mr Timbrill, may I be honest?'

'Go ahead, and for God's sake call me James. I could do

60

with talking to a person who has a grip on reality.'

'Why on earth did you accept? You're not cut out for this kind of pressure.'

'I was given little choice.' James paused, frowning as he recalled the interview. 'Actually, I was given no choice at all. The PM expressed his complete confidence in me.'

'He would have to.'

'Thank you, Angela.' James enjoyed her sarcasm and decided to tell her straight away. He had an embryonic plan forming in his head and wanted to hear her opinion. 'Since I am now in charge, I'm going to do something no one has anticipated.'

'Invade Poland?'

'Sorry, but some painter with a major personality disorder beat me to it.' He liked her spontaneous humour. 'No, what I was going to say is that firstly, I want you to move with me.'

There was a stunned silence. 'Me? But I'm not qualified to be a Parliamentary Private Secretary.'

'You are now. Call it a battlefield promotion.'

'Well, OK, thank you. You'll need all the support you can get if you're going to take on that lot.' She waved dismissively in the general direction of the upper floors, areas brimming with staff whose actual function seemed to be unknown but whose job descriptions inevitably incorporated the word 'secretary'. Frankly, there were more secretaries in the building than soldiers; Private Secretaries, Principal Private Secretaries, Under Secretaries, Assistant Secretaries and Assistant Under-Secretaries. There were legions of Deputy Secretaries, Deputy Under-Secretaries, Permanent Under-Secretaries, Parliamentary Private Secretaries, Parliamentary Under-Secretaries and Parliamentary Private Under-Secretaries. Rumour had it there was, somewhere in the vast building, a Permanent Principal Private Parliamentary Deputy Assistant Under-Secretary, but the unfortunate who held the post had long since been crushed under the weight of his ID badge.

All James needed was an honest-to-God, down-to-earth, tell-it-how-it-is, no-nonsense, politically incorrect secretary. One who could type. Like Angela, for instance.

'Like I said, leave it to me. I'm in charge now, although it pains me to say it.' He leaned forward, suddenly serious. 'Listen, I know why I got the job. If it's obvious to you I'm fairly useless then it's certainly so to Downing Street. Don't underestimate the PM. He's a shrewd man. He obviously wants a night-watchman, a nonentity who will provide a bit of stability, someone to tide them over at least until the next election. If there hadn't been an embarrassing shortage of suitable candidates I wouldn't have stood a chance, but it's too late now – the announcement's been made and they're stuck with me. He would never sack me so quickly after my appointment because that would make him look like a right donkey, so here I am in a sudden position of strength, and as well as taking you with me, I'm now going to do something entirely unexpected.'

Angela struggled. 'What?' She just couldn't imagine James doing anything noteworthy – he was an accountant from Gloucester, for Christ's sake, a place she suspected had only just begun to enjoy the benefits of electrification!

'The PM suggested I take a look at cutting costs. Sure, every new boy gets told the same, but he's also promised any savings we make will be ploughed back into the department and not collared by Social Security. I suspect he made his promise lightly without actually expecting to have to honour it. However, I've been given a real opportunity to achieve something in the short time that's available to me, and even though I'm likely to go down in history as one of the most ineffective ministers this century, and let's face it I'm up against some stiff competition there, I still want to achieve something. I have got a little pride, you know.'

'So what are you going to do?'

'Commission a review of all the associated agencies and administrative sections in the MoD, but this time to be carried out by a fully independent non-governmental inspectorate. An impartial team from the private sector. They'll have unlimited access and three months to identify the dead wood. I'll then go to the PM and insist on a great big wad of cash on top of what we can squeeze out of the ministry. If he refuses, I'll just resign.

He won't want that, so the extra money should come our way.

'My goal will be to cut all the scandalous spending on things we don't need any more. Did you know we've recently spent two million pounds on doors for this place?' he suddenly fumed, waving a hand around to signify the surrounding building. 'That's an awful lot of bullets and boots! The forces are there to defend us and that's where the resources should be concentrated. I don't think anyone would argue with that, so I'm going to hack away at the pen-pushers and layers of pointless management. Any savings will be used to provide better equipment, training and salaries and certainly much better pensions. We'll buy a few frigates, get the shipyards going again, or something like that.'

'And you think you'll succeed?'

'Probably not, but I hope to expose such outrageous profligacy that whoever comes after me will have to do something. I don't care who gets upset because I haven't got a career to defend. Whatever happens, I'll be out at the next election, so what have I got to lose?'

'A fat pension?'

'My dear, they'll fall over themselves to give me a pension just to get rid of me.'

'I don't believe I'm hearing this,' said Angela faintly.

'Wake up! This is the way things are run. Politicians bide their time in ministerial posts knowing that they'll be moving on as soon as something more succulent turns up. They pick at a few problems, play the media game and swan off after a couple of years. It's the professional civil servants who actually govern each department because they represent experience and continuity. I thought everybody knew this. Our civil servants do a magnificent job but they are devious little sods when it comes to expanding their own bureaucracy – the bigger the better because it looks like they're needed.'

'Of course everyone knows the civil servants run everything. It's just you don't hear that from anyone at Westminster.'

'That's not the only thing you'll be hearing from me, I can assure you.' James stood up and assumed an earnest air, slipping one hand into his trousers pocket to give himself an aura of casual gravity. Angela recognised his authoritative House of Commons stance. He had become James Timbrill MP, Secretary of State for Defence, projecting the quiet confidence she knew he never felt. 'Mr Speaker, many before me have merely tinkered before moving on, but I plan to be remembered as the first post-war minister who actually made a difference.' James paused theatrically and glared pugnaciously around an imaginary Commons. 'Our forces will be armed to the teeth with everything from chilli-dipped suppositories to this department's weapon of choice, nuclear powered pencil sharpeners!'

'You're bloody mad,' she giggled.

'So was George the Third – and he had blue wee-wee.' said James, glad to see he'd managed to put a smile on her face. 'And now I'm going to hide under my desk. Only the important calls, please.'

James couldn't settle. He sat for a few minutes, toyed with the idea of calling Celeste, then decided to freshen up and stepped into his private bathroom to rinse face and hands, but when he returned to the office an unexpected visitor loitered by the window.

'Hello, James. I hope you don't mind me dropping in like this, but I'm rather pressed for time.' Austerly, despite the devastating events of the day, still managed to convey just a trace of supercilious arrogance. How the hell had he got past Angela?

'Not at all.'

'Something of a surprise, no doubt.'

James felt sufficiently vindictive enough to reinforce their dramatic change in circumstances by sitting behind his desk and deliberately closing a manila folder stamped *Restricted*. Actually, it was next week's menu, but since almost all paperwork in the department had a *Restricted* rating at the very minimum, even the menu was regarded as an official document, fully protected by the Official Secrets Act.

MoD documents are, as one would expect considering the subject matter, invariably sensitive, and this being a bureaucracy honed to perfection over many years and by two first-class, no-holds-barred world wars, there had long been an approved hierarchy of document classification. Unsurprisingly, the actual document establishing this classification remains, in itself, classified.

Firstly, at the very bottom of the pile, a few lowly documents fall into the *Unclassified* category These can be safely left on tube carriages or restaurant tables without any undue fuss. The next upward level of classification is *Restricted*, covering such important documents as the week's menu. Leave one of those on public transport and you can expect a reprimand at the very least. One above that is *Confidential*, and the inadvertent loss of a *Confidential* document in British Home Stores can put an embarrassing dent in your career. Then comes *Secret*, the spook's favourite There are two categories in this well-known classification; plain, ordinary, good old bog-standard *Secret* and the critically important For-Heaven's-Sake-Don't-Tell-The-French *Secret UK Eyes Only*. This category is normally reserved for anything the MoD wants to keep from Britain's staunchest allies. In other words, anything that's been a tad embarrassing or a bit of a cock-up.

Finally, at the top of the pile, and this is where the loss of a document can really land you in some major trouble – as in prison time – comes the infamous *STRAP* classification. STRAP is an acronym for Signature Transfer Required from Authorised Personnel. These documents come with a minder and must be signed for at all stages of use. They are never left unattended. They are never removed from the building. They are never lost or mislaid. You sign your life away when you take charge of one of these. The staff joke that STRAP documents are so called because you have to literally strap them to your body at all times.

Thankfully, the canteen menu, certainly the most carefully scrutinised document in the building, remained comfortably within the *Restricted* classification, but that didn't stop James from concealing its contents from unauthorised eyes. Austerly bridled at the unspoken insult but said nothing. James, fortified by the thought of all those missiles now under his control, gazed at the disgraced minister and waited. This should be very interesting. In what form would the bribe be offered? Would subtlety be exercised or would the man get straight to the point?

Quentin Austerly was a smooth bastard. Real smooth. Smoother than Captain Smooth of the Smooth Team at the University of Smoothness in Smoothville. He always dressed immaculately in regulation pin-stripes and waistcoat, possessed a widow's peak of very dark hair which for some inexplicable reason made him highly attractive to the opposite sex, and was as dishonest as the day was long. Essential requirements for an ambitious politician. His biggest hero was Richard Milhous Nixon.

'So, what can I do for you, Quentin?'

Austerly chose his words carefully. 'Firstly, despite what has happened this morning, I hope you'll remember I was always fair in our dealings. I regarded you as an equal. You are an excellent minister.'

James knew when he was being lied to – Austerly had been an abrupt prig who barely acknowledged his existence, and even when he did, was overtly rude. Well, two could play at that game. 'Thank you, Quentin, that's refreshing to know. What about the time you made me take the train to Glasgow while you and Sharples chartered an RAF jet, you oleaginous, follically challenged knob?'

'Still haven't let that go, have you.'

'Nope. Listen, old bean, let's cut the mutual admiration crap. We both know I would have gotten nowhere under you and Sharples so don't shovel that pile of stinkies in my direction. Just tell me what you want.'

In an instant, the oily friendliness dropped from Austerly's manner. His voice was flat and hard. 'Special consideration for defence contracts for my companies.'

Aha! The direct approach after all.

'Get out!'

'But Jimmy boy, I offer you something in exchange.'

'Exactly what part of "get out" don't you understand?'

'Poor James, you just don't know when an opportunity comes your way.'

'I don't give a rat's arse about you or your opportunities, but here's some free advice. If you sling your hook now I'll spare you the ignominy of being thrown out. I believe there are still a few camera crews loitering around outside waiting to catch something juicy for the one o'clock news. My boot up your pinstriped backside should suffice.'

'All right, I'm going.' Even now it annoyed James he was still being made to feel guilty by Austerly. 'Just remember, I could have helped you make some obscenely large amounts of money.'

'Money? Is that all you're interested in?'

Austerly sneered. 'Money's all that's ever mattered. I'm surprised. I thought you, of all people, would have understood that, but apparently not. You need a brain for this job!'

James had never been one for violence, but even he could be tested. The stapler hit Austerly square on the back of the head even as he dived through the door!

'And so, Mr Speaker, my tenure as Defence Secretary will be characterised by a vigorous drive towards greater efficiency, accountability and value for money. So often in the past we have seen an almost criminal wastage of resources. I duly give notice that this will stop!' James paused theatrically. The Commons was unusually full for his speech, which was something of a novelty for James – he was well acquainted with vast acres of empty green leather.

He felt nervous, as he always did when addressing the motley hordes and their snobbish, carefully cultured indifference, but that nervousness was admirably concealed behind a mask of supreme confidence. Only Angela and Celeste knew how he really felt. He imagined his Mistress sitting alone on the back-benches in her very finest strappery, a coiled whip hanging from her belt and Bertie perched at her shoulder. James slipped a hand in his trouser pocket and took comfort fingering the concealed outline of his tight leather punishment briefs. Goodness, his middle regions really were wrapped in a deliciously warm and snug embrace!

It had been a good speech, and the PM showed full support

by sitting beside him, smirking at his main adversary across the dispatch box, the formidable Vivian Bell.

Bell fully justified his position as Her Majesty's Leader of the Opposition. Strangely for such a high profile member from the other side of the political divide, he was also one of James's regular drinking partners, or at least he was when he could give his termagant wife the slip. Clara Bell possessed a tongue that could split tree trunks at three hundred paces, and there was an unofficial parliamentary committee fully engaged in thwarting her energetic ambitions to become an MP.

It was chaired by her husband,

There was a guarded murmur of approval. James's sudden appearance on the front bench was treated with caution. It was obvious they didn't like strangers. Strangers! What a joke – he'd been an MP for years – the fact was they didn't like nonentities, and the distressing truth was that as a nonentity, James qualified admirably.

'With this aim in view, I am initiating an urgent financial review by a small and flexible group of independent experts assisted by the Treasury.'

The PM nodded authoritatively. This was baloney, but nobody ever remembered what was said in the House.

'My aim is to transform the armed services into a modern, efficient, and flexible organisation.' Surprisingly, the speech was rather good. Much was in the general vein of what James was going to say anyway. Except for the last few lines, of course.

'Hear! Hear!' murmured the Premier dutifully. He scribbled a few notes on an order paper with his famous gold pen, a gift from the American Senate, only half aware of what James was saying. After all, the speech had been produced by his own talented writing team, so it was not surprising he was completely unprepared for James's bombshell.

James took a deep breath, shuffled his papers and promptly departed from the notes prepared for him by No. 10. 'The viability of major defence establishments located in central London will also be reviewed and if cheaper accommodation can be found elsewhere, then departments will be dispersed, and the huge amounts of money saved will be ring-fenced to buy state of the art equipment to support the finest forces in the world. British weapons and British technology to defend British interests!'

The PM looked up and frowned. He didn't remember this bit. Still, it sounded good. Nice to know Timbrill actually had some inventiveness. 'Very good, James,' he murmured, perfectly happy to encourage this minor streak of independence. 'Keep going.'

'The review will be led by three fully independent city auditors who have already been charged with the task. They have been granted unrestricted access and will report directly to me and I will present their findings to the Cabinet. Reviews have so often in the past been diluted by internal politics and diverted by vested interests, but I can assure you no such prevarication will occur this time. I have asked for a meticulous investigation into the costs of running *all* Ministry of Defence administrative departments and operational agencies, starting here in Whitehall, and those that cannot justify their existence in these rapidly changing times may well fall by the wayside.'

The Prime Minister dropped his files in shock, a reaction not entirely lost on the Opposition, nor missed by the cameras. Viv Bell perked up and grinned like a Cheshire cat. James forged on regardless. This was his moment. 'Since the end of the Cold War, the continually swelling levels of expenditure of these shadowy departments have remained largely unchallenged, but for no longer. This penetrating examination has already begun and will concentrate on identifying those areas where profligate bureaucracy runs unchecked, and will commence with – Ow!'

James jerked to a halt with a squeak of surprise at the sharp pain in the back of his thigh. There was a sudden collective gasp of shock in the chamber followed by a deathly silence. James looked down and to his utter amazement discovered he'd been stabbed.

By the PM!

Nonplussed, he gaped at the magnificently engraved golden shaft of the pen protruding from his thigh, then raised his eyes and stared into a face white with fury.

Chapter Six

'So what happened next?'

Celeste relaxed on the sofa with Bertie perched behind. He sat quietly with eyes half closed, floating along in that deliciously pleasant limbo-land between consciousness and slumber, a wing occasionally twitching.

'Well, there was a bit of a stunned silence,' said James.

'I can imagine.'

'Unusual for the House of Commons – more often than not there's some pompous twit shouting his mouth off or blustering in outraged froth about something pointless.'

'That's so true.'

'The PM literally dragged me back on to the front bench. He nearly pulled my trousers down in his haste!'

'How embarrassing. Were the cameras rolling?'

'Absolutely. I take it you missed the evening news?'

'Yes. Sebastian sneaked in to frighten Barnstaple and Bertie caught him red-handed. It took a while to calm things down.'

'Pity. It was the main headline. I hate being so high-profile. Anyway, Viv called the serjeant-at-arms, which created no end of fuss and a fair amount of shoving and gesticulating in the lobbies.'

'Not gesticulating in the lobbies!'

'I'm afraid so. He seems to think I should prosecute the Prime Minister for assault with a deadly weapon.'

'The pen is indeed mightier than the sword.'

'But not as pleasant as the whip, and losing my trousers would have been particularly humiliating since I was wearing a nice pair of leather briefs.'

'You do enjoy yourself at work, don't you?'

'In addition, the stripes from my last visit were still proudly flying their banner.'

'Yes, I recall I was rather keen with the crop.'

'I've no complaints, Mistress.'

'I should hope not!' Celeste protested with mock severity. 'Did the official Parliamentary nurse get your trousers off?'

'She did, but fortunately I managed to change out of my leathers and into something more conventional before reaching the medical room.'

'That was lucky.'

'Hello,' Bertie said cheerfully, emerging from his snooze and hopping down onto the sofa arm. 'I'm a plumber.'

'Is he on twenty-four hour call-out?' asked James, accustomed to such genial interruptions.

'This is BBC One,' the macaw announced gravely in received English. 'And now the news.'

'Bertie, do you want some nuts?'

'Ah,' murmured James. 'Blackmail, the last resort of the desperate.'

'Nuts, Bertie. Do you want some?' Celeste opened a drawer, extracted a few Brazils and let them clatter onto his feeding tray. Bertie looked around, his attention drawn to the familiar sound. 'Well? Do you?'

He knew the answer to this one. 'Yes, I do!' he chirruped, and scrambled back along the top of the sofa like a mountaineer negotiating a Himalayan col. A hop brought him back to his perch and he bent to inspect the bribe. It always worked. He knew if he pestered in a nice way he'd always manage to extract some small treat from his mum.

With Bertie's attention diverted, Celeste sat again. 'So what happened after the Prime Minister stabbed you? Now there's a sentence I never thought I'd ever utter,' she added dryly.

'I had a blazing row with him in his Commons office. He wanted to know what the hell I was trying to do. I told him I found the speech prepared for me appeared to be lacking in certain areas and so I rectified the omission, assuming this review covered all areas in the ministry.'

'Hence the references to all those anonymous departments in

the MoD.'

'Yes. Despite reminding him he'd assured me of his full support, it now appears he wasn't exactly planning to go that far and berated me soundly, at which point I felt a little righteous anger come to my rescue.'

'Oh dear!'

'I was quite impressive, even if I say it myself.' Celeste smiled at his ironic tone. 'I waved my ink and blood-stained trousers at him, accused him of an unjustified attack and threatened to resign on the spot. That blasted pen really hurt. Anyway, he backed off quicker than the Italian army in full flight, at the mention of resignation! The spectre of another departure from the MoD had a remarkably soporific effect. I was offered tea, the ultimate sign of reconciliation, and things progressed in a more civilised manner. The matter of my possible resignation was quietly shelved, which confirmed my assessment of the situation. Then I got to wondering why such an investigation should provoke so a violent reaction, after all, any ministry must, in the end, be accountable to Parliament.'

'James, has anyone ever told you how wonderfully innocent you are? I remember the way things were run in Brazil – what makes you think Britain is any better?'

'I'm sure corruption isn't as widespread in this country with our system of checks and balances, but at the same time if there are factions with their own agenda then I just want them rooted out, and an investigation into the accounts is one of the best ways of revealing what nasty little insects are scuttling around under the carpet. Suddenly, I realised how truly worried he was. I'll bet some of these covert agencies have secrets worth telling and the PM must have had involvement in some of them.'

'You'll get sacked or discredited before anything hits the newspapers. Or worse. Can you imagine what they would make of us?'

'The thought has crossed my mind, but as I've already pointed out I'm going to be out of a job after the next election anyway so I've nothing to lose by rocking the boat. Rather the opposite, actually; the public do like to see a minister doing his job. The press are definitely on my side for this one.'

'Will you retire?'

'That's the plan. My financial interests are just about sufficient to see me through to old age and I figure I can maybe boost my income with some memoirs if things get really desperate. I've seen some amusing things at Westminster over the years.'

That was another thing that Celeste liked about James. He wasn't greedy. 'But you'll get bored.'

'Hardly. I'll be far too busy looking after my cottage. I've always been a country bumpkin at heart. You can come to stay with Bertie, so what could be boring about that.'

'Country bumpkin!' announced Bertie from his perch. There was no telling what phrases appealed to that extraordinary mind. Celeste waited for a few moments but the macaw had nothing more to add so she returned her attention to James, adopting a more formal pose. 'Enough chat, now. You may begin.'

'Yes, Mistress.' He removed his jacket and hung it over the back of the chair. Tie, shirt, and socks followed. He folded his trousers neatly and stepped out of a pair of bright red silk boxers.

'Those are new.'

'Camden Market. Bargain pack of three. The others are in black and British Racing Green.'

'How appropriate.' Well-off by most standards, James still refused to pay the ridiculous prices demanded in the more popular West End stores. She appraised his naked body, pleased the easy life had not been entirely detrimental to his waistline. An embryonic erection nosed forward like a retriever scenting a fallen duck. James always began each encounter completely naked – a powerful reminder of his subservience – yet he had, and never would, he knew, see Celeste in any advanced stage of undress. 'Turn around.'

A line of fading stripes latticed his rump, purple and green on pale ivory. Each parallel line was deep and thin, barely a quarter of an inch from its neighbour. Sitting on a scalding hot Venetian blind would have created an almost identical pattern! She had been particularly fiendish during their last session and beaten him with more than her usual vigour. James had suffered his punishment with the stoicism of a true masochist, panting and puffing in the aromatic darkness of his smothering leather helmet.

His need for release was much greater now he had responsibility for the nation's defences, and Celeste had adjusted her chastisements accordingly. She noted with satisfaction the puncture in his thigh was properly dressed; however, the inadvertent injection of ink would certainly leave a permanent reminder of his encounter with the prime ministerial pen.

'You may dress.'

'Thank you, Mistress.' She noticed with satisfaction the angle of his erection had increased significantly.

James brought forward a heavy portmanteau from its place beside her bureau, unbuckled the lid and pulled out a great armful of black leather clothing. Items were laid out reverentially in a crescent at Celeste's feet like a ritual offering. She sat in silence, then pointed. 'This, the open hood, and your full suit.' James set aside the selected ensemble, its straps writhing like a nest of snakes. More often than not she preferred the simpler items of restraint that took just a few moments to render him helpless, but it was a Friday evening and they had plenty of time.

James tugged, laced, and buckled himself into his leather body suit, always conscious of her critical gaze. He swept back his hair and slid the strange helmet over his head, drawing the rear laces closed with gloved fingers to complete his encapsulation. Eyes peered out owlishly from oval apertures above a similar opening for his mouth. Silver poppers surrounded these openings, allowing a gag and blindfold to be snapped on easily. After minor adjustments, he knelt before his mistress in humble prostration and laid his face on the floor.

Celeste watched the entire procedure with a regal expression. James was good at dressing himself – heaven knows, he'd had enough practice! She stood and walked around his silent form. Needle-tipped stiletto heels clattered delightfully on the parquet. His eyes, now encircled by leather, followed the progress of her gracefully arched feet, so perfectly presented in polished grey patent court shoes with slender ankle straps.

'Trust me, I'm a doctor,' said Bertie, for no discernible reason. 'Can I wax your legs?'

'Hush, my love.' There was always a danger of the macaw interrupting the delicate atmosphere in the salon, but both Celeste and James would never dream of banishing him to another room. In an odd way, his occasional comments added a touch of normality to the proceedings. 'Eat your nuts like a good boy.'

'Yes, mummy.' Bertie lost interest in them and turned his attention elsewhere.

Celeste pointed at the floor. 'Down!' she ordered. James lay on his belly spread-eagled, arms and legs pointing to the four corners of the room, his body held rigid. Celeste tapped a light dusting of talc over his fingers and toes. 'I'm now going upstairs to dress. Don't move. Understood?'

'Completely, Mistress. Please, feel free to take your time.'

'Indeed I shall, and when I return we'll get those laces really tightened up!'

The door shut quietly leaving James on his own, his chin resting on the floor. It rarely took Celeste less than an hour to prepare for the evening. He held himself perfectly still since the slightest smudge in the talc would betray any movement to her eagle eye, and that would, perversely, result in her not punishing him – and he did so want to feel her whip. It was bondage without the bonds. He shut his eyes and dreamed of his beloved mistress, acutely aware of a stiffened erection jabbing against his belly.

Bored with eating, Bertie preened for a while, cleaning his cobalt wing feathers fastidiously, chattering and whistling to himself. Once satisfied with his appearance, he let his mind wander in an aimless fashion. The room was warm and quiet, so it was not surprising a light snooze took him unawares.

Some time later, he awoke with a start from a delicious dream in which he soared effortlessly over the green crowns of an endless forest. He picked at an apple in a half-hearted way then, refreshed from his slumber, suddenly felt in need of some mental stimulation. He cocked his head to one side. Now what was that? Surely it was a new carpet in front of the sofa. Bertie scrambled from his perch and hopped down off the sofa to take a closer look.

James, too, had sunken into a meditative trance and was startled out of his own sublimely erotic fantasies by the sudden scratch of claws on wood. He peered out through the oval eye openings in the leather helmet. A pair of scaly feet appeared, advancing with the curious waddling gait characteristic of macaws. Sickled talons clacked on the polished floor. A long tapering tail swished along behind, sweeping from side to side like a bright blue besom.

'Oh, no,' he sighed. The last thing he needed was the attention of a clever and mischievous macaw. The blue-trousered legs came closer. Those barbarous claws looked absolutely lethal. It would have been easy just to sit up and fuss Bertie, perhaps even persuade him back onto his perch, but doing so would irritate Celeste. She expected him to remain absolutely motionless. Besides, he knew from past experience his chances of controlling the macaw were practically zero – Bertie was a good boy and never listened to anyone except his mum.

'Shoo!' prompted James hopefully. The exclamation made no impact at all. He watched with a sinking heart as the pacing legs appeared first on one side of his head and then the other. Bertie circled warily, then closed on his target. A brightly coloured face suddenly popped into James's view, curious and attentive, with large brown eyes encircled by sunshine yellow spectacles.

Dipping forward and with tail lifted high, Bertie dropped his head to the floor, twisted his neck and peered upside-down at the hooded features. An eye glared back at him surrounded by the strange black skin.

'Scat! Scram! Skedaddle!' hissed James. Normally so polite to the bird, he felt that he could, under the circumstances, be excused for a temporary lapse in manners.

'Hello,' said Bertie cheerfully. 'Who are you?'

'Pope Pius the Fourteenth,' replied James sarcastically.

'Really? I'm a coastguard.'

'Congratulations. Filey's nice at this time of year!'

Bertie didn't understand, so he reverted to a well-proven approach. 'Nice hat.'

'Thank you.'

'I like hats,' the macaw announced firmly.

'I do, too.'

'I like pears. Do you have any pears?'

'Not on me, oddly enough.'

'Do you have any nuts?' This was one of his favourite phrases.

'I have two and you're definitely not going anywhere near them!'

'Nuts. I like nuts,' confirmed Bertie in the tone a small child would use when describing its favourite food.

'I know. You keep telling me every time I come here. There are nuts in your tray, why don't you go and see,' added James hopefully.

Bertie straightened to peer up at his stand. He knew all about his tray. Tray was a simple word, often spoken, and he made the association between it and the food it so often contained. James held his breath and fervently hoped the macaw would return to his perch but after a few moments consideration the blue face reappeared once more, upside-down, feathered crown pressing on the parquet, neck twisted and eyes bright with impishness. He showed no inclination to comply with James's request. 'Banana, perhaps?' he enquired politely.

'Sorry, fresh out,' mumbled James. 'Please, be a good boy and leave me alone.'

Bertie scampered around James's head to peer in at the other eye. James decided not to answer any more questions. It only encouraged further conversation. 'Hello? Anyone home?' When this brought no response Bertie moved a step closer. James stiffened. God, the damned bird was huge. The two stared at each other in silence while ten seconds expended themselves in a leisurely way, then Bertie suddenly lunged.

'Oi! Get lost, Bertie!' James protested angrily. The macaw

grabbed at a popper, obviously attracted by the shining steel. He tugged hard as if pulling up a worm, but his feet skidded on the smooth floor and he lost his grip. Claws clicked like castanets swinging in a gale, scrabbling for a hold. James resisted stoutly, still determined not to disturb the delicacy of his talcum powder prison and cursing the playful bird silently. One had to be careful what one said to such a perfect mimic.

Suddenly tiring, Bertie released the popper and scuttled away out of view. Not seeing where he was going proved even more disconcerting for James. Vague noises betrayed the macaw's circumnavigation around his rigid form. Bertie hopped over one outstretched arm and decided to test the new rug for comfort. With a flash of blue he settled on James's arse.

Unsurprisingly, the rug flinched.

Equally unsurprisingly, Bertie consolidated his grip to ensure his balance.

An urgent need for complete immobility swept over James. He froze. Needle-tipped claws grazed his buttocks, tightening reflexively at his slightest movement. Bertie walked from cheek to cheek, testing each globe for resilience by bobbing up and down, but he seemed doubtful as to which of the two was most comfortable and so waddled up James's spine to perch on his head. The leather helmet, although substantial, offered very little protection. Sweat dripped from the end of James's nose and collected under the hood. He desperately hoped the macaw would tire and return to his perch, but Bertie seemed perfectly content and settled down to roost. Unfortunately, as with all birds, the tendons in his legs automatically tightened his grip when he sat.

James groaned softly, not daring to startle the macaw. His head felt like it was clamped in a vice. Deadly claws grazed his skin through the leather. There was no doubt the slightest movement would now draw blood, so he gritted his teeth and prayed for Celeste's speedy return. Apparently satisfied with his new nesting spot, Bertie began to purr, the vibrations rattling James's teeth.

Oblivious to the drama unfolding downstairs, Celeste was in no hurry to dress. Sebastian sidled in while she was applying make-up and rubbed against her legs before meandering away to some private corner for a preparatory snooze in advance of his main sleep of the evening. The Persian approached the door with increasing trepidation and peered timidly around the corner before hurrying on furtively. Celeste had never discovered what particular incident precipitated this cautious behaviour but she was sure Bertie was at the bottom of the cat's nervousness. The macaw, as one would expect, had been entirely uncommunicative on the subject.

'Well, what shall it be?' she asked nobody in particular as she stood naked before the mirror. She tossed her luxuriant copper locks about her shoulders in the way shampoo advertisements intimated was irresistible to men and smiled coquettishly at herself. 'Something stern, I think. I believe my poor slave downstairs has had a busy week ordering new missiles for the navy.' She smiled at the thought of James still lying on the floor trying to bore his wayward stiffy through her parquet.

The cream leather catsuit fitted perfectly, accentuating her silhouette, her waist narrowed by a wide corset belt. She eased on thigh-length boots, tied off the red silk laces in big bows, and paced back and forth, entirely comfortable in the towering heels. She then decided on a helmet. Normally content to tie her hair up, she knew James would respond more if she was hooded. The helmet was open-faced and framed her features in an oval border trimmed in black piping. She tugged her copper pony-tail out through a short vertical funnel at the crown and let it tumble freely.

Celeste nodded satisfaction at her dramatic reflection while slipping on a pair of thin kid gloves. She exuded that aura of authoritative competence and overt sensuality which James desired so much. She checked her appearance carefully, turning this way and that, her tumbling ponytail draped over one shoulder, then gathered up her crop, bullwhip, several pairs of handcuffs, and sauntered downstairs.

'Oh, Bertie, you little scamp, what are you doing?'

She found him perched on James's head like a blue phoenix sitting on an ebony gargoyle, the span of his claws easily enough to embrace the entire crown. It was a comical sight. James opened his eyes at the sound of Celeste's chuckle, his concentration so great he had not heard her approach.

'Help!' he squeaked. 'Please!'

Claws still clasped his head, but the grip suddenly loosened as Bertie hopped down onto the floor and ran towards her like an eager pirate in baggy blue breeches. Still determined not to move, James could just see the macaw standing in front of a pair of cream stiletto boots. 'Mummy,' the bird said, looking upwards. 'I love you.'

'I know, my precious, and I love you, too. Here, on your perch.' There was a flutter and Bertie swept upwards, disappearing from James's truncated view. 'Now be a good boy and keep quiet,' she cooed.

'Yes. Be quiet. Watch TV.'

'Later.' Celeste fussed over her beloved pet until he settled, then returned to James's prostrate form. She examined the talcum powder for signs of disturbance. 'Excellent,' she murmured. 'Very impressive – under the circumstances.'

'Thank you, Mistress. I had a powerful incentive to keep very still.'

'So I saw. How is your head?'

'I think the bleeding's stopped.'

'Considering the damage those claws can do, you got off lightly. Why didn't you just put him back on his perch?'

'And move? No – he wasn't too heavy. Besides, in a perverse way, I quite enjoyed the companionship. He's always such an amiable chap.' James still lay stretched out on the floor gazing in adoration at the slender heels of Celeste's boots not twelve inches from his face.

'I have to say it did look amusing.'

'Things like that only happen to me,' he complained with a sigh. That was true enough – she sincerely hoped he had more luck with Britain's nuclear trigger. 'Bertie's very inquisitive, isn't he?'

'Yes, he is.' Celeste bent to tighten laces and jerk straps a notch tighter before snapping one pair of handcuffs around his ankles and the other around his wrists, his arms settling in the small of his back, fingers curled like black claws. He struggled briefly to test the extent of his bondage, but then Celeste brought her riding crop down on his buttocks without warning, the flat crack of leather on leather instantly answered by a startled squeal of pain and shock.

Too stunned to speak, James fought to contain the searing line of fire planted across his seat. He jerked spasmodically and screwed his eyes shut against the tears as the burning peaked before slowly subsiding into a wonderfully effusive glowing.

Jesus, that felt good!

All the problems and dilemmas at work, the careful mediation between pompous civil servants and belligerent staff officers, the tiresome compromises and endless massaging of egos, the political machinations and back-biting in Cabinet, all of it simply melted away, purged by the exquisite sensation flooding through his body. Serenity descended on James like a balmy mist floating down from heaven itself.

Celeste sat on the sofa, composing herself. She placed her booted feet together and tapped the polished tips with her crop. 'Come! These need cleaning,' she announced primly.

'Yes, Mistress.' With an occasional creak and rattle, James levered himself forward on his belly like a great stiff slug and kissed one toe with profound reverence. A pink tongue wriggled out of the hole in his helmet and skipped over the instep before running up and down the heel. The cream leather was already immaculate – Celeste had never worn them outside the house – but the ritual was crucially important, reinforcing the nature of their curious but profoundly fulfilling relationship.

Celeste watched negligently while each boot was lovingly licked. James performed his task with joyous humility, but was aware of the limits placed on his attentive osculation. Everything up to the calf was, as always, his territory, but anything above remained strictly out of bounds. He glimpsed up at her shapely legs. The glorious mysteries found between those soft thighs would always be denied him, but no matter. James was utterly content with the situation. He idolised Celeste with every fibre of his body. She enchanted and bewitched his soul, yet he had no desire to be anything other than her slave. In turn, she found his attentive submission, humour and high pain threshold rare qualities and perfect for her own unique desires.

Celeste massaged his face with her feet. He rolled on to his back and lay supine, arms and legs still bound. The smooth tan soles rested on his cheeks and forehead, blocking his vision. She noticed the silhouette of a splendidly stout erection tenting the leather over his belly and tapped at it with the crop. James started violently and one of her feet slipped from his face.

'Clumsy!' she muttered in mock irritability. 'I'll have to bind you properly. Get the harness!'

He crawled across the floor, inching forward by twisting from side to side, and gripped the writhing mass of strappery in his teeth before returning, dragging the harness behind him to lay it at her feet like an obedient spaniel presenting a stick. She took the harness from him and pressed down on the back of his head with one foot, squashing his nose against the floor. 'Tell me, why should I bother to use this harness?'

'Mistress, I might not be able to help myself moving, so I need to be restrained properly. Tightly.'

'Well, I must confess this does look good on you. I do like the neatness of the straps and the way they divide up the target area. It helps me to be more accurate.'

'The patterns you draw are aesthetically pleasing,' agreed James, sniffing her parquet. He recalled the slovenly stripes of some of his former acquaintances. There was no artistry from a working girl – the marks on his bum sometimes looked like the scribblings of a drunken spider.

Or a Jackson Pollock!

'I agree it's important you can't move,' she said. He heard the jingle of the handcuff keys as they skittered across the polished floor. Celeste had tossed them into a far corner. 'Fetch!' she ordered. 'Then we'll see about getting you properly restrained.'

James found his head released and set off once again, shuffling forwards in a serpentine manner. Bertie watched him pass by. 'Fetch!' he repeated faultlessly.

'I am,' muttered James, throwing a sideways glance at the macaw perched above him.

83

'Hush, Bertie,' murmured Celeste. James retrieved the keys with his teeth and returned, gazing in adoration at her leather-shrouded form. The hood framed her face, accentuating her intent stare and flushed cheeks. Copper hair sprouted from the funnel at her crown like a burnished fountain before cascading in glorious waves over one shoulder. She looked magnificent beyond measure. No woman could be more self-assured, more confident, more powerful, more puissant. She was a goddess and he worshipped her without question.

Celeste removed the handcuffs and sat back, one gloved hand draped over the arm of the sofa. James knelt to kiss it humbly before slipping into the harness. He secured his legs together at ankle, knee and thigh before buckling the waist and chest belts and fastening a deep collar around his neck. The broad bands crimped his leather suit. Celeste waited until he had finished, then turned him around, took his arms and fed them through a series of loops behind his back. The buckles were tightened with a jerk. She uncoiled her bullwhip, stepped back a pace, and struck him across the rump with no mean vigour.

James shrieked. Impressively.

Bertie started at the sudden sound and watched him crumple to the floor. Fortunately, the house was detached. Their kind of foreplay tended to be sprinkled with such auditory outbursts and these would certainly have attracted neighbourly attention had Celeste lived in a tower block.

'Now we can't have you making a noise, can we.'

'N-no, Mistress,' he panted querulously. 'Please, I beg you to silence me.'

'As you wish.' Celeste extracted a ferociously large gag from the portmanteau, knelt beside him and forced it into his mouth, poppers snapping to hold it in place. A blindfold covered his eyes. Now totally helpless, he jerked and writhed on the floor under the accurate rain of blows extravagantly applied by his beloved mistress, breath rasping. She wielded the whip with skill and verve, planting its stinging tip all over his bottom.

And all the while his excitement grew.

Bertie watched the ritual with casual interest, noting with approval Celeste's enthusiastic chastisement. She dominated The Kneeling Man in much the same way he dominated Sebastian, and as such her actions seemed quite natural to him. It appeared his mum was experiencing no difficulty with her guest and would not be requiring his help again, so he sipped a little water and settled down for a nap, flinching in unison with James at the crack of well-aimed rawhide on leathered buttock.

Presently, judging that her slave had suffered enough, Celeste tossed the whip onto the sofa, attached a leash to his collar and jerked him towards the door. His sinuous movements enchanted her. Writhing like a snake on his belly, he strained from side to side, puffing and panting like a bronchitic steam locomotive with a leaky boiler. They meandered out of the salon and across the hall to the cellar door. She slid James down the wooden stairs head first, holding on to his ankles to stop him falling uncontrollably, each undignified bump accompanied with a heavily muffled grunt. From there it was only a short crawl to their goal.

The wardrobe stood tall and broad, a monument of Victorian confidence in solid English oak, ornate and impossibly ugly, with Gothic influences in its soaring columns and grotesquely intricate carvings. To James, it was a dark box of mystery and delight.

Celeste took the key from a hook beside the stairs and unlocked the full-length double doors. The insides were heavily padded. Even the doors were covered in thick panels of buttoned black leather. A sweet aroma wafted out. She dragged James to his feet, reversed him into the welcoming darkness and secured him upright with a great host of supple straps. He struggled a little, as he always did, but it was just a token effort – he would have just as happily jumped inside of his own accord. Celeste folded a pair of long leather flaps together over his feet, joined them with a zip and tugged slowly upwards. The flaps enclosed James in a cocoon from toe to neck rather like a bizarre sleeping bag, snugging tightly to his form, wrapping, concealing, submerging.

'Comfortable?'

'Mmmmph!'

'Is that a yes?'

'Mrrmmph!'

'Or a no?'

'Mmm! Grruummm!'

Celeste chuckled at the little interchange. The bag was checked again, then she slipped a matching hood over his head and tied off a drawstring, leaving just an open circular ring over his nostrils for breathing.

How splendid he looked!

Celeste's compulsion to place men into positions of respectful subservience had grown inexorably over the years. She never doubted the path she'd taken, never felt for one moment her pursuits were in any way aberrant. Her desires remained an abiding passion, introducing structure and meaning into her life. It was a calling which continued to give her endless pleasure and each time she mummified James she experienced a deeply spiritual satisfaction. The beauty of her creation engaged all her senses; the aesthetic symmetry of his gently bulging body, snug and secure in its womb-like enclosure, the accompanying creak of tensioned strapping, and the sweet, earthy odour of warm leather wafting gently around the cellar.

The double doors swung shut. Bolts slid home. The key turned with a well-oiled click. She hung it on the hook again, took one last look at the silent wardrobe and its blissfully contented package, then slowly climbed the stairs. Her breasts felt heavy. Heat between her legs betrayed a profound excitement. Nimble fingers promised repeated pleasures. Thank heavens for Purple Pippa, her intimate buzzing buddy.

'Good night, James,' she said softly, pausing on the threshold, then turned out the light and locked the cellar door.

Chapter Seven

'Will you stop your damned fidgeting!' grumbled Coberley. He sat in the back of a nondescript white Transit van staring at a sophisticated military thermal imaging monitor. Pritchard was barely able to shuffle past him in the cramped interior. 'This thing is tricky enough to operate without you bouncing around looking for your stupid sandwiches.'

'I'm sure I put them down the back of the seats.' Pritchard finally squeezed behind his partner and, stooping to avoid banging his head on the roof, reversed himself to sit on the Elsan chemical toilet bolted in one corner. He looked around, continuing his search, but there weren't too many places of concealment inside the cluttered vehicle. Without much hope, he picked up a cardboard box and rummaged inside amongst the jemmies, Slim Jims, latex gloves, Tasers, and CS gas canisters, generating furtive rustling sounds in the dimmed red light. 'Goddammit, how can they just disappear? Are they by your feet?'

'No,' replied Coberley without moving.

'You didn't even look!' Pritchard objected peevishly.

'Give me a break, Bob. I'm actually trying to work here.'

The two men had spent all day and most of the evening parked a few hundred yards down the road from Celeste's house, so little wonder they were finally getting on each others' nerves. Greenwich did that to some people. Neither liked using the van much, although both had to admit it often proved to be extremely handy as a mobile base of operations when out conducting their nefarious deeds.

Strange scarlet shapes floated before his eyes. The actual

detector head transmitting the colourful image had been stuck on the salon patio doors earlier that morning while Celeste was still asleep. The tiny probe was encased in a protective blob of silicone superbly camouflaged to resemble a dollop of bird droppings, so it was no surprise the device was designated with the appropriate MoD acronym, CRAP – Counter-surveillance Remote All-weather Probe. The probe was easily sensitive enough to detect a thermal gradient through the double glazing and curtains inside, converting a heat signature into a graduated spectrum of colour. Cooler temperatures appeared in blue and green, warmer in yellows and reds, and this rainbowed image gave them a clear view of what was happening inside the salon, while an astonishingly sensitive micro-microphone picked up any sound.

The CRAP was supplemented by UDDERS, a Ultra-high Definition Digital Electronic Reconnaissance System comprising a powerful night vision camera lodged under a leafy shrub on the edge of the lawn. Operated remotely from Coberley's control panel, UDDERS provided an excellent overview of the rear of the property via an ultra-high definition digital signal. He sat at the cramped console fingering a joystick gingerly. The camera responded to his commands and played slowly from window to window before returning to the larger full-length double doors leading into the salon. Although pitch black outside, it, too, was still capable of providing an extraordinarily sharp image. With the camera outside and the ingeniously disguised probe covering the interior, Coberley was satisfied he had all angles covered, and everything CRAP and UDDERS saw was digitally stored on a hard drive at his elbow, ready for later analysis if required.

The grubby white Transit, despite its scruffy appearance, had nonetheless been tweaked by some serious petrol-heads, with extensive carbon fibre bulletproofing, big fat tyres, upgraded suspension and brakes, Kevlar racing clutch and a supercharger the size of a beach-ball strapped to the bored-out, nitrous-boosted engine, a combination of which provided performance straight from the Scalded Cat Institute of Motoring. Although almost new, the van had been expertly "distressed" to help it blend in more with its urban surroundings. Darkened rear windows fitted with armoured one-way glass allowed the occupants to see out while at the same time discouraging external inquisitiveness, and a number of small projections spaced along each side panel might have looked like the former fixings of advertising signs but were, in fact, a combination of fish-eye camera lenses and nozzles for spraying tear gas. The interior, although uncomfortably cramped for the operators, was fully equipped with all the latest real-time surveillance and satellite communication hardware the advanced technical sections of GCHQ could provide. In addition to the Elsan, of course. Some things never change.

Coberley had confirmed Celeste was the only human occupant of the house, but she was not alone. Several smaller heat sources occasionally moved. He identified the parrot immediately, primarily because the report stated it would be there, but it took him a while to figure out the tiny infra-red signal appearing intermittently in one corner was likely to be a sleeping hamster or some other such nasty little rodent. All seemed tranquil, then the heat signature of another creature appeared, one that scuttled hurriedly across the room towards the patio doors.

'Hey up, Bob, she's moving,' he murmured. 'Coming directly towards us.' Both men were far too experienced to allow Celeste's proximity to the CRAP to rattle them. It was highly unlikely she'd notice the minuscule probe nestling in the centre of its silicone bird dropping. Coberley switched to UDDERS just as Celeste drew back the curtains and opened the door. 'How sweet, she's putting out the cat.' He witnessed her actions with perfect clarity. Celeste held the door ajar and a fluffy bundle scampered outside. Coberley zoomed in. 'That's interesting.'

'What is?'

'The cat.'

'Why? Does it have two heads?' The door closed and the curtains were drawn again. Celeste left the salon for a moment and so Coberley, for want of something better to do, continued to track the Persian as it strolled insouciantly across the lawn towards the shrubbery, no doubt to seek out its favoured loo stop.

'Well, come on now, that's not really very likely, is it!'

'I'm ever hopeful.'

'Sorry to disappoint. My point is that the cat's one of those long-haired types.'

'So?' snorted Pritchard dismissively. He was a top-class field operative with the most secretive agency in the United Kingdom, a man with the highest possible security classification, an unobtrusive visitor to many of the more troublesome countries around the globe, an expert in a wide range of espionage techniques, black belt in any number of obscure, oriental fist-flailing Grasshopper martial arts and totally fluent in Russian and German, however, his interest in the nocturnal habits of cuddlesome domesticated quadrupeds was, it had to be said, minimal.

'So how do they wipe their bums with all that hair?'

'How the hell should I know?'

'Must get a bit messy.'

'I sincerely hope your observation isn't based on personal experience.'

'A mite gooey, wouldn't you say?'

'Oddly enough, I'm not interested.'

Coberley smiled. 'I'll bet Bloxham suffers from the same problem.' Rod Bloxham was another JSON operative and the only officer in the department to sport any facial hair. A broad isthmus of black beard connected each ear via a forested crescent around the jaw, knitting everything together into one unbroken hirsute jungle through which appeared only eyes, nose and, just occasionally, lips. Coberley guessed that, when it came to matters of hygiene, his colleague and the cat quite possibly shared the same logistical problems of cleanliness.

'Call me provincial, but it's a thought I find strangely repellent!' said Pritchard, pulling a face.

'That's the one thing separating us from the lower species, you know.'

'What is?'

'We can't lick our own backsides!'

'You really are truly horrible at times.'

'Although I believe there's a girl in a brothel in Hamburg who can disprove that theory.'

'Really? Is there a website?' The Transit had full roaming broadband capabilities and some clever software patches allowing them to bypass all known password protection systems. Just the ticket to access the occasional smutty porn site to while away the hours when things got really boring.

'How should I know?'

'Well that's no good.'

'Did Bloxham ever tell you about the time he hid a micro flash card in his pubes?'

'No, and please, for the love of all that's good and holy, don't elaborate further.'

'Couldn't find it.'

'What?'

'He lost it. He had to be scanned with a metal detector. Migrated around to his back hair.'

'Are you serious?'

Coberley chuckled. 'Nah, course not. Wasn't his back hair at all – it was hidden in his navel!'

Pritchard sighed heavily. 'Listen,' he said in a pained voice. 'I know you like to pass the time bringing up these little anecdotes, but could you please pass the next ten minutes bringing up some silence. Please? Just for me?'

'Sure. No problem,' replied Coberley. There was a five-second pause, which appeared to be the absolute limit of his resolve. 'Anyway, going back to Hamburg, they reckon there's a higher concentration of contortionists in the brothels there than anywhere else on earth. Fancy that.'

'Great,' said Pritchard dryly. 'Just get on with it, will you.'

'You're unusually tetchy tonight.' Coberley shifted UDDERS again with a touch of the joystick and saw Sebastian's head jerk around. 'Damn! The cat's heard the motor drive. It's coming over.' He watched the image wax in size. Sebastian ducked under the leafy bush and bent to sniff at the compact camera. Coberley saw its nose loom larger and larger until it was so close the lens was unable to focus.

'Oh, cock, no!'

'What's going on?' Pritchard asked sharply.

'I don't believe it. The blasted cat's just taken a leak over my UDDERS.' He recoiled with a jerk as Sebastian's copious spray hit the lens. The Persian appeared anxious to smother the alien scent of carbon fibre and plastic with his own ammoniac odour and watered with vigour, tail vertical, rear end trembling and head turned to check his aim was true. When finished, he looked back with what Coberley swore was a smug catty grin on his furry face before strolling away to start his nightly patrol.

'Cobblers!' exclaimed Pritchard with real feeling. 'Now that's going to stink! One of us is going to have to sneak out and clean the damned thing.'

'Too right. That's a valuable piece of kit. Hugo will have a fit if some congealed cat's pee gums up the works.'

'Yeah, but who's going to do it?'

There was an awkward silence. Both were unwilling to volunteer. Both knew exactly what the other was thinking. 'We'll toss,' suggested Coberley amiably. He had a good record against Pritchard and fished into his pocket. There was a spinning flicker of metal. 'Heads!' he called. They both bent to examine the coin in the faint red illumination.

Pritchard's shoulders slumped. He muttered a heartfelt imprecation under his breath.

'Don't forget your tissue,' replied Coberley with a prim snigger, pleased he'd avoided that distasteful little job.

'It's not bloody fair,' grumbled Pritchard, like a pensioner opening his council tax bill.

'I believe we applied a mathematically sound principle of selection via a commonly agreed democratic decision.'

'Yeah, right, you conceited sod!'

'You always were a bad loser.' Coberley returned to his task, switching from the somewhat degraded image provided by the dripping UDDERS back to the CRAP. Using some clever filtering programmes, he was able to smooth out the distortion created by the curtains and focussed on the stationary figure. The woman quite plainly sat at a bureau. After a few moments, Coberley realised she had started to write. 'Like puppy dog's noses,' he said softly.

'Now what are you dribbling on about?'

'Her nipples. They're cold!'

'Trust you to notice that.' There was a faint air of disgust in Pritchard's voice. The thought of handling the soiled UDDERS had dampened his enthusiasm for the mission.

'She's got nice round tits, certainly big enough to keep your ears toasting on a cold winter's morning!'

Pritchard exploded. 'For God's sake, you're using state of the art equipment the Russians would sell their grandmothers to copy! Each piece of CRAP is a tour-de-force of emerging nanotechnology and can switch from infra-red to image intensifier to normal vision at the flick of a button. It's completely undetectable, remote controlled up to a distance of six miles, can laser range for precision targeting and was developed after years of painstaking research at the cutting edge of data processing miniaturisation. It is the ultimate in sophisticated surveillance equipment and costs the best part of ninety grand a pop. It's the first device sensitive enough to see clearly through curtains and runs indefinitely on a solar powered battery that is in itself too damned clever for its own good – and all you can use it for is to satisfy your unwholesome perversions! There are times when you really do make me puke!' be fulminated bitterly.

'So you don't want a peek, then?'

'Don't be a prat, shift over!' sniggered Pritchard immediately. The two men swapped places in a jiffy. The CRAP was extraordinarily sensitive and gave an excellent image. 'Oh, yeah, I see what you mean. Lovely. Erect and very kissable,' he murmured with obvious appreciation. He had no difficulty in identifying Celeste's contours. She sat with legs crossed, chin in cupped palm, and wrote with quick certainty. Occasionally, she paused with pen between lips and looked up as if for inspiration. Because the CRAP was working on infrared and consequently sensitive only to heat, the colour gradient revealed that indeed her nipples were colder than the rest of her body, as were her fingers and the tips of her ears and nose. 'She should be going to bed soon. What's the time?'

'Ten fifteen.' Coberley had finally located Pritchard's supper lurking behind a fire extinguisher. There was a faint crackling of cling film and an odour of tuna filled the van. 'Bloody Norah, Bob, this is disgusting! Can't you get your missus to put something less rancid in your sandwiches? These smell like a prossie's gusset.'

Pritchard smiled. They always needled each other out in the field. It relieved the tension and made the time pass more enjoyably. Perhaps that was why they worked so well together. 'If you think that smells, get a load of this!'

He farted. Spectacularly. Three bars adagio, followed by a brief but entertaining encore. It was a full-on anal *a cappella* of which any man would have been proud. Swift revenge for losing the toss.

'Bugger me!' protested Coberley, waving his hands about to disperse the unwholesome odour, but there wasn't much chance of escape in the back of the van. 'That's a bit evil, you dirty-arsed bastard!'

'Went down the Bombay Duck last night. Tucked into a beef phal with sag aloo and two Peshwari nans, all washed down with three pints of gut-rot, make-you-blind cider,' announced Pritchard proudly. 'Bloody gorgeous it was, too, a fine example of traditional English cuisine.' He concentrated on Celeste's image and ignored Coberley's gasping protests as something truly deadly wafted through the Transit, curling paint and corroding unprotected metal surfaces. What was she doing? Who wrote nowadays when you could easily pick up the phone or send a text? He continued to watch intently, then the answer hit him. 'Greg, I think she's writing her diary.'

Coberley instantly forgot his complaints. 'Sure it's not a letter?'

'Yeah. She's just finished and is flicking back through.' Both men knew such journals were a fertile source of information. A woman's diary reigned supreme because it was so much more expressive than a man's. Women opened their hearts to their diaries in a way that often made for torrid reading. It was a genetic thing. Like shoe shopping. 'What's the betting Dickless Jimmy's in there.'

'More than evens. Call him!'

Pritchard punched up a number on his mobile. It was a very special mobile, keystroke scrambled and encrypted. Even GCHQ couldn't eavesdrop on conversations from this phone. Chaplain answered before the second ring.

'Yes?' It was a bit terse. Perhaps he'd been trying to hump his wife again. Chaplain may be just about the most powerful man in Britain but it was well-known around the office he couldn't get a stiffy!

'We think she has a diary.' There was a pause while this information was absorbed. Pritchard continued to stare at the screen, the phone held to his ear. The woman finished reading, placed the book into an internal drawer and shut the bureau. She then stroked the parrot from neck to tail, fussing it lovingly. Soft murmurings of endearment were duly recorded by the micro-microphone, as was a strange muted resonance that sounded suspiciously like purring. The image was so detailed he could easily see her lips moving.

'What do you think, Bob?'

Pritchard knew exactly what Chaplain meant. He flipped over to UDDERS again and scanned the walls and roof carefully for some minutes through the soiled lens. Chaplain waited in silence.

'I can't see any alarm on the house. Odd for this neighbourhood. The patio doors are the standard wooden rubbish. Checked them out this morning when we put in our CRAP. I figure we should be in and out in two minutes, twenty to photocopy the diary and a few minutes to tidy up. This'll be a doddle. There's nobody else about.'

What he meant was that there was nobody else *human* about. Pritchard, of course, completely dismissed Bertie's presence. The curious absence of an alarm should have been ample warning.

Chaplain sighed. He wasn't concerned about the legality of his actions – JSON operatives had burgled numerous houses, tapped countless phones, intercepted sackfuls of mail, and threatened, assaulted, and blackmailed sundry unfortunates over the years with complete disregard for any law. No, it wasn't a sense of moral outrage that made him pause, more a premonition of doom. He trusted his instincts, and for some inexplicable reason his instincts screamed at him. However, his desperate need to dispatch Timbrill before the auditors knocked on the door overcame his caution. This was an unmissable opportunity.

'OK. Go ahead. When you've finished, bug out and set up outside Timbrill's flat.'

The phone went dead. Pritchard stared at Coberley's faint silhouette and nodded. The other man switched on the portable laser scanner, leaned back in his chair and put his feet up on the console. 'Anyone for a tuna sandwich?' he asked.

They waited nearly two hours before changing into black coveralls. The image of Celeste had long departed the salon, leaving the signatures of the parrot and hamster alone in the room. A bedroom light had glowed for a while, then been extinguished. The house lay in darkness. Outside, the neighbourhood was silent and deserted. At just after one, the two men slipped out of the Transit, took a long, hard look in every direction, then stole along the empty street, over the wall and into Celeste's garden. Pritchard retrieved the soiled UDDERS camera, wrapped it in a plastic bag and stowed it away. He grimaced in disgust at the lingering miasma of stale tomcat.

They paused for a moment to check over the house again. There was no cry of warning and so, hugging the deeper shadows, they trotted around the edge of the lawn with backs bent and crept up to the salon doors. Both pulled on balaclavas to complete their trendy outfits in burglar black, and each wore two pairs of thin latex gloves, well aware that fingerprints could still be deposited through a single glove thickness. Neither intended to leave any traces of their visit. Pritchard peeled the CRAP detector off the glass pane and slipped it into his pocket, keeping watch as Coberley picked the lock in under ten seconds. The door opened silently and the men glided inside like spectral shadows.

The only sound was the regular ticking of a clock.

Pritchard left the door ajar but ensured the curtains were

fully drawn to seal in the light, then flicked on an LED pencil torch. They threaded their way around the furniture to the bureau. He lowered the lid and played his torch over its neat innards. Assorted bills were slotted into a series of small compartments. A battered sweet tin held a bundle of twenty-pound notes wrapped in an elastic band. Coberley ignored this and continued to search swiftly. He opened an inner drawer and smiled. Celeste's diary lay inside with some letters. He saw the House of Commons crest and took them without bothering to check the contents, then reached towards the precious book.

''Ello, 'ello, 'ello – what's going on here, then?' Lights flared, the sudden brilliance dazzling both intruders. They whipped around, stunned by the curiously throaty male voice behind them. Automatically, Coberley separated from Pritchard to divide the attention of the man, snatched a telescopic baton out of his pocket and snapped it open in a lightning defensive sweep, crouching with legs planted wide for balance. Expanding out to its full length, the steel bar gave him confidence. It was an excellent weapon and he was skilled in its use. He possessed no moral qualms over using it and both of them would certainly drop any person trying to prevent their escape. They had done so in the past with clinical brutality. No prisoners were taken when burgling for No. 10.

Bertie sat on his perch, his claw still covering the special light switch attached at one end. Celeste had fitted it so he could stay up if he wanted. He wasn't the sort of namby-pamby macaw who cowered under a towel draped over his cage every night. Actually, the towel trick would have been a little difficult since he didn't even have a cage. He glared suspiciously at the two men dressed in black who crouched on either side of the bureau. This was his territory!

'Sweet Jesus!' whispered Pritchard querulously, having just experienced a brief attack of bubbling flatulence that, distressingly, wasn't wholly gaseous in nature. A momentary weakening in the bottom department had allowed some of his curry to reappear. Perhaps he wasn't cut out for all this espionage stuff any more.

'It's the sodding parrot.' Coberley straightened cautiously

and looked at Bertie through the cut-outs in his balaclava. The wool stuck to his perspiring face and itched like crazy. His mouth was as dry as a desert. He, too, had been completely unnerved by the bird. His heart hammered in his chest, thumping out an adrenaline accelerated tattoo of churning fear.

'Book 'em, Danno!' said Bertie, not liking the look of the two men at all. Something told him these two weren't invited guests. Visitors always entered through the front door with his mummy. Perhaps this pair were related to The Kneeling Man – they were certainly the same colour – but even he never entered unaccompanied and always brought a small offering of tasty goodies. Since they were dressed in a familiar manner, Bertie was willing to give them the benefit of the doubt. He waited expectantly for his nuts. He quite fancied an apple, if truth be known. There was a pause, during which an unbelievably foul smell began to permeate around the room. It seemed to rise like an awful rotting mist from the taller man.

Pritchard pulled off his hood and wiped his face with the back of his sleeve. Suddenly, he laughed softly, but its quavering brittleness had an edge of hysteria in it that made Coberley's hair stand on end. 'Greg, I don't believe it – that goddamn bird's made me crap my pants! This is Chaplain's call – he better cough up for my laundry bill.'

'Yeah, you bloody stink!' muttered Coberley, lowering the baton. He felt distinctly queasy himself. Sweat streamed down his face. He, too, risked removing his balaclava to mop his forehead with a grubby handkerchief. Bertie eyed them both with suspicion and decided he did not like them at all. Their black bodies and pale, scrawny necks reminded him of vultures. Ugly birds with disgraceful table manners. Nobody liked a cannibal!

'Come on, Bob, let's grab the book and get out of here.' Pritchard turned back to the open bureau.

'Stop!' shrieked Bertie. He was quite prepared to tolerate the men so long as they stood still, but the moment they moved …

'Jeez!' gasped Pritchard, clutching his heart and staggering back. The diary and letters dropped from his grasp and fell to the floor. More curry threatened to squeeze its way to freedom.

Bertie's yell was as piercing as a train whistle.

'For Christ's sake, Bob, will you shut it up!' hissed Coberley.

'How? I'm not bloody David Bellamy!' In a desperate attempt to placate the bristling macaw, Pritchard made a catastrophic error. He held out one hand and made a soft clucking noise with his lips. It sounded like a toothless old crone trying to French kiss. 'Who's a pretty boy, then?' he twittered hopefully.

Oh dear.

Oh dear, oh dear!

'I AM NOT A PRETTY BOY!'

It seemed inconceivable such a small larynx could generate so much noise. Bertie's incandescent fury at this inane phrase caught them both completely by surprise. No, he decided, these men weren't guests at all. Their intrusion was unacceptable. The time for action had come. His home needed defending. His mummy had to be protected. He gathered himself and hurtled forward off the perch, wings beating and buffeting. Coberley gargled in his throat as a huge blue gargoyle swept down onto his head, vicious claws stretched wide, needle-tipped bill darting toward his face. He dived to the floor as talons raked through his hair, scattering an occasional table. Executing a tight turn, Bertie returned to scythe off the top of his left ear with a single deadly strike. Pain lanced into the side of his head. He watched in sheer horror as the severed lump of cartilage plopped onto the floor beside his knee. Blood spurted down his neck and spread in pools on the parquet.

Aroused by the sudden commotion, Barnstaple poked his head out of his den to see what all the fuss was about, took one look at the scene of carnage and wisely scurried for cover.

Fortified by the success of his initial attack, Bertie swooped again and again, terrifying the burglars with his shrieking ululation, hacking at them, his wings beating powerfully. He had them cornered and there was no escape.

'Bertie! Stop that at once! What –?'

'Bugger!' swore Pritchard, and turning away from Celeste, tugged the hood back over his head, but in his haste pulled it on back to front. Tufts of damp hair poked out of the eye and mouth holes at the rear of his head. He could still see her through the stretched wool – just. She stood in the open doorway dressed in emerald silk pyjamas, legs braced apart, her face contorted with anger and outrage. There was not one jot of fear or timidity in her aggressive pose.

'Who the frigging hell are you?' she yelled, and snatched up her bullwhip and riding crop. Celeste, fortunately, was well provisioned with such useful items. Without waiting for an answer, she lashed at Coberley's prostrate form as he, too, struggled to replace his balaclava.

Considering the practice she'd put in over the years, it was hardly surprising the whip found its mark.

Coberley screamed. A scalding fire cut across his thighs and lower back, bringing sudden tears to his eyes. The shock and pain were indescribable! He raised his baton to ward off her second stroke but the whip struck with a crack, excoriating his knuckles. He yelped like a wounded puppy and snatched his injured hand back, the baton spinning wildly through the air before clattering to the floor and rolling under the sofa. She caught him for a third time as he nursed his injury, the braided rawhide savaging his shoulders. He convulsed, shrieking in agony, and Celeste threw her head back and laughed with wild abandon, her eyes shining. At that moment, Bob Pritchard seriously wondered about her sanity; no normal woman would have dared attack two such sinister intruders and then enjoyed it so much! In a way he quite admired her bottle.

However, admiration would have to wait for another time. Satisfied she'd now destroyed any enthusiasm Coberley still had in the proceedings, Celeste turned her attention on Pritchard. Her arm swept back ready for another deadly lash, the whip coiling and writhing about her feet like an angry black serpent. Still half blinded by the woollen hood, Pritchard leaped into action before she could strike. He dived over the sofa and tackled her around the waist. Celeste deployed her short-range defences and flogged him viciously hard across the neck with the riding crop. He grunted in pain but the blow was not forceful enough to deflect his dive. With arms wrapped around her body, they both crashed against the wall as one. Pritchard relied solely on his bulk and inertia, using Celeste as an air bag to cushion the impact. He felt her crumple.

The wind was driven from Celeste's lungs. Something cracked with excruciating agony in her shoulder and she lost the strength in her arm. Pritchard's weight drove her to the floor. She collapsed with a gasp, knocked her head against the door jamb and lay stunned, struggling for breath. He wrenched the whip out of her inert grasp and tossed it into a corner, then heaved Coberley to his feet and headed for the exit, his mind now so set on escape he completely forgot about the diary lying on the floor.

He also overlooked Bertie.

A sudden, unbelievable pain seared across the top of his shoulder. It felt as if a surgeon's scalpel had cleaved through his flesh. He tried to shield his eyes with one arm but Bertie, driven into an uncontrollable rage by the attack on Celeste, hacked and clawed at his hidden face with razor claws. The woollen hood proved no protection against such ferocity and the skin over his cheek parted like ripping paper. Blood exploded, streaming down his neck, warm and frightening in its volume. Using close quarter tactics perfected on Sebastian, Bertie lunged again, this time on Coberley, slashing at him with frenzied hatred, driving him back down to his knees. The struggling trio staggered towards the patio doors. A desperate blow from Pritchard almost broke one of Bertie's wings, forcing him to wheel away from their ducking heads, but the respite was momentary and he turned in a flash to dive again as they tumbled forwards, moving in to unleash yet another weapon in his formidable armoury.

A glutinously liquid weapon! Very offensive. His shower was copious, pungent, and accurate, spreading impressive pools of white faeces over Coberley's hunched back and shoulder. 'Yes!' he crowed triumphantly.

Pritchard, now almost blinded by sweat under the balaclava, charged at the patio doors – and missed. He slammed into the wooden frame at some considerable velocity, breaking his nose, and rebounding back into the room, tripped over Coberley's prostrate body with arms swinging wildly. Unceremoniously dumped on his rear beside his partner, he landed heavily on his tail bone, grunting at the sharp stab of pain. Now both of them were down again and Pritchard was beginning to panic. They had to get away. Fast! He rolled over onto his knees, suddenly conscious of much more blood, this time gushing down his throat. Bertie exploited this momentary hiccup in their escape by attacking again, but spurred on by the proximity of the doors and a desperate need to flee into the darkness beyond, both men managed to scramble to their feet and with a final lunge, burst out into the garden side by side. Carried forward by his own momentum and unable to pull up in time, Bertie crashed into the partly open curtains and swinging doors. There was a frantic flapping, the sound of feathers scraping against wood, then silence.

Still slumped against the wall, Celeste opened her eyes. The world remained stubbornly unfocussed, whirling in jagged confusion. She shook her head and fought the disorientation with sheer willpower, fighting for equilibrium until, mercifully, the spinning slowly eased. Clutching at her side with one hand, she climbed painfully to her feet, suddenly aware the salon was ominously quiet. Staggering to the patio doors, she swept the curtains aside just in time to see the two desperate men vault over the garden wall and make off up the street at a run. The effort of standing made her cry out; something deep in her shoulder hurt horribly. Agony accompanied each breath. Her ribs felt crushed, her chest unbearably tight. She squeezed back her tears and stumbled into the darkened garden. 'Bertie! Bertie! Come back!'

But Bertie was gone.

Chapter Eight

Bertie soared up into the night sky, reaching a zenith before swooping back down. A tree loomed up and he landed a little clumsily, one wing draped over a branch. This had been even more exciting than his attack on Sebastian. He had no idea who the black men were, but they'd been repelled. One was also scent-marked so Bertie knew he'd scored psychologically as well. There was nothing more gratifying than defecating on characters you didn't like. Sebastian, for instance. Having discovered just how absorbent his fur was, Bertie now showered him on a regular basis, and the cat's obvious distress at having to lick himself clean only added to his inclination to continue his campaign of bombardment. He had only just begun to recover his equilibrium when he spotted two figures fleeing down the street and without hesitation, launched himself in pursuit, dropping like an apocalyptic demon out of the darkness.

'Christ!' Coberley panted, holding a handkerchief to his horribly mutilated ear in a futile attempt to stem the flow of blood. 'What a cock-up!'

'Just keep running. I think we're –' Pritchard screamed in pain, a girlish, shivering cry of absolute terror as Bertie's claws raked the back of his neck and shoulder again, drawing fresh lines of agony. He looked up to see a shadow twist in mid-air with astonishing skill and return swiftly. The speed of the attack was terrifying. Screeching like a banshee, Bertie swept in from the front, a shadowy Titan with sickled claws thrust forward, bloodstained and murderous. The two panicking men dived to each side as the bird flashed between them, wing tips hissing over their heads. They put on a final spurt to the Transit. Both were now bleeding profusely from numerous wounds to the face and head. Pritchard's broken nose was blocked and congested. Blood and snot slid down his throat in a coppery trickle. Neither had ever faced such a furious and deadly assault.

'Quick, get in!' gasped Coberley unnecessarily. It was doubtful any other course of action had entered Pritchard's head. He beat off another attack with a swing of his arms, flung open the door and dived inside. The powerful engine roared into life, Coberley hit the laughing gas boost and howling tyres laid enormous streaks of smoking rubber down the road. Bertie still attacked gamely, gripping the wipers and buffeting the windscreen with his wings but Coberley switched on the wiper motor, jerking the macaw from side to side. They both laughed hysterically as Bertie was swept back and forth across the glass and in a fit of diabolical sadism, Coberley doused him with a generous squirt from the washers. He struggled to maintain his grip, hissing at the men through the glass, but Coberley switched to fast wipe and Bertie was suddenly swept off to one side and spiralled into an uncomfortably prickly hedge like a fighter downed by a missile, droplets showering from his nether regions. He heaved powerfully against the twigs but the van had accelerated around a corner with another tremendous squeal of tyres and was gone by the time he managed to extricate himself.

Silence fell.

'Mummy?' He didn't recognise a single landmark. Every house looked strange and unfamiliar, stark in the harsh orange light. 'Mummy?' he called again nervously. Bertie gazed up and down the street, but there was no sign of Celeste. This disturbed him a great deal. They'd never been parted before and the thought of her loss welled up to smother him in a frightening blanket of anxiety. His agitation grew. 'Mummy?' The call was pained, like that of a lost and confused child. Bertie desperately needed the comfort of Celeste's presence, but the street was utterly alien. Eventually, because there was nothing else to do, he flew up above the houses and circled several times nervously before setting off towards the great flood of lights to the west.

A net curtain slipped back into place as he disappeared. After a moment's hesitation, a liver-spotted hand with arthritic joints fumbled with a pen and carefully made a note on a jotting pad beside the phone.

Bertie flew for what seemed an age, gliding over endless buildings. Street lamps necklaced the roads, inviting him to follow, but they only led to a greater confusion of highways. Some of the larger routes were clogged, despite the early hour. Cars and vans followed each other dutifully, the serpentine streams of trudging traffic well-spaced while they moved but then bunching together again at the next junction like a vehicular concertina.

The vastness of the city was disorientating, but instinct took over and guided by a pale moon – the only light shining above him – and an untested homing instinct, he toured the delights of Millwall, circled the glass-glittering arrogance of Canary Wharf and, crossing the dark ribbon of the Thames again, completed an erratic tour of the East End. The City still beckoned away to the west, bright and twinkling, but it seemed too far away for comfort. Eventually, tired with trying to find his house and now in desperate need of human companionship, he dropped lower, aligning himself along silent streets, searching for a roost. A tree loomed up and he slowed, altering the angle of body and tail before landing with a final sweep of his wings. Unfortunately, this disturbed a colony of starlings who complained vociferously at the intrusion, shrieking and lunging at him with testy aggression, their raucous cries inviting him to push off out of their tree, so he swooped into a nearby garden, spotted the illuminated square of an open bedroom window and executed an immaculate landing on the wooden sill.

Bertie poked his head inside. A small girl lay asleep on a cot bed surrounded by untidy clutter, her cherubic face illuminated by a night light on the bedside cabinet. Bertie looked about in interest. The room was awfully pink, with matching wallpaper, curtains and carpet. Posters and pictures hung on the walls, some skewed as if the room had just experienced a minor earthquake. He hopped on to the pink foot board and regarded the sleeping girl with curiosity. She was very pretty, with chubby red cheeks and a messy tangle of pale blonde curls spread in coiled disarray over a My Little Pony pillow. His movement disturbed the girl. She stirred, opened her eyes and stared directly at him, blinking rapidly.

There was a long, long silence.

Bertie didn't like silences. They made him uncomfortable. His cheerful nature demanded at least some token attempt at communication. 'Hello! My name is Bertie and I'm very pleased to meet you. Who are you?' His diction was perfect. This was what he had been taught to say and it usually got an answer, but the girl looked strangely shocked. She shrank back in stunned disbelief under the protection of her equine-spattered duvet, pulling it up to her widened eyes and hugging a large, one-eared teddy bear for moral support. Bertie tilted his head to one side. 'Hello? Anyone home?'

This eventually got a timid response, muffled by the covers. 'Pleased to meet you, Mister Bertie.' The girl's voice was faint and tremulous – after all, it wasn't every night you woke up to find something huge and violet perched at the bottom of your bed. On the whole, showing the remarkable resilience native to children, she seemed to be coping rather well. 'I'm Mary,' she said after an awkward pause.

Splendid! This was a major breakthrough between the two species. Bertie liked Mary's oratorical style. Short and simple. Keep the words to a couple of syllables each and he could, with luck and concentration, strike up quite a conversation. However, social niceties could wait. There was something much more important on his mind. 'Mary, I'm hungry. I want nuts.'

'Pete, are you awake?'

'Mmmmm?'

'Pete!'

Something shook Peter Osborne out of a warm and pleasant slumber. 'Not now, Cath. I'm tired.' It was an automatic response to a request that had become depressingly rare in the last year or so.

'Pete, I can hear Mary downstairs.'

'So what!' This came in Limbo Language, that slurred, in-between-consciousness mumbling which afflicted humans who had just checked out of the real world and were galloping headlong towards the delicious other-universe of sleep. His lack of paternal concern over the welfare of his daughter annoyed Cath.

Actually, quite a lot of things about Pete annoyed Cath.

Catherine Osborne sometimes wondered why she bothered any more – her husband had definitely not turned out to be the man she thought he was when they performed the church aisle shuffle six years ago. She persisted doggedly against his somnolent indifference.

'But Pete, I can hear her talking.'

There was a non-committal grunt shot through with impressive quantities of disinterest from the vague hump on the other side of the bed. She waited, but the hump showed little inclination to move further and its breathing settled back into pre-snoring mode. Exasperated, she suddenly kicked him. Hard.

'Wha – what?' A light flared. Pete winced and sat up rubbing his eyes with the heels of his palms. 'For God's sake, Cath, what are you doing? It's the middle of the bloody night!' There was that distinct note of irritability in his voice she knew so well. Under normal circumstances it would have been best to leave him be, but Cath could not let this rest and was already out of bed and pulling on her dressing gown. Mary was their only child – and if the frequency of their coition was anything to go by, that situation was unlikely to change.

'I told you, I heard Mary talking downstairs.'

'Yeah? Big deal! She's been able to talk for years.'

'Moron! Cretin!' she ground out. 'So who's she talking to? Who's answering?' Cath picked up a heavy vase and stole towards the door. As she cracked it open, Pete heard furtive voices downstairs. One was definitely Mary's, but the other most definitely wasn't. Suddenly very awake, he leaped out of bed and looked for a suitable weapon. With rising panic, he jerked open his wardrobe door and after a moment's rummaging, extracted a golf club. A seven iron. Virtually unused.

Pete's painful attempts to master the noble game had cratered Shooter's Hill golf course with divots of varying sizes. Despite overwhelming evidence to the contrary, he remained convinced that one day he would be able to strike the ball straight and true without showering his playing partners – and any casual observer unfortunate enough to be within the immediate vicinity – in a generous cascade of stones, shredded turf, and very surprised earthworms. An optimist by nature, Pete was one of those men who firmly believed that if aliens were prepared to travel truly colossal distances across interstellar space only to kidnap and impregnate astonishingly ugly American women with bouncing triplets, then they could also teach him to play golf.

It was all really rather sad.

He padded after Cath, relieved her of the vase and pushed her behind him. Together, they stole down the stairs and along the gloomy hall. Ahead, the kitchen light shone brightly. Mary's voice filtered through the half open door.

'More?'

'Yes please.'

Cath clutched Pete's arm as they inched forward. There was a sickening, stomach-churning crack. Like bones breaking. Mary giggled. 'I don't know how you can get those out without breaking them. Daddy can't.'

'Easy-peasy.'

Pete took a firm two-handed grip on the club and slowly pushed the door open with its head. They stared into the kitchen. Mary was perched on her stool by the breakfast bar, dressing gown on inside out and legs swinging in mid-air, one slipper dangling from her toes, the other lying abandoned on the floor. Something vast and weird and covered in blue feathers was perched on the back of the stool next to her, gripping the pine backrest with one foot, its steel-coloured claws so sharp little shaves of varnish curled off the wood. Worryingly, those needled tips also seemed to be stained with what looked suspiciously like dried blood. In the other foot it held a Brazil nut to its viciously curved bill. As they gaped in utter disbelief, the armoured husk was effortlessly crushed and the fleshy nut neatly extracted.

'Wow, that's great,' breathed Mary, lost in wide-eyed admiration. 'Here.' She pulled another from the packet and held it out.

The big blue thing took the friendship offering and said, 'Thanks.' Casually. Conversationally. In perfect English.

'Holy Mother of God!' whispered Pete. Both Mary and her new companion looked up at the sound of his voice.

'Hello, Daddy.' She wriggled off her stool, ran forward and pulled him into the kitchen by the seven iron. Cath was spot-welded to his back, fists knotted in his pyjamas. She peered over his shoulder with frightened eyes at the huge bird. They both edged nervously towards the breakfast bar. By contrast, Mary showed no fear at all.

'Hello, Daddy,' repeated Bertie faultlessly. 'My name is Bertie and I'm very pleased to meet you.'

'Bertie's my friend. He's something called a highniclinch macaw and was lost and flew in through my window and was *so* hungry we came down here and I gave him some of your nuts and I hope you don't mind, Daddy.' It all came out in one excited, breathless rush. For a moment, Cath observed in a totally detached manner that Bertie's use of grammar was far superior to her daughter's. She didn't know whether to laugh or cry.

'No, I don't mind, poppet.' Pete's faint voice still reflected his confusion, after all, it wasn't every day you were awoken from a deep sleep to find your daughter carrying on a conversation with a bird the size of a cooker! On the whole, he thought he was coping magnificently. There was an uncomfortable pause. He didn't want to act the twit in front of his family, but it became very obvious his wife, his child – and probably the macaw as well – were waiting for him to say something. Discounting his simian supervisor at work, it was the first conversation he'd ever attempted with a non-human life form.

'Bertie?' he asked hesitantly.

'Yes, Daddy?'

'His name is Pete, silly,' interjected Mary.

'Yes, Pete Silly?'

'Do you have an owner?'

Bertie considered this thoughtfully. He had a mummy. 'No owner.'

'Are you lost?'

'Lost. Yes.'

'Do you have a mummy?' interjected Mary with a theatrical sigh, hands on hips, obviously much more at ease than her father and impatient to take charge of the situation. Her acquaintance with Bertie was more extensive than his – by about ten minutes. She showed a confidence Pete could never hope to match.

'Mummy. Yes. Celeste. Bertie loves Celeste. Nut. Please.'

Mary obliged.

'Thanks.' Bertie was impressively polite.

'He's very hungry,' said Mary. 'Perhaps he's been flying all night.'

'I think he must have escaped,' observed Pete. 'Pity there's no ring on his leg.'

'I've never seen such a beautiful creature,' whispered Cath. 'Could it harm Mary?' She remained safely behind her husband's back. Yes, that was definitely blood on those claws.

'No, I don't think so. Look at the way he is with her. This bird has been around people all its life – how else could it talk so well?'

Bertie craned his neck to one side at the sound of Cath's voice and peered at her partially concealed face. She saw an intellect in his steady brown eyes which shattered for ever some of her basic assumptions on life. 'Hello,' he said amiably, 'I'm Bertie.'

'Hello, Bertie,' replied Cath nervously. 'I'm Cath.' Like Pete, the thought that she was holding a rational conversation with a fully sentient creature was simply overwhelming. She struggled for equilibrium.

Mary clambered back on to her stool, losing her remaining slipper in the process. She dipped into the pack for another nut and passed it to Bertie, oblivious to the petrified amazement of her parents. To her, it seemed natural to make friends with

110

Bertie. He spoke to her, she spoke to him. Simple. The fact he was a macaw didn't bother her in the slightest. Mary's childish trust gave Cath a sudden lump in her throat. How long would it be before that wonderful innocence was lost for ever? 'What shall we do?' she asked nervously.

'Well, he must be very valuable so we better phone the police and get them to collect him.' Pete and Cath looked at each other. They both knew the effect this would have on Mary. She had been pestering them for a new kitten since last Christmas when Rooster, her fat ginger tom with the zig-zag tail, had been found crumpled on the patio with a broken neck. Having indulged generously in the remains of Cath's Yuletide sherry, he'd staggered outside for a seasonal wee, but an ill-advised stroll along the top of the fence had been inevitably doomed. With his normally urbane feline poise suffering significantly under the influence of Spain's most famous export, he'd succumbed to gravity, with fatal consequences. Although Bertie was short of a paw or two and definitely the wrong colour, Mary obviously considered his arrival as a timely gift from the gods to ease her loneliness.

There would be heartache.

'I'll do it now.' Pete abdicated his paternal responsibilities with typical alacrity and disappeared upstairs to make the call leaving Cath, as ever, to deal with the difficult situation. There were times when she could gladly strangle him. Her daughter fussed over the macaw as if it were a baby. The bird lapped up the attention, closed its eyes and began to purr, impressing Mary mightily. When the inevitable question came, Cath knew it would be the hardest of all to answer.

'Mummy, can I keep him?'

Pritchard parked the car and walked the few yards to his flat still smarting from the humiliation of the abortive burglary. His desperate call to Chaplain resulted in a torrent of vitriol, followed by a stony silence even more difficult to stomach. He and Coberley were ordered to dress each other's wounds and make their way home. Coberley's ear was a mangled mess requiring a little home surgery to tidy up. Fortunately, the van was equipped with an excellent first aid kit, including powerful sedatives as well as a range of recreational drugs generously donated by HM Customs, all stored in handy self-seal plastic bags ideal for planting on innocents and other folk of a similarly awkward disposition.

Jesus, his face hurt! The swollen skin felt tight and buzzy under the dressing and itched abominably. Nearly two-thirty – with luck, his wife would be asleep. Sadly, his hopes were short-lived. Despite the lateness of the hour, a light still burned in the lounge. 'Suzy?' he whispered tentatively. Pritchard was a man fearless in the face of danger, but he was most certainly frightened of his wife. Suzanne Pritchard rivalled Xanthippe with PMT. The wife of Socrates was a woman of legendary shrewishness, and no doubt this fact was instrumental in old Beardy's decision to take refuge in philosophy!

His shoulders slumped when he caught sight of her on the sofa, head turned away in a gesture of rejection and fluffy dressing gown wrapped tight like chain-mail armour. Her body language revealed less of a welcome than he was hoping for, her aura bristling with anger.

'Hi,' he said, placatingly, and headed straight for a comforting shot of whisky. Silence. Damn, now he was in some kind of pretty poo! That particularly haughty disdain was reserved for only very special occasions.

'Still up, then?' For a man who possessed a degree in psychology, he was, nonetheless, still capable of uttering the most breathtaking banalities.

'How remarkably observant.'

He grimaced at her tone. It was as cold as a banker's conscience. A riptide of hostility swept across the room. 'Sorry I'm late. Bad night at the office.' Despite the rigours of the Official Secrets Act, Suzy knew exactly what he meant. That damned man again! She'd met Chaplain on only one occasion and found him utterly repellent. The man oozed about as much charm as a disease-ridden swamp full of interesting forms of death.

'What was the date yesterday?' she asked stiffly, still staring at the wall.

Pritchard froze, the cold hand of panic massaging the back of his neck. How many husbands throughout the land have suffered a sudden and total breakdown of bowel control on hearing that phrase? He quickly reviewed the essential dates upon which his life depended; their wedding anniversary, her birthday, her mother's birthday, her aunt's birthday, her sister's birthday, her other sister's birthday, her other sister's disturbingly masculine lesbian lover's birthday. The list was apparently endless and only included one person who needed to shave every day. No, he was confident he was in the clear.

'Wednesday?' It was a feeble and wholly inadvisable attempt at humour.

'Don't be facetious,' she snapped tartly. 'You know damned well we were supposed to go to the cemetery.'

The bitch!

No, not his wife – their dog, or rather, their ex-dog.

Missy Wah-Hey had checked out this time last year after a terminal encounter with a speeding lorry loaded to the gunwales with toilet seats. The toilet seats were purely incidental to the proceedings, but Pritchard liked to think there was a deity with a delicious sense of humour up there somewhere. Suzy had arranged to have Missy's pulped remains interred at the Cricklewood Memorial Pet Cemetery with as much pomp as a state funeral.

Missy Wah-Hey! Damned stupid name. Pritchard felt sure that had Missy Wah-Hey been Mister Wah-Hey, his demise would have been catered for with far less ceremony, probably something involving a bin liner, a dust cart and the local landfill site. He considered this a much more fitting end to a deeply unpleasant, inbred shih-tzu imbued with a pathological compulsion to scent-mark his shoes.

'Oh, yes, sorry,' he mumbled. Suzy had wanted to put flowers on Missy's plaque, which seemed an odd offering for an untrainable, half-savage, hirsute pissing machine. A side of freshly slaughtered buffalo, still warm and dripping with blood, would have been far more appropriate. 'We'll go this evening.'

'This evening is too late. You should have remembered. Really, Bob, you're worse than useless – I don't know why I married you! You've turned out to be nothing but a disappointment.' Having vented her wrath, she pulled the lapels of her dressing gown together beneath her chin in symbolic denial and stood, turning to glare at him for the first time with bitter disapproval. Her eyes narrowed. 'What's that on your face?'

'A broken nose.' Pritchard gave up any attempt at humour. Experience had taught him nothing he now said would make one iota of difference.

'I'm not interested in that.' Sympathy was not one of Suzy's more endearing qualities. Not with him, anyway, which was why, under no circumstances, would he ever tell her about his recent distressing loss of bowel control.

'Thanks for the concern.'

She pointed at his cheek. 'What happened?'

'I was attacked by a parrot.' It was the truth, of course, but his weary resignation gave the statement a hollow ring. Suzy stepped closer. She saw a trio of parallel scratches disappear under a great slab of dressing and without warning, ripped it away with furious wrench. Pritchard screeched spectacularly. His hand flew up to protect his cheek, but Suzy had seen enough.

'You despicable little man!' she hissed venomously. 'You've been with another woman, haven't you?' Until that moment, it had not even remotely occurred to Pritchard that the marks of Bertie's claws closely resembled those from human nails.

'Don't be so ridiculous – it was a parrot, I tell you! A bloody big blue one!' He felt the first stirring of anger arrive to bolster his arguments, anger which gave him the courage to offer up a spot of mild swearing in her presence. His wife strongly disapproved of all cursing. She felt any intelligent person should be able to communicate their feelings without the use of profanity.

Suzy went ballistic. 'That's a crock, you cretinous oaf, you foul faecal scraping, you snivelling blob of rectal discharge! You work in London, not Africa, so don't you dare lie to me, you vile, suppurating, loathsome pustule!' Still no swearing –

but he had to admit she got her point across.

'Dammit, Suzy –'

A stinging slap silenced his protestation. It was delivered without inhibition, her muscular arm swinging back to get maximum acceleration before arcing forward in a blur to deliver a full, open, scything palm strike that hurt. Considerably. She chose his lacerated cheek as her target and whilst his attention was distracted by the pain, closely followed up her tactical advantage with a technically perfect knee to the scrotum.

Pritchard's legs finally called it a day.

He folded to the ground and watched his wife storm out of the room. She took the stairs two at a time, marched into the bedroom and slammed the door so hard their wedding photograph fell off the wall.

Wracked with agony, Pritchard sagged forward on his knees, hunched in a ball with chin resting on the carpet and eyes closed, hands clutched over his groin in the time-honoured traditional manner. All he wanted to do was retreat from a world of hurt, to escape just for one minute from the worst evening of his life. Wrapped in a haze of suffering and throbbing pain, he shook his head gently in denial. 'I suppose that means sex is out of the question,' he mumbled finally.

Ellen Coberley lay in the darkened bedroom listening to the small noises of the night. Sleep was far from her mind. Suspicions did that to you. Greg had wandered before. Just once. But once was enough. She'd beaten the crap out of him, sentenced him to six months sexual denial and ordered a humiliating check-up at the STD clinic. Since then he'd been, as it were, on probation. Had Marks & Spencer offered a male chastity belt, Ellen would have been first in the queue with her credit card. Small size, of course. Something uncomfortable in rusty iron with studs on the insides and tasteful barbed wire trimmings.

She sighed heavily. He was never this late without calling. To put her mind at rest. To check in. To report. Not this time, and as the hours dragged on, doubts inevitably began to coalesce once more. After discovering him humping that cow

Muriel, she could never quite get out of her mind the nagging thought he was dallying with some strumpet, but then again that unpleasant salamander, Chaplain, was just as likely to get Greg working on something at the last minute. She, too, was perhaps more acquainted with the nature of JSON than Chaplain would have liked, but there it was. Pillow talk was a natural consequence of being married – and she was now, by bitter experience, an unusually inquisitive woman.

Suddenly alert, she heard a stealthy step on the stairs. The bedroom door cracked open. His careful approach was charted by the faint rustle of clothing. Ellen shot out an arm and switched on the bedside lamp to reveal her husband frozen in the act of removing his trousers, one leg raised like a renegade nocturnal morris dancer caught in the glare of passing headlights. Ellen was far more observant than Suzy. The missing half of his ear was a dead giveaway. So was the bizarre patchwork of plasters covering his neck and face. She spotted them and what they failed to conceal immediately, and like Suzy Pritchard, also leapt to the wrong conclusion.

Her formidable temper ignited quicker than a rocket heading for Mars and she was on him in a flash. Handicapped by entangling trousers, Greg Coberley went down under a savage barrage of blows and kicks. Her screaming fury knew no bounds, and he found himself under merciless attack for the second time that night.

Chapter Nine

Wilfred Thompson had become a worn round peg in an increasingly rigid square hole. Once, and how long ago it now seemed, he'd been an ambitious and respected member of the Metropolitan Police Force, but a succession of indifferent transfers had left his career in a shaky condition. Wilf was a good copper all right, it was just that he was a bit – well, boring. And grumpy. Very definitely grumpy. Now bitterness tinged his personality like a tea stain on granny's best tablecloth.

An air of melancholy followed him around as if something unpleasant was stuck on the sole of his shoe. His record as a Detective Constable stationed at Greenwich was solid, which was the kindest possible description for unadventurous, unlucky, and unambitious. He was very much of the old school, a man of the beat who had cautiously worked his way into CID, promoted when there was no other option available to his superiors. Wilf would never make his mark, and that rankled. The Met had become a promising career area for pushy graduates breezing in from trendy universities with their obscure degrees in exobiology and Etruscan pottery. They hated the compulsory two years on the beat, regarding the time as an impediment to their management aspirations. These were officers who climbed the corporate police ladder in effortlessly energetic leaps, sprinting past him at frightening speed with their high-profile crack busts and televised gun sieges while he struggled valiantly with vandals and teenage shoplifting gangs. Important, yes, especially to those on the receiving end of such low-level crimes, but not really important enough to warrant any close attention from the promotions board. They were looking for drive, for ambition, for sexiness, and if there was one thing Wilf certainly was not, it was sexy. So, as time passed, he slowly became resigned to the fact he'd never become a Detective Sergeant – and, frankly, you had to be pretty awful not to make DS.

It really cheesed him off.

He hung up his favourite gumshoe mac and sat down. Affairs looked pretty depressing, as usual. His minuscule empire comprised a cluttered mountain of files supported by four wooden legs. He looked around, gave a weary sigh and decided to fortify himself with a coffee, but never made it to the machine.

'Got something for you.'

Detective Chief Inspector Tristram Yates dropped a folder onto the chaos, glancing sourly at the untidiness. Yates was young and dynamic. He had been in the force just nine years and already well outranked Wilf. Yates was going places. There were fast-track plans for him of which Wilf could only dream.

Bastard!

For his part, Yates had ambivalent feelings towards Wilf. Some days he thought the older man should be demoted back into uniform because of his surly insubordination, other days he though Wilf was OK, especially when a little tenacity and honest hard work had paid off and another gang of juvenile carjackers found themselves packed off to court. Wilf was an odd character and preferred his own company. Dour, uncommunicative, acid-tongued and bitter, yes, but – and Yates would rather poke out his own eyes with habanero-dipped porcupine needles than publicly admit it – he was also one of the most tenacious and intuitive detectives he'd ever met and just too damned useful to discard. All it needed was a niche which Wilf could fill, and Yates had finally found one; he used Wilf as a vacuum cleaner to clear up all the odd little incidents which were so time-consuming for his more able officers.

So, naturally, this new case fell into his jurisdiction.

'Morning, Tris.' Now what kind of a name was that? Sounded like a proprietary brand of suppository. Wilf smoothed back the scanty remnants of his grey hair and silently cursed the

118

genetic inheritance that had left him monastically bald from the age of twenty-six. 'What pleasures do you bring this morning, O Mighty One?' Git!

Yates had long ago given up reprimanding Wilf for his mildly irritating facetiousness. It was a complete waste of energy. 'Can't you keep your desk tidy?' he admonished for the umpteenth time. There was not a hair out of place in Yates's aseptically clean office. He hated mess. Wilf knew he hated mess. Wilf cultivated messiness. Cause and effect. Childish, Wilf knew, but satisfying.

'I'll tidy up later,' he lied genially. 'What's on your mind?'

'Jailbird. Came in last night on a wing and a prayer.' There was a stifled titter around the office. Wilf felt a sudden sinking feeling. Not another infantile prank. 'I'd like you to take it up. Talk to him and see what flies out of the cupboard.' More covert giggling. Wilf opened the folder. Every block on the enquiry sheet was empty except the Christian name.

'That's all you got? What's up, Tris, interview technique failing you?'

'No, but I'm sure you'll make him sing like a canary.' This time the snorts of laughter were unmistakable. Wilf scowled. Life was difficult enough without this tosser yanking his chain. 'He's in cell four. See what you can get out of him – it'll be a feather in your cap.' Yates sniggered nastily and disappeared into his office.

Wilf shook his head and wondered how such a monumental dickhead could get by without being filled in on a regular basis. He glared at the grinning faces and stalked down to the cells.

'Morning, George.'

'Morning, Wilf.' Sergeant Phillips knew Wilf too well. It was inevitable who he had come to see. 'Number four?'

'Yeah. Guess so.'

'I thought Yates would put you on this case. Strange fellow, this one. I hope he doesn't come up before the beak.' Wilf waited, but the custody sergeant was not forthcoming. He sighed heavily, stalked down to the cell door and flung it open.

'Bugger me!'

Wilf jumped back in shock. The cell was filled with

119

something big and blue. Very big and very, very blue! As big as a B-52! Bigger! He turned to find half the station crowded at the end of the corridor and laughing like idiots. Tears were trickling down Yates's cheeks. 'All yours, Wilf,' he gasped. Wilf gave them the finger and girding his loins, stepped back into the cell with no small apprehension.

Bertie finished stretching the stiffness out his wings and tucked them away. He shook his long tail a few times and stared at this new companion. The man was very old, with patchy silver plumage. He also seemed a little nervous, unlike Mary, who had displayed the easy confidence of youth. Still, his face looked kindly enough. Time to make friends.

'Hello. My name is Bertie and I'm very pleased to meet you.' He was glad Celeste had taught him that difficult sentence and really appreciated the way people responded. He'd employed it before on many occasions and as a result, his diction was near perfect.

Wilf raised an eyebrow. The words were clear and concise. He became aware of that appraising stare which Cath and many others found so disconcerting. Wilf's police training took over. The art of interviewing now came as second nature after seventeen years in the force. Rule one: act cool. Always.

'Hello, Bertie. I'm Detective Constable Wilfred Thompson.' Bertie sat in silence, perched on the back of a chair weighed down with several hefty legal tomes stacked on the seat. A saucer of water and a digestive biscuit lay on top of the books. Bertie had ignored the biscuit. He only liked the chocolate ones. Jammy Dodgers were another favourite, but it appeared the station catering budget didn't stretch to anything so exotic. 'You can call me Wilf.' Wilf emphasised his name, repeating it several times. He felt a complete tit interviewing a parrot. Yates was going to suffer for this.

'Wilf. Your name is Wilf. My name is Bertie.' This came back straight away, spoken again with cheerful competence. Amazing!

Wilf slid onto the hard bunk and thought for a moment. He knew very little about parrots but this bird was bright, that much was immediately apparent. He'd seen Attenborough on

TV, crawling around in some bug-infested jungle, inveigling the viewer to observe some bizarre, multi-legged mating ritual which always ended in a spot of post-coital cannibalism. The man was undoubtedly the greatest voyeur on earth! Still, he made some damnably interesting programmes and Wilf vaguely remembered one on parrots. They had a keen intellect and some were excellent mimics so with careful questioning he might – just might – get all the answers he needed to enable him to return Bertie to his owner. Now wouldn't that just wipe the smile off dear Tristram's vacuous face.

'I'm going to ask you some questions,' he enunciated slowly. 'Who owns you?'

Bertie regarded him with a doubtful eye. 'I'm Bertie.'

'Yes, I know.'

'Bertie.'

'Good. Great.'

'Wilf. Your name is Wilf.'

'That's right. Now Bertie, tell me, who looks after you?'

Silence.

'An owner? The name of your owner?'

'No.'

Wilf pursed his lips. That was obviously not true; someone cared for this bird, and cared very much. He was in beautiful condition.

'How about a mother then?'

Bertie tipped his head on one side and regarded him with an unwavering stare. Wilf was conscious of a sharp intelligence dwelling behind those lively brown eyes; his formal introduction proved he was able to speak complex sentences. It was more than a little unnerving. 'Yes,' he said eventually.

'You have a mother. Excellent.'

'Pieces of eight,' said Bertie dutifully, embarking on a familiar course. People always seemed to expect this inanity. Sometimes, they clapped.

'Quite.'

'Land Ho!' Another favourite.

'What a relief.'

'Shiver me timbers. Pirates off the starboard bow!' This,

121

being his third nautical offering, completed the trilogy of topical parroty phrases he'd gleaned from the television. Members of his species tended to be typecast by Hollywood.

Wilf waited to see if Bertie trotted out any more gibberish but the bird now seemed content. He started again. 'Bertie?'

'Hello.'

'Tell me about your mother, your mum.'

'Mummy?'

'Yes, your mummy. You have a mummy?'

'Mummy. Oh, yes.' Bertie's head bobbed vigorously up and down and he chuckled and trilled away to himself quite happily at the comforting thought of Celeste and her beautiful copper plumage.

'What's she called?'

'I love Mummy.' This was delivered with certainty. 'Oh, yes, I love Mummy. Mummy. I love.'

There was no doubt Bertie loved his mummy.

'Mummy,' he repeated again. To Wilf it seemed he drew great comfort from the word.

'Yes, wonderful.'

'I love Mummy best.'

'Great! What's her name?'

'Name?'

'What do you call her?'

'Wilf?'

'No, no, my name is Wilf.'

'Bertie?'

'No. You are Bertie, remember?'

'My name is Bertie.' Bertie was beginning to enjoy himself immensely. Here was someone new to dominate, someone so dense he couldn't see he was being played. Celeste would never fall for a trick like this. Having established a satisfactory psychological ascendancy, Bertie pressed home his advantage. 'Nuts. I want nuts.'

'Are you hungry?' Wilf took the untouched biscuit, broke off a piece and popped it in his mouth. He offered the remainder hopefully, holding it up gingerly between finger and thumb, well aware such a viciously hooked bill could do some serious damage. Bertie reached out and with infinite gentleness, took the biscuit with his claw, then crushed it and scattered the crumbs onto the floor with disdain. 'Yes. I want nuts,' he announced firmly. Then remembered his manners. 'Please.'

'Oh, very well.'

A packet of Brazil nuts arrived ten minutes later. The cell echoed to the steady cracking of shells. Wilf was fascinated by the expert co-ordination of claw and bill; Brazils possessed iron-hard husks and were notoriously difficult to extract without breaking, but what Wilf witnessed was impressive; the big macaw juxtaposed both strength and dexterity to a delicate nicety.

'Do you prefer Brazil nuts?' asked Wilf. Bertie favoured him with a glance and did not reply, so Wilf urged on him a little. 'Well? Do you?'

This was a phrase he'd heard plenty of times before. 'Yes,' he replied automatically, 'I do.'

'That's nice. So, can you tell me about your mother?'

'I love my mummy.'

'Good. I'm glad to hear it.'

'Good. I'm glad to hear it.' Bertie's mimic of Wilf was perfect in accent, diction, and pitch. If nothing else, it indicated to Wilf the bird was linguistically accomplished, but he was also like a headstrong child and ignored all questions for several minutes while he preened and took a drink. Wilf sat with calm patience, intrigued by the macaw's fastidiousness. This was an interesting diversion from the normal events of his day and Yates could hardly berate him for ignoring more important work, having set Wilf the task of interviewing Bertie himself. Now determined to conclude a successful interrogation, he was quite happy to wait until the bird was ready. After a final shake of his wings, Bertie gave his full attention to the detective again. He stared steadily at Wilf and announced casually, 'Mummy. Her name is Celeste.'

A major breakthrough. 'Celeste. Great, now we're cooking.' Wilf scribbled the name on his form.

'Celeste, Celeste,' he chirruped happily, exfoliating another Brazil with merciless precision.

'Do you have a father?' asked Wilf.

'A father.' Bertie seemed momentarily confused. He knew Celeste once had a father, but Ray had gone away a long time ago, before they came to this grey, treeless land of chills and noise and miserable crowds.

'Yes, a daddy.'

'No.'

'Only a mummy.'

'Yes. Celeste.'

'Does your mum have another name?' Wilf had to repeat this several times. It was like trying to coax information out of a very small child. Or an inebriate. Both seemed to have a similar attention span.

'Another name?'

'Yes, Bertie, another name.'

'Mistress.' The Kneeling Man used that one quite a lot. Wilf shook his head sadly and tried a different approach.

'Where do you live? Where is your home?'

'Close.'

'I know it's close. How close, do you know?'

This was a trifle too abstract for Bertie, who had better things to do than master the topography of London. He gave Wilf what could only be described as a withering look. 'Don't know.'

'Is it a flat? A house, perhaps?'

'House.' He pounced on this quickly. 'Yes. Big house. Big and warm.' He thought fondly of his home, and of those who lived with him. 'Barnstaple.'

'Barnstaple! Good grief, you've flown a long way – no wonder you're so hungry; I'm surprised your bloody wings haven't fallen off.'

'Yes. Barnstaple.'

'Barnstaple in Devon,' scribbled Wilf. He was getting somewhere at last.

'Devon?' Confusion again. Bertie tipped his head to one side and looked at him. What on earth was he talking about?

'Yes.'

'Hamster.'

'Oh.'

'Nice guy. Friend.'

Bertie didn't even bother to mention Sebastian. The cat was the most contemptible form of life in the universe. He idly picked at another Brazil while Wilf sadly scratched out his notes.

'I'm getting nowhere,' he muttered, looking at his watch. Despite his desire to annoy Yates, he regretfully decided there were more urgent cases than having to grill a recalcitrant parrot just to satisfy his boss's perverse sense of humour. Pity really, it would have made a pleasant change to cheer up this Celeste by returning her bird.

'Bertie, I'm going now.' He headed for the cell door.

'Going? No. No. Where?' Bertie asked suddenly. He was a sociable chap and didn't like being on his own. Perhaps he'd overplayed his hand tormenting Wilf.

'To get a cup of coffee and arrange for you to be taken to the zoo.'

'Zoo?' Bertie found most of the sentence too difficult to understand, but zoo was a great new word. Monosyllabic. Easy to say. 'Zoo,' he repeated thoughtfully.

'Yes, the zoo. Maybe you'll meet some other parrots.'

'Not a parrot.' The answer came back immediately and was very clear. Wilf could have sworn there was more than a trace of annoyance in Bertie's answer.'

'What are you then?'

'A macaw. A hyacinth macaw.'

'Well I'll be damned!'

'Now we're cooking,' said Bertie amiably.

An hour later, Bertie was taken by police van across the river to Regent's Park. Wilf carried him gingerly using a thick Kevlar gauntlet borrowed from one of the dog handlers, glad of the protection from those deadly claws. Bertie was, to his great relief, pleasantly docile during the journey. They were met by a darting, nervous little man with a knife blade for a nose and restless brown eyes. He reminded Wilf of a sparrow, so it was no real surprise he turned out to be head keeper for the bird houses.

'Good morning, Detective Constable Thompson. Allow me to congratulate you on a remarkable find.' He seemed unusually excited. Bertie looked bored.

'Mr Keynes?'

'Colin Keynes, yes. My, what a magnificent specimen.'

'Thank you. I work out, you know,' replied Wilf.

Colin hooted with laughter. 'Very witty. Actually, apart from our Millicent, he's the only other fully grown hyacinthine we've had here for some time.'

'Millicent?' The two men walked together past cages and on through the gardens. Children crowded around the enclosures, chattering and pointing at somnolent, spectacularly uninterested creatures. A few turned to follow their progress, goggle-eyed at the sight of Bertie.

'Yes, our own resident and, to my best knowledge, one of only a handful of unattached females in the country. She's just reached maturity and we hope to breed her soon.'

Bertie turned and stared at Colin. Hello, this sounded interesting. He knew exactly what a female was, even though he'd never actually seen one.

'So come on, tell me about these birds. Why are they so rare?'

'The usual reasons, destruction of habitat and so on, and even those remaining areas are now being rapidly cleared for agriculture. If we don't stop soon we'll lose a lot more than these beauties.'

'What do they eat? I've been feeding him Brazil nuts. Is that OK – I haven't poisoned him, have I?'

'They're fine. Any fatty or oily nut will do. You can tell by the condition and colour of his plumage he's had a good diet.'

Bertie rather hoped the conversation would return to Millicent.

'I have to admit I don't think I've seen anything quite so blue in all my life – apart from some seized DVDs from Amsterdam.'

Colin chuckled. 'I'm sure I don't know what you mean, Detective Constable.'

126

'Wilf.'

'Tell me, Wilf, did Bertie say anything to you?'

'More than I get out of the usual occupants of our cells. He was quite the chatterbox.'

'That's not unusual. They're great mimics and in rare cases can have well-developed vocabularies, although not nearly as good as the African Grey parrot. Now they really are astonishing talkers!'

'I've got to tell you, Colin, I found it pretty weird at first.'

'Yes, well, that's understandable. We expect intelligence from chimps and the like, but not from birds. It can be a bit of an eye opener on your first encounter. Macaws, in particular, are extremely bright and very, very inquisitive. Cranial size doesn't equate here because their brains, although not much larger than a big walnut, appear to be structured in a unique fashion.'

'A bit like teenagers.'

'Tell me about it – I've got one of those at home. Anyway, they're equally as clever as dolphins and certainly much more so than dogs. I'm sure it'll come as a shock but I can assure you some parrots can understand in excess of a thousand words. Not bad when you consider the average human has a vocabulary of only about six or seven thousand words. Even budgerigars have been trained to repeat up to five hundred words and can perform surprising feats of eloquence.'

Colin's enthusiasm was delightfully infectious. It was such a pleasant change to be in the company of someone absorbed in a field of expertise that didn't involve ram raiding or spray-painting underpasses.

'Most people simply cannot accept a lower creature has cognitive powers but I can assure you it's true. Macaws are extremely long-lived and you simply can't go through an extended lifespan relying purely on instinct on a day-by-day basis. There must be some accumulated powers of understanding and reasoning in there that slowly build up over the years.'

'Makes sense. So, tell me more about Millicent,' enquired Wilf. It was a question Bertie was on the point of asking himself.

'She was a gift from the Brazilian Government to help with a world-wide breeding programme and has developed a significant relationship with us. She's mastered all the important words, such as "cold" and "hungry" or "thirsty", but we haven't quite got on to *War and Peace* yet. Macaws have the lowest threshold of boredom of any animal and need constant stimulus or they begin to develop severe behavioural problems. It's cruel to keep solitary specimens unless you can devote hours of constant attention to keep them occupied. That's why we try to pair them as soon as they reach maturity. Once they've mated they stay with the same partner for the rest of their lives. It's all rather sweet, when you think about it.'

'No divorce?'

'Not with these blue beauties. Hyacinths are compulsively social and live in large family groups in the wild, communicating with such a complex range of sounds it can really only be described as a language. Obviously with our limited resources we can't devote individual attention to Millicent so we had a radio installed in her aviary. I can tell you she's quite well up on classical music, can whistle snatches of Mozart, and simply adores the shipping forecast.' Colin grinned at Wilf's sceptical glance. 'It's the clear enunciation and repetition, you see. Easy to pick up.' Wilf couldn't figure if he was being ribbed or not, but having spent some time with Bertie he could quite believe what he'd just been told. 'What surprises me is that he is not ringed. It's not exactly against the law but it certainly helps identification.'

'We ought to ring some of the nasty little specimens I have to deal with,' observed Wilf dryly.

'Around the ankle?'

'Well, I can think of somewhere much more interesting.'

'Ouch!' Keynes winced. He was glad Wilf declined to explain further. 'It seems strange Bertie has been unable to tell you his address. Most owners teach their birds that right at the start. Ah, here we are.'

Address! Now there was a word Bertie instantly recognised. If only Wilf had asked the right question. Of course he knew his address, but he wasn't going to tell them just yet, not until he'd seen Millicent anyway – what did they think he was, stupid?

Wilf had been conscious for some time of a rising background cacophony of cheeps and tweets, chirrups and twitters, hoots, squeaks, trills and screeches that signified the approaching aviaries. Colin led him to an extremely capacious enclosure perhaps twenty feet high and more than three times that in width and depth. The interior was filled with luxuriant foliage and numerous wooden perches. Plump, colourful ground birds strutted around on spindly legs amongst the bushes and bamboos, pecking at the soil with jerky movements like epileptic robots. Above, sitting here and there on sturdy branches, a number of large parrots observed the newcomers with interest and squawked discordantly at their approach. Some sat in solitary splendour, others squeezed against each other like pensioners cuddling up on a sea front bench during a February gale.

'We've got a good selection in here,' said Colin. 'They're very sociable and all get on well together.'

'What are those?' Wilf pointed to a restless group of spectacular multi-coloured birds – vibrant blue, yellow and red.

'That gang of delinquents? They're scarlets. Quite something, aren't they? Absolutely beautiful, but full of mischief.' Colin peered into the aviary. 'Now then, where is she? Up there, somewhere, is *Anodorhynchus hyacinthinus*.'

'Who?' Latin was not one of Wilf's stronger subjects.

'The hyacinth macaw. Ah, there she is, behind that big branch.' All three craned their necks and peered through the wire. There was a distant flash of deep blue amongst the leaves, but no more.

'Millicent! Come here, sweetie!' Colin called, scratching at the wire. 'Come on, Milly! Show yourself.'

'Dogger! Irish Sea! Fair to moderate; falling slowly!' was all Millicent deigned to utter from her lofty perch, despite Colin's entreaties.

He shrugged and apologised. 'Sorry, but you can't force her to come,' he said, and began to walk away.

'Hang on, aren't you going to put him in with her?' asked

Wilf. It was a question of burning importance for Bertie as well.

'Good Lord, no!'

'What! Why not? If they're that rare, surely this is a golden opportunity to increase the species.'

Too right it is. Bertie glared at Colin.

'Wilf, we would have to make all kinds of preparations before we could mate them, not even counting the formal permission of Bertie's owner. There would have to be tests to check both birds were completely healthy and DNA testing to ensure the widest spread of the gene pool to keep the species viable. Other zoos may have more suitable partners for Bertie. With so few hyacinths in captivity we must get the very best breeding match possible. You have to understand this is a very delicate matter.'

Bertie wished they would stop talking and just let him get on with it; all he wanted to do was woo and hump her! A minute, maybe two. Tops!

Wilf's reasoning was roughly analogous to Bertie's. 'I'm sure they don't wait for the results of gene testing in sunny Brazil, so why don't you just let him have a go?' It appeared Bertie's chances of a jump were substantially more rosy than his had ever been. Anything he could do to help, he would.

'Sorry, but we simply can't risk it. What if they fight, or Millicent gets injured? No, it could be disastrous without detailed preparation. We're not even sure if she's receptive.'

She is, you idiot!

'Pity.' Wilf really felt quite sorry for Bertie. He followed Colin through a gate marked "Private" to an area segregated from the public by a tall wooden fence. There, a few sheds contained feed and tools and all manner of sundry items required to keep the aviaries clean and well-stocked. They passed an access door at the rear of the macaw enclosure, hidden from public view by foliage. Bertie stared long and hard at the receding aviary. He'd be back. An empty holding pen stood nearby, a temptingly short distance from the maidenly virtuous Millicent. Wilf climbed inside carefully and looked around, nodding with approval at the spacious cage. 'Nice billet.' He gently urged Bertie onto a perch. 'See you, kid.'

'Goodbye, Wilf. Thanks for the nuts.'

Colin's eyebrows shot up in surprise. Wilf gently stroked Bertie's neck and grinned. 'I told you he was sharp.' He slipped a tangerine and the remaining Brazil nuts into a feeding pan attached to the perch and levered himself out of the door.

'How long will he be with us?' asked Colin, securing the latch.

'Difficult to say. We'll continue with our enquiries, but I have to tell you this is pretty low priority stuff. We know he lives around Greenwich somewhere, has a hamster pal called Barnstaple and his owner's name is Celeste, but that's about it. Our best bet is when Celeste reports him missing, which she must surely do. She obviously loves him because he's so attached to her. With a spot of luck, we might have him home by tomorrow.'

'Good. This must be quite disturbing for him. Meanwhile, I'll check up with the local bird societies to see if they can trace him. Have you thought about approaching your pals in Customs? If he's been brought in legally then they'll certainly have a record of his entry into the country.'

'Exactly what I'm going to do when I get back to the station.'

'The import regulations are unbelievably strict concerning endangered birds, but if it can be proved he's been hand-reared and a pet for a significant period of time then there wouldn't have been any trouble getting him into the UK, although I suppose he could have come to Britain long before we had the regs.'

'Is that likely?'

'It's certainly possible. Bertie's in his prime and could already be well over thirty. That's another wonderful thing about macaws. Once you have one, you literally have one for life – they can live for up to sixty years!'

The gate closed again and the two men disappeared, leaving Bertie to sit in silence. He waited until he was thoroughly alone and hopped over to examine the door lock. He didn't like cages very much. Having bonded to Celeste as a chick no cage was ever needed to keep him by her side as they cruised the rainforest rivers. He followed her everywhere, waddling up and down the wooden deck like an obedient dog, chattering away to the amused crew.

The latch was a ludicrously simple affair, the kind he learnt to pick while he was still a fledgling. This was going to be easy. An examination of the aviary floor produced a twig of the necessary size and strength. He climbed up the wire, hooked his claws into the grille beside the door, gripped the twig in his powerful bill and threading it through the mesh, neatly releasing the latch with a controlled flick of the head – and those arrogant monkey boys thought they had a monopoly on the use of tools! He flew to the back door of the other aviary. Again, the bolt succumbed to his expert manipulation and he scampered eagerly into the enclosure.

'Hello, Millicent. My name is Bertie. I'm going to jump your bones!' The television provided a rich source of material for these romantic occasions.

Millicent's head appeared from behind a bushy branch. She peered down to see a very handsome boy standing inside her cage. Inside! The other birds looked on, amazed at Bertie's sudden reappearance. One trilled a greeting, which, although the accent was unfamiliar, Bertie understood. He responded with his own formal call, a melodic screech that, although unintelligible to human ears, carried in its multi-layered harmonics information of his breed, status, sex and intent. As a youngster, Bertie had naturally learned how to communicate with many other species of birds, chattering across the still evening waters of the Madeira from the deck of the *Esmeralda*, learning both the human tongue from the girlish Celeste as well as his own language from his cousins swarming in the distant trees. All birds, having a common ancestry, understand the basic calls of almost every other species, even if the accents were sometimes atrocious, a linguistic feat of which humans remained blissfully ignorant.

The resident macaws responded politely to Bertie's greeting, bobbing heads and welcoming him with a nod and a whistle. Bertie stared up at Millicent for a few seconds, then spread his wings and displayed magnificently, a glorious violet splash, dazzling in its majesty. His audience cooed appreciatively and settled themselves down to watch the inevitable shenanigans with lively interest. If they'd had popcorn, it would have been passed around!

'Rockall, north-north west, twelve miles.'

Bertie was forced to consider the possibility that Millicent's conversational skills were somewhat limited. However, talk could wait until later. He felt an uncontrollable stirring in parts which had never stirred before and launched himself with a wild cry of passion.

'Forties! German Bight!' There was now an element of panic in Millicent's voice.

There was no thought of DNA testing. None. Nature took its course, if not entirely willingly, then certainly noisily, and was accompanied by agitated news of deteriorating weather conditions in Fastnet and a storm warning in Finisterre.

All told, it took him a little less than twelve seconds.

That's a man for you!

Chapter Ten

'Your blasted macaw has raped Millicent!'

'What?' Wilf cradled the receiver on one shoulder while sorting through the usual untidy pile of folders stacked precariously on his desk, an early morning sourness lending his face more than its usual hang-dog expression of melancholy. Colin Keynes was spitting blood on the other end of the phone. 'What on earth are you talking about?'

'Bertie! Surely you haven't forgotten that macaw you brought out to us yesterday.'

'I'm hardly likely to, am I?' This delivered with all the compacted sarcasm of a worldly-wise, long-serving police officer.

'Nor am I! He picked the lock of his cage and got in with our Millicent.'

'So?'

'So he's bloody well shagged her!' Keynes fizzed like water splashed on a hot plate. He really was rather upset. Outraged, to be honest. Wilf tossed the files, leaned back in his chair and smiled broadly. Good old Bertie. Nice to know someone was getting their claw-over.

'Oh, dear,' he said mildly,

Keynes went critical, like a badly maintained Russian reactor. '"Oh dear!" Is that all you can frigging say?' he shrieked.

Wilf held the phone away from his head to protect his eardrum and covered the mouthpiece. 'Bertie's humped that girlie parrot!' he announced to no one in particular. 'They're not happy campers over at the zoo.' There was a ripple of

135

laughter around the office.

Yates passed by and grinned. 'Nice one, Wilf. That's made my day. Damned bird gets more sex than I do.'

Wilf considered his senior's statement while Keynes continued to fulminate and came to the conclusion no woman in her right mind would want to come within a million miles of Yates. She'd have to be on some sort of powerful and thoroughly illegal mind-altering substances to find him even tolerably pleasant. He returned to the splenetic keeper, still in a state of utmost agitation.

'Mr Keynes,' interposed Wilf firmly. 'Colin, calm down. I cannot see your problem. Does it really matter if Millicent is covered by Bertie or another male? If chicks hatch, does anyone really give a toss who's the father?'

'But you don't understand,' Keynes yelled. 'These macaws only mate with one partner. Milly now won't breed with any other male. She and Bertie are an item. Don't you get it – they've bonded. For life! That's truly knackered our breeding programme. God knows what's going to happen when Bertie is returned to his owner – poor Milly will be heartbroken. She'll pine.'

'For the fjords?'

'Don't get smart with me, Thompson,' he snarled. 'This is a catastrophe.'

'Come on, Colin, surely it's not that bad. Treat their encounter as a blessing in disguise. *Brief Encounter* in feathers.' Wilf idly speculated on how macaws mated. Noisily, in all probability. Have to watch the claws. Still, not as dangerous as porcupines or tarantulas, and they manage without too many problems. Plenty of them mooching about in the wild. Keynes was still blathering on interminably when a passing constable slipped a note onto Wilf's desk ...

Wilf coaxed Bertie out of the police van, again thankful for the protection provided by the thick gauntlet. Bertie's claws easily encircled his wrist. He could feel their tips indent the glove like hypodermic needles. Collecting him from the zoo had been a little awkward. Keynes was like a father who'd just discovered his virginal daughter had spent a weekend on enthusiastic sausage manoeuvres with the Parachute Regiment. Wilf and, it has to be said, Bertie, were both entirely unsympathetic. However, for a species noted for its uxoriousness he had been less reluctant to be prised away from his new amour than might have been expected. Wilf guessed Millicent's limited meteorological vocabulary probably had something to do with it, but at least the macaw gave him no trouble on the short trip to Greenwich.

He looked fondly at the big bird. It was so difficult not to like him. 'Is this home, Bertie?'

'Home. Yes.' There was a note of distinct excitement in the musical voice. He bobbed his head and began to trill loudly. An ivory Persian curled up on the mat opened an eye and instantly leapt to its feet as if it had been juiced with several thousand very unwelcome volts. It hissed menacingly with fur raised before pelting for cover in the bushes. No love lost there, observed Wilf.

'Good.' He always knew it would be a simple problem to solve. Bertie's disappearance would inevitably be reported so all he had to do was wait. If only every case was as easy to solve.

'Wilf?'

'Yes, Bertie?'

'Thank you.'

'My pleasure.' He rang the bell. A few moments later, the door swung open.

'Bertie! My darling!'

'Mummy!' There was a sudden rush of blue as Bertie swept up from Wilf's arm and turned full somersaults above their heads, singing in an exuberant paean of joyful happiness. Celeste grabbed a leather gauntlet from a table beside the door and slipped it on, calling to him. Bertie trilled wildly and with a fluttering sweep of wings, settled on her arm like a giant feathery gargoyle. She was overwhelmed, kissing and stroking the macaw, her eyes streaming helplessly. Wilf was surprisingly moved. In a job not noted for many genuinely happy moments, this was a sight to savour. For some strange reason, Bertie began to purr very loudly.

'Oh, Bertie, you naughty boy, where have you been?'

'Zoo. With Wilf.'

Celeste seemed to notice Wilf for the first time and wiping the tears away, smiled with obvious embarrassment. 'Detective Constable Thompson? I'm sorry about the blubbing, but Bertie is, well, he's someone very special.' The macaw was most definitely much more than a mere pet.

'A pleasure to meet you, Miss Gordon. I can see I've come to the right house.' Bertie rubbed cheeks with Celeste and chattered like a small child.

'Please, call me Celeste. I can't thank you enough for finding him. Do come in and have a cup of tea. I want you to tell me all about his adventures.'

Wilf hesitated for a moment. There was an ever-growing mountain of urgent paperwork back at the station, but Celeste *was* a very attractive woman. Rich copper hair gleamed around her shoulders. He'd never seen such a unique shade of glowing ginger. 'Thanks, Celeste, I'd love a cup. My name's Wilf, by the way.'

Wilf despatched the van driver back to the station and followed Celeste indoors. She led him into the salon and urged Bertie on to his perch beside the sofa where he immediately bent to investigate the contents of his food pan. The tea took a few minutes to arrive, giving Wilf time to examine the room. After so many years in the force, he couldn't help himself. There was a definite foreign theme in the decor, exotic, Latin, and brilliantly colourful. Indian artefacts lined the walls; bows and blowpipes, feathered head-dresses and rainbowed hangings. Brightly patterned rugs were scattered over the parquet flooring while various paintings and photographs depicted native village scenes and landscapes of rugged mountains, dense forests and broad, lazy rivers. One in particular caught his eye and he peered more closely. He recognised Celeste as a young girl with long ginger pig-tails surrounded by the cheerful crew of a river steamer, the laughing group standing under the shade of an awning stretched over its stern. An infant parrot sat on her shoulder, awkward and blue, and he realised with some surprise

138

it was Bertie. Judging from Celeste's age now, that meant the macaw must be almost thirty years old, possibly more!

Wilf's attention wandered from the photo. He picked up a wooden effigy and stared at its outsized erect phallus. The figurine was coarsely carved in mahogany, but the unfeasibly engorged genitals were exquisitely detailed and anatomically perfect in every way. Celeste bustled in and noticed his interest. 'It's a tribal fertility icon from Brazil,' she said without embarrassment. 'I lived in the heart of the Amazon Basin until my parents died. As you can see, I brought much home with me.' She nodded at the decorations around the room. 'A lovely reminder of an extraordinary country.'

'Is this modelled on a real man?' Wilf felt a depressing wash of inadequacy on being confronted with such enormous tackle.

She smiled at his mock indignation. 'Now then, Wilf, in all honesty do you really think I would've come home had the men of Brazil been so sumptuously endowed?' Wilf decided he liked her sense of humour. He threw his mac over the back of a chair and sat down. Celeste poured and Bertie whistled happily like a milkman going about his morning round on a sunny summer's morning.

'You have some lovely things here.'

'Thank you. Brazil is a wondrous country, full of cultural and artistic delights.'

'Too many bugs for me.' Wilf was not an acolyte of exotic travel. Ramsgate pushed all his buttons, thank you very much.

'There are creatures much more terrifying than the bugs, believe me.'

'Such as?'

'Snakes, for instance.'

'Yuk!'

'And caimans.'

'That's a sort of dwarf crocodile, isn't it?'

'That's right, but in the deep jungle rivers they run up to a size big enough to take a man.'

'Nasty. Ever see a piranha?'

'My favourite psycho-fish. Sure, I've seen plenty and things can get ugly if you come across a big shoal.'

'Good lord,' muttered Wilf, pulling a face. 'What an awful place.'

'Not so, it's astonishing, despite the occasional viciousness of its flora and fauna.'

'Then why have you returned to boring old Greenwich?'

'I suppose I just wanted to be back in England. Nothing forced me home. I had a very nice villa in Manaus, but I got lonely after Dad died. We kept each other company when Mum passed on, but Brazil was something I shared with my parents.' Celeste neglected to mention that, in fact, the real reason she'd returned to Britain was to search out the very sort of man she'd found in James. It had taken many years, but eventually it dawned on her that if she stayed in South America then she would forever remain sexually unfulfilled. However, although she already liked this policeman, she certainly did not like him enough to tell him that!

Wilf seemed satisfied with her answer and moved on to another topic. As a copper, it came as second nature to be always asking questions. 'So tell me, Celeste, why did Bertie escape? I can't believe he left you by choice.'

'Defending me against burglars the night before last.'

'Burglars!' Wilf looked up from his cup, his professional interest sharpening considerably. 'What happened?'

'Bertie woke me at about one in the morning. There was a hell of a row coming from downstairs so I went to investigate. I thought he was attacking Sebastian again.'

'That wouldn't be the cat, by any chance – the Persian I saw scuttling for cover?'

'Yes. They don't get on too well.'

'He did seem keen to avoid Bertie's company.'

'But when I got downstairs I found two intruders in here standing beside my bureau.'

'Has this been reported?'

'Yes. I've had no end of visits from the police since. It's considered a serious crime because of my injuries.' She nodded at the sling supporting her arm.

'Were you visited by a SOCO?'

'A what?'

140

'Scenes of Crime Officer.'

'Ah, yes, you mean Debbie. She came just as I was taken to hospital and was still here when I got back. Everything had been photographed and she was busy looking for fingerprints. A constable explained everything.'

'His name?'

'PC Drewing. Do you know him?'

'Yes. Ian's a good lad. I'll pull the file when I get back to the station, but please go on. Do you think you could recognise the men again?' He sipped his tea and eyed her over the top of his cup. She really was quite gorgeous. Lovely legs – and those glorious emerald eyes!

'No. They were wearing black overalls and rubber gloves, but for some reason both had taken off their hoods. Bertie had switched on the light because they were just standing there looking dazed. One turned away and pulled his hood back on just as I came into the room, so unfortunately I never managed to see his face. The other was grovelling on the floor. Bertie had already removed half his ear by this time – I found it beside the sofa after they'd gone.'

'That should help with a DNA identification. I'll also make sure we check out the local hospitals for anyone admitted with an incomplete set of ears. Was there anything else? I know it's probably all in the report, but I'd really like to hear everything you remember.' Wilf just wanted to stay there and listen to her all day.

Celeste sat back and appraised the detective. He was tall and stringy, but doubtless tough, a trifle sad and grey, a threadbare man whose age appeared to be lost somewhere in the mid-forties, but there remained a deep warmth to his eyes which reminded her of James – and his astringent humour was definitely appealing. Her woman's instinct was sure; here was a man of capability, determination, rectitude and loyalty. Being a detective suited him. He'd found his calling and obviously loved his job, even though he tried to project an air of worldly-wise weariness.

'It was all over so quickly. I lashed out and caught One-Ear across the back with my whip –'

Wilf spluttered into his cup. A trickle of tea escaped epiglottal control and headed off to explore his lungs. 'Whip?' he coughed noisily.

'A memento from Brazil,' said Celeste smoothly. 'He squeaked a bit, then the other dived over the sofa, slammed into me and knocked me to the ground. I was stunned for a while. Can't really remember what happened next. The doctors say I've broken a collar-bone and two ribs, hence the sling.'

'Looks to me like a case of Actual Bodily Harm, as defined in the oft-used Offences Against the Person Act 1861, Section 47. I think your injuries fall under ABH, don't you?'

'You know your laws, Wilf, that's for sure. I'm impressed.'

'Thanks. I've had occasion to use that one before and I'd certainly go for ABH in this case. These two are in real trouble if we find them. They'll be looking at a custodial sentence even if they have no previous. Go on.'

'Debbie found something called a telescopic metal truncheon under one of the chairs and Constable Drewing told me it's regarded as an offensive weapon.'

'True enough. We're issued with them. A pocket-sized piece of unpleasantness. They're much more effective than the old hickory sticks and can give you a very serious injury. The telescopic definitely makes it Aggravated Burglary at the very minimum. That's burglary with an offensive weapon.'

'Which is covered by?'

'Theft Act 1968, Section 10,' replied Wilf promptly. 'A burglary where the offender uses any firearm, imitation firearm, weapon of offence, or explosive, blah, blah. Kinda buddies we are, me and Section 10. Seen a lot of action together over the years.'

'Then Bertie rejoined the fray again. It was – well, pretty spectacular!'

Wilf reviewed his knowledge of the macaw. 'I can imagine.'

'He simply went crazy. I never realised until then just how formidable he is. It must have come as a shock when blood started spurting everywhere. He chased them to those patio doors and was dragged outside in the struggle. The last thing I saw was the pair of them leaping over the garden wall and running away up the road. Bertie was nowhere in sight. I called but he never came back.'

Wilf put down his cup and went to examine the double doors. 'Were these locked?'

'Of course.'

'Interesting. There's no damage to the locks or hinges.'

'Constable Drewing mentioned that.'

'Ian's a bright boy. He'll have told you it means the lock was picked, not forced. These guys were professionals. I'd be very surprised if they left any fingerprints. What's this mark here?' The wooden frame was crushed slightly at eye level.

'The man who hit me ran into the door. I think there was something wrong with his hood.'

'That must have been quite an impact. Probably broke his nose.'

'I sincerely hope so,' said Celeste warmly.

Wilf slowly walked around, looking at the room from every angle, then stared out across the garden for a few seconds before returning to his seat. 'What I find mystifying is that all these lovely antiques were ignored. This is a fencer's dream, yet none of it was touched. You say the two men were at this bureau. What's in here?'

'Papers, bills, some petty cash. The usual sort of thing.'

'How much cash?'

'About two hundred pounds in a tin.'

'Gone?'

'Actually, no.'

'Really! Now that's significant. They were smart enough to pick the lock but too dumb to take the cash.'

'Well, it does seem they only touched my diary, although I doubt there's anything in it of much interest to anyone. I found it on the floor beside the table with some letters. Nothing else was disturbed or stolen.'

Wilf sat down again and wondered if he warranted an entry in her diary. The thought of her description of him made him cringe. He finished his tea and held the cup out for a refill. He wanted to stay very badly indeed.

'You look puzzled,' said Celeste, topping him up. 'I'm no

expert but perplexity in a detective implies not all is well.'

Wilf pursed his lips. Something definitely wasn't right here; his instincts, honed by years of experience, were up in arms. 'There's something strange going on here. I'll look into it when I get back to the station and let you know if we have anything.'

'Thanks, Wilf. I appreciate it very much.'

'In the meantime, I'm ashamed to have to tell you Bertie has not exactly behaved himself while he's been on the run …'

'What have you got on the Gordon burglary, Ian?'

PC Drewing looked up and grinned. Wilf was OK by Ian. Despite his grumpiness, the older man had taken pains to ease him into the hectic routine of the station, helping immensely with his superior experience, local knowledge, and dry, unruffled approach. Ian thought it grossly unfair Wilf's promotion had been overlooked for so long.

'Here's the report, Wilf. Miss Gordon gave as good a description as possible, but these two definitely weren't any of the local boys. I don't see we have much to go on.'

'What's new.' Wilf studied the file for a few moments and checked over the computer entries. Drewing was right – they stood no chance of solving this one. Debbie had done her usual thorough job, but the burglars had used gloves. There was the ear, of course, now languishing in the forensics freezer with other assorted body parts carelessly abandoned at various crime scenes around the borough. Unsurprisingly, no one had come forward to claim it, and hospital enquiries had also drawn a blank.

'No prints at all. These guys were careful,' said Drewing.

'Not all is lost, my boy. Don't forget the ear itself.'

'I love DNA.'

'Exactly. Let's see if the appliance of science can provide us with anything.' The ear provided ample material for the lab boys, along with samples taken from the wide selection of bloodstains thoughtfully garnered by Bertie. 'We'll definitely get DNA for both men. It's up to the guys in white coats now.'

'Persons in white coats,' corrected Drewing. 'Don't forget we're equal opportunity employers now.'

'Smart arse,' muttered Wilf. 'This political correctness crap gets on my tits. Sorry – my non-male infant-feeding orbs!' He knew in such cases the results could take up to a month to arrive. He closed the file and sat staring into middle distance. The whole affair didn't sit right. 'I don't like the use of the truncheon. That's nasty.'

'Not as nasty as a knife,' reflected Ian. Cutting crimes were becoming disturbingly common. 'She was lucky in a way; she was only in her jim-jams – things could have got a lot worse.'

Wilf nodded in acknowledgement. Now that was an uncomfortable thought. 'Why would two professional burglars go to the trouble of picking the lock and then ignore wads of ready cash, not to mention the antiques?'

'Perhaps the lights went on before they had chance to pocket the goodies.'

'Maybe. But thieves rummage real quick. If I was doing a house, I'd grab the cash box even if I had to leave the rest. It was plainly visible in the bureau, yet untouched.'

'Which leads to an unusual conclusion.'

'I have to agree with you, Ian,' said Wilf. 'Perhaps they *were* actually after the diary. I think I'm going to have to see Miss Gordon again.'

'You lucky old bugger!'

'Privilege of age, Constable Drewing,' Wilf grinned smugly. He threw the file on top of an unstable stack of folders and turned his mind to the next in an endless line of tasks when the sounds of an irate conversation floated across the office.

'I've told you before, sergeant, don't encourage the old bag. I won't have her taking up valuable police time. Get rid of her. Now!' Yates turned on his heel and flounced into his office. Wilf and Drewing looked at each other.

'Daisy?'

'Got to be. No one else induces that distinctive whine of exasperation in our dear leader's voice.'

'I'll go.'

'No,' said Wilf. 'You better get on with those statistics for our beloved Tristram.' Drewing flinched at the note of scorn in his voice.

Wilf made his way down to the front counter. The sergeant on duty nodded towards a figure straining to read a notice exhorting vigilance against pickpocketing. 'It's all right, Phil, I'll look after her. Hello, Daisy, how are you today?' He clasped the hands of a shrunken old woman and led her gently to a nearby seat. She seemed unusually cold even though the weather outside was pleasantly mild. Her limp was obviously painful. Wilf ordered tea straight away.

'I'm troubled, Mr Thompson, very troubled.' Daisy Jeffries had lived in the borough all her substantially long life, but had become disturbingly vague in the last few years. This made her vulnerable, and so gave Wilf cause for concern. Despite the outward eccentricity and frailty, he knew Daisy still had a lively mind in there somewhere and her incalculable local knowledge had been useful on more than one occasion. For that alone, as well as for simple compassion, he always tried to find the time to chat whenever she made the effort to hobble the half mile from her home to the station.

The tea arrived courtesy of Sergeant Phil. Daisy's transparent hands hardly seemed strong enough to grip the plastic cup. She sipped noisily. Her dentures required major renovation. She was a tiny woman with a few sparse wisps of white hair sprouting from under her red bobble hat. She wore her favourite heavy brown coat made shapeless by several thick jumpers and a host of thermal vests. Knitted stockings completed her trendy nonagenarian outfit. *Haute couture* had passed by Daisy decades ago but at least she kept herself warm.

'So what's been keeping you awake this time?' asked Wilf.

Daisy slurped like a council lorry flushing out a recalcitrant drain. 'I found a crisp packet in my front garden yesterday. It's a disgrace, that's what it is. We never had these problems when there was National Service.' Daisy had a thing about litter. Well, more than a thing – perhaps an overwhelming compulsive obsession was a more accurate description.

'Salt and vinegar, it was. I don't even like salt and vinegar, and cheese and onion always gives me uncontrollable wind,' she added in a conspiratorial whisper, as if imparting some dreadful secret. At the desk, Phil stifled a chuckle. Like Wilf, he had known Daisy a very long time and thought she was great. Sadly, Wilf didn't have time to list the extensive range of foods that gave him the bottom burps. Curries hovered somewhere near the top of the premier league, a trait he unknowingly shared with Bob Pritchard.

He sighed inwardly. Yates would go supernova if the entire force was called out on litter duty. It looked like Daisy was settling in for the duration. Time to execute a discreet tactical withdrawal. 'Listen Daisy, you just stay here and finish your tea. I'll ask Constable Drewing to tidy up next time he's down your way, OK?'

'Blue it was.'

She wasn't listening to him. Daisy's grip on reality seemed to be fading completely. Phil raised a helpless eyebrow. Wilf looked at his watch and hoped in vain Daisy would get the hint.

'What was blue, Daisy, the crisp packet?'

'Yes. Beautifully blue. Like the sky. How do they print them in such lovely colours?'

'I don't know.'

'On plastic as well.'

'It's a mystery.'

'Yes, the bluest thing I've ever seen.' The old lady suddenly looked up at Wilf and the vagueness melted from her eyes like mist on a sunny morning. 'Mr Thompson, the crisp packet *was* blue, but not as blue as that wonderful bird!'

Wilf's jaw dropped. Daisy sniggered suddenly. 'You look like you've swallowed a frog.'

He shut his mouth with a snap before Phil noticed. 'You saw a blue bird – a big bird?' He held his hands wide apart.

'Oh, yes. Quite as big as that.'

'Daisy, now this is very important; when did you see it?'

'Night before last.' No hesitation. 'I couldn't sleep because of my hip so I went downstairs to make a cup of tea. Tea and two aspirin. The soluble ones are the best. From the Co-op. All those bubbles fizzing in the glass, then it goes clear and ...'

'The bird, Daisy, let's concentrate on the bird.' Wilf gently steered the conversation back on course.

'The bird? Yes, sorry. Anyway, there was a noise outside so

I peeked through the window and saw two men running down the middle of the road.'

'Two men. Are you sure?'

Daisy nodded with surprising vigour. A cervical vertebra cracked ominously. 'All in black, they were. I could hardly see them at first because it was so dark, then they got closer. It all seemed a bit strange so I watched them some more. I hope you don't think I'm a nosy person.'

'Of course not.'

'I'm not like that Mrs Henry,' she said tartly. 'Always poking about in other people's business. I was very happy with my packed lunch.' Daisy and Alice Henry both vied for the coveted *Lived Longest in the Street* award. They'd been needling each other on and off ever since a minor altercation blossomed into full-scale thermonuclear war over the choice of sandwich filling during their visit to the Festival of Britain in 1951.

Wilf nudged her in the right direction again, like a collie shepherding a gaggle of hallucinating sheep. 'Never mind Alice. Just tell me what happened next.'

'Well, we should have had sardines, but she insisted on Spam.'

'No, no, Daisy, calm down. I don't mean about the sandwiches. Can we stick to the men.'

'Oh dear, I'm getting diverted again, aren't I. Anyway, they ran towards my house waving their arms above their heads. It looked very odd. Quite comical. It reminded me of Max Wall. I saw him once at –'

'The bird, Daisy,' said Wilf firmly. 'Let's stick to the bird, shall we?'

'Um, well, OK. Where was I? Ah, yes, then I saw the big blue bird suddenly appear. It was swooping down on them and screeching. I'm surprised it didn't wake the whole neighbourhood.'

'Go on.'

'Can I have another cup of tea, please?'

'Sarge, do the honours again, would you?' The drink arrived quickly enough – Phil was now keen to lend an ear to the

148

conversation – and Daisy wrapped her gnarled hands around the cup, sipping steadily. Her need for warmth seemed endless. 'So what happened next?'

'They had a van. It was parked by the post box.'

'Can you remember the make?'

Daisy shook her head slowly. 'No. They all look the same to me, but I remember it had two headlights,' she added helpfully.

'I'm afraid they all have two headlights.'

'Oh.'

'What colour was it?'

'White. It was a bit dirty.'

'Any writing on the side? Any signs?'

'I don't think so.'

'How long had it been there?'

'A long time. All afternoon and evening, which struck me as odd.'

'Why so?'

'Well, if they'd been hiding in the van all that time then how did they go to the loo? Men need to go more often than women,' she added in a knowing whisper.

'Daisy, that's an excellent point. You would have made a great policewoman.'

She blushed and hung her head. 'Go on with you, you're just saying that.'

'No, I'm serious. This means they came prepared. They just ran out of luck coming across such a good guard bird.'

'Yes, I can see that.'

'So the men jumped into the van and drove away?'

'Jumped?' Daisy laughed so much she almost spilled her precious drink. 'Lord! Mr Thompson, you should have seen them. What a panic, just like the Keystone Kops.'

'I can imagine.' Bertie was a formidable opponent – and a good shagger, by all accounts. 'Can you remember anything else?'

'Well, let's see. Yes, the bird was still attacking the van when they drove off. It was all over the windscreen. They came towards my house and turned towards the shops. The tyres made a horrible squealing noise around the corner just like an episode of *The Rockford Files*. The poor thing was thrown off and landed in Mrs Walton's firethorn hedge. She always gets a lovely show of berries every autumn, doesn't she.'

'That's true.' Even Wilf knew all about Mavis Walton's legendary hedge.

'Anyway, the blue bird sat there for a few minutes and then flew away. I went back to bed after that because I was cold.'

Wilf's initial excitement evaporated. Apart from identifying the getaway vehicle as a white van, not exactly uncommon in London, Daisy had merely confirmed Celeste and Bertie's account of the burglary. Interesting that they'd spent so much time waiting. This was certainly not a spur of the moment job. Whoever the pair were, they had definitely targeted Celeste's house. He'd check the local CCTV cameras to see if any picked up the van. He patted her on the shoulder. 'Well, thank you very much, Daisy. You'll be happy to know the bird was found and returned to his owner this morning.'

'What sort of bird is it? I've never seen one like that in the park.'

'You won't. He's a hyacinth macaw, from Brazil.'

'He's a long way from home. No wonder he looked lost.'

'Not lost at all. He actually lives just around the corner from you, not quarter of a mile away.'

'Really? How lovely. I'd like to see him again. So who were those two men?'

'Burglars.'

Daisy suddenly became quite agitated. 'I thought they were up to no good. Very suspicious, they were, all dressed in black. Very furtive.'

'It's a good job you kept an eye open.' Wilf held her veined hands, happy to feel a little warmth finally returning to the leathery skin. Daisy was such a sweet old lady. 'I wish everyone was like you – it would make our job a lot easier.' Daisy managed to vacuum up the last few precious drops of tea like an asthmatic Hoover. 'You just sit here and I'll get the constable to come down and take a statement. Just tell him everything you told me and we'll pop it in the computer.' A statement would make Daisy feel she had accomplished something and that her difficult journey to the station had been worth the effort. She laid arthritic fingers on his arm as he rose. 'Oh, there's one more thing I remember about the van, Mr Thompson.'

'What's that?'

She rummaged in her Co-op plastic carrier bag and pressed a scrap of paper into his hand. 'The registration number.' Her eyes were bright and sharp. Daisy fully understood the significance of this and Wilf could not entirely suppress the vague feeling he'd been toyed with for the second time in the past twenty-four hours. He unfolded the paper and smiled broadly. 'Daisy, I love you!'

Her face glowed.

Chapter Eleven

'Now that's odd.' Wilf sat back and frowned.

'Trouble?' asked Drewing.

'White Transit van fits the bill perfectly, but it's registered with the Ministry of Defence and the rest of the details are sealed.'

'You're joking!'

'Look for yourself.'

Drewing peered at the screen. The two men glanced at each other for a moment. 'That's it then, game over.' Both knew any further enquiry would be pointless. A well-rehearsed policy of non-co-operation would swing into action, and even if they did finally manage to identify the culprits, a message would come down from on high ordering them to forget the whole affair.

Wilf was genuinely nonplussed. 'Why?' he asked softly. 'Why on earth is Celeste Gordon of interest to the MoD – or more likely one of its murkier sections?'

'Well, their world is not quite as clear-cut as ours. Perhaps they've something on her we don't know about,' suggested Drewing.

'Possible, but she just doesn't fit the profile.' Both men knew such covert surveillance operations went on all the time. Normally, the special services were extremely proficient at these clandestine activities, but that didn't mean things always went to plan. Coming across Bertie must have been a hell of a shock. Drewing shrugged and looked at his watch. 'Looks like we'll have to chalk this one down to experience. Fancy some lunch?'

'What possible connection can there be?'

'Best to drop it before Yates finds out. He doesn't like visits from New Scotland Yard. Again, what about lunch?'

Wilf felt a sudden stirring of rebellion. 'I can't drop it,' he said quietly. 'Protecting her is why we're here.'

Ian sighed and shook his head. Wilf's inflexible idealism was well known around the station and had proved a major liability to his career. 'Has anyone ever told you why you're still a detective constable after all this time?'

'Frequently.'

'Well then listen to them.' Drewing levered himself out of the chair, patted Wilf on the shoulder and turned his body towards the canteen and his thoughts to a pie sandwich.

Wilf abandoned lunch and returned to Celeste's. She was obviously pleased to see him again. So was Bertie. He waited in the salon while tea was prepared. Bertie bobbed up and down in a clear display of pleasure, chirruping happily. Wilf remembered how to get on the macaw's good side and produced an apple.

'Wow! Thanks, Wilf.'

'That's OK, Bertie.'

'Apple. Lovely.' He held it carefully in one claw and sliced with surgical precision, parting the ruddy skin to get at the white flesh beneath.

'My pleasure.'

'Now we're cooking.'

Wilf had mastered the art of conversation with Bertie. Short and monosyllabic. Celeste appeared with the tea. 'An apple. How kind. What do you say, Bertie?'

'Thank you, Wilf,' said Bertie dutifully.

Wilf nodded and turned to Celeste. 'How are the injuries today?'

'Still painful, especially my ribs. Any news?'

'Well, yes and no.'

'That sounds enigmatic. Let's have tea and you can tell me more.' Bertie abandoned the apple and hopped onto the sofa. Food could wait for later. Here was a chance for some attention. He sidled up to Wilf, purring loudly, nudging at one hand with

154

the side of his face.

'Why does he do that?'

'He mimics Sebastian. I have to say it's a pretty good impersonation.'

Wilf obligingly tickled the beautiful blue feathers under his chin and stroked down the length of his muscular back.

'That's nice,' said Bertie. 'More!'

'No, Bertie.' Celeste was firm. 'We have to talk. You watch the television.' She pressed the remote and the screen flicked into life. She patted the arm of the sofa beside her and Bertie waddled over, settling himself comfortably. His attention was soon captured and Celeste turned back to Wilf. 'There, that should do it. Now then, you said there was good news and bad.'

Wilf sipped his tea and nibbled a Garibaldi. 'Well, a witness has corroborated your story and also provided the registration number of the van they used.' Bless you, Daisy.

'Excellent. That should identify them.'

'Normally, yes, but not in this case.'

'I don't understand. Was the van stolen?'

'No.'

'So what's the problem?'

Wilf shifted uncomfortably in his seat. 'I have to ask you this,' he said with obvious embarrassment, 'but is there any aspect of your life which may excite official interest?'

Celeste sat back and gazed at him for a long moment with steady green eyes. Wilf squirmed. That cool stare made him feel unclean. 'This may concern my relationship with James.'

'James? James who?'

'James Timbrill, the new Minister for Defence.'

'Oh, God,' muttered Wilf. He shook his head in weary disbelief. 'The man who got stabbed. That explains everything. The van is registered with the MoD.' They looked at each other in silence. Pieces of the jigsaw fell into place with distressing clarity. 'Let's do some original thinking,' he said eventually. 'You and Mr Timbrill have a close personal relationship, yes? Right. Last week, we had that major reshuffle in the MoD. Matters must have been more serious than they appeared on the surface.'

'Believe me, they were. It doesn't take a genius to guess from where I get my information, but James is entirely discreet regarding matters of national security.'

'Not in question, Celeste. I don't doubt Mr Timbrill's honesty and patriotism for one moment, which is more than can be said for his two predecessors. So, up he pops, gets poked in the leg by the PM and yet somehow still retains his job. Now why is that?'

'They can't sack him,' said Celeste. 'The Government is shaky enough as it is. Another round of resignations would fatally damage its credibility, so despite angering the PM he's relatively safe for the moment.'

'I see. So we have an unknown catapulted into a position of authority who immediately shows an unexpected streak of independence. That announcement of a financial probe must have sent a few shivers of fear running through Whitehall. I can just imagine those cosy clubs full of mandarins seething with rage when your boyfriend puts the squeeze on them.'

'James rarely discusses his work, but it strikes me what he's planning to do should have been done a long time ago.'

'I agree completely, Celeste. However, I think someone has decided Mr Timbrill needs to be put on the end of a tight leash.'

Celeste's lips twitched with a knowing smile.

'It's all a question of control and they can't control Mr Timbrill because there's been no time to collect the dirt on him, so it looks like we're not dealing with an ordinary burglary. I believe this was sanctioned by somebody who wanted information to apply as a lever, hence their interest in the diary. You said you found some letters on the floor as well. May I see them?'

Wilf nodded when he saw the House of Commons crest. 'That confirms it. This was no petty theft. You had a visit from spooks, my dear. So I'm asking again, is there anything I need to know?' Wilf took a sip of tea and balanced the cup and saucer on his knees.

'No.' The answer was firm. 'James and I have a confidential and stable relationship which in no way compromises his duties at Westminster.'

156

'It appears someone is intent on finding out whether that's true or not. Let me give you a tip – these people may well come back, so take whatever precautions you think might be necessary. Uncomfortable evidence sometimes turns up in the strangest of places and at the most inconvenient of times. It's the best way to control officials in exalted positions. If it hadn't been for Bertie, your papers and diary would have in all probability been spirited away, photocopied, and returned without your knowledge. Think on that!'

Celeste did, and the thoughts were disturbing. Although her diary was not particularly graphic a perceptive reader would immediately surmise the, ah, binding nature of their peculiar friendship. Wilf displayed a tactful concern, but she was determined to protect James at all costs. 'There's nothing I can possibly imagine would be of interest in my diary. I'm much more concerned about the legality of their actions.'

'Be assured, this particular burglary is as thoroughly illegal as any other.'

'So what's stopping you from arresting the two men?'

'Technically, nothing. Everyone is subject to the law, but I would have to rely on MoD co-operation to supply me with the names of the operatives, and that information, I can assure you, will be classified. So, no names, no case.'

'Can't you press them?'

'I could if it was important, but it's not.'

'It's important to me.'

'And to me as well. If I pushed, we'd still get nowhere. If I pushed hard, my future in the force would become mysteriously precarious. Sooner or later, I'll be told very firmly to stop my investigation. The establishment will close ranks to protect itself and we'll just get nowhere.'

'But you're a detective.'

Wilf laughed softly and shook his head. 'Sorry, Celeste, flattered as I am in your touching faith in my abilities, the plain fact is my position won't make any difference. Orders will come down from on high.' He took another sip of tea and regarded her with a shrewd eye. 'There is perhaps one way we can force things along.'

'What have you got in mind?'

'Tell the press.'

'Is that wise?'

Wilf shrugged. 'The trouble with the media is control. Once you've gone public you have to accept whatever they unearth. They're good diggers so it could get embarrassing. Messy. However, scandals like this gather pace and cannot be swept under the carpet, but you have to count on them discovering if there's anything embarrassing lurking in the wardrobe.'

Celeste thought Wilf would be very surprised indeed at what lurked in her wardrobe! 'Well, before we decide to go down that route I'll need to talk to James.'

'Naturally.'

'Please excuse me.' Celeste spoke to James from her bedroom. Wilf waited patiently, content to sit with Bertie. The macaw remained engrossed in the TV, his head angled slightly as he gazed in rapt attention at the screen. Wilf purloined another Garibaldi and ruminated quietly until Celeste returned.

'Well?'

'This puts James in a very awkward position. He's furious the burglary seems to have been organized from within his own department, but knows even he will never find out who's responsible. He's adamant the police should handle everything and will co-operate fully with you. He feels it's important for the investigation to remain under independent police control as a demonstration of impartiality and fairness.'

'Absolutely. And the press?'

'Do what you have to, Wilf. We both want the men who assaulted me brought to book.'

They sat in silence for a moment. Bertie was still watching the television and Wilf glanced over at the screen. The lunchtime news was just finishing. 'And finally,' said the newscaster, 'Regent's Park was thrown into confusion yesterday when a rare macaw was brought to the zoo having been found by the police. Displaying remarkable skill, he managed to open –'

'Milly!' shrieked Bertie without warning. His cry was as piercing as a whistle. Wilf started violently, the cup went flying and scalding tea cascaded into his crotch. A frightening elevation in the temperature of his testicles also produced a scream of equally respectable loudness. Celeste completed the triplet with her own soprano shriek of shock and surprise, then lunged for Bertie, who, in a moment of consuming passion, launched himself at the screen like a blue rocket.

It really was a very big mistake.

He knew the television wasn't an open window to the outside world, but in an instant found himself overwhelmed by the miraculous appearance of his amour. There was a flash of azure across the salon followed by a hollow thump as he hit the screen at considerable velocity. The impact squashed him to the glass in a feathery blue ball, then he slid slowly downwards and collapsed in an unconscious heap on the carpet.

The salon had been transformed from a haven of domestic tranquillity into total chaos in less than two seconds!

Celeste, although grateful to Wilf for all his efforts, was rather less interested in the state of his broiled bean bag than in the extent of her beloved Bertie's injuries. She fell to her knees and touched him carefully, but there was no response. Bertie lay flat on his back, wings folded and claws closed, his head lolling to one side. 'Oh God, no, he's broken his neck!' she quivered.

By necessity, Wilf needed to act fast. He whipped a bunch of flowers out of a vase and swiftly doused his sautéed happies with cold water. The smarting brought tears to his eyes, but the pain subsided slowly as his glowing love spuds managed to cool. 'Is he breathing?' he croaked, still clutching his groin.

Celeste bent closer to the supine macaw. 'I – I don't know.'

'Let me have a look.' Wilf was a veteran of numerous emergencies. He knelt gingerly, wincing at the scraping of sodden underpants against freshly steamed plums and straightened Bertie's head. 'I'm sure he's still alive. Yes, there's a pulse.' The regular tripping under his exploratory fingers could only be a heart. Celeste slipped her injured arm out of its sling and gently lifted Bertie onto the sofa. A few moments later, a wing twitched and he stared up with unfocussed eyes. She fussed him outrageously while Wilf sponged away some of the excess liquid from his regions. He looked like a man suffering from an extremely distressing incontinence problem.

'Bertie, are you all right? Come on, my darling, speak to me.'

'Dark,' mumbled Bertie. 'Light. Men.'

'What's he saying?'

'No idea.' Bertie was normally so eloquent his disorientation was immediately obvious to Wilf. 'Perhaps he's concussed.'

'"It's the sodding parrot!"'

Celeste recoiled at the strident male voice. She stared at Bertie with hands held to her mouth to stifle a sob. Wilf's eyes widened in sudden comprehension. He thrust his hand into a pocket, pulled out a pencil and notebook and bent down beside the semi-conscious macaw, scribbling furiously.

'"Greg, bird me made crap pants!"' intoned Bertie, this time in a different voice. '"Chaplain cough bill."'

'"You stink Bob get out of here."'

'This must be –' gasped Celeste, but Wilf shushed her into silence with an angry gesture.

'"Greg shut it up who's a pretty boy then."' Bertie suddenly tried to sit up. '"Who the frigging hell are you!"' he shouted, then rolled over and sat on his belly, scaled legs splayed awkwardly to each side. He shook his head and tried to compose himself with almost human embarrassment.

Celeste blushed furiously at the perfect imitation of her voice. She looked sheepish. 'Sorry about that.'

'Hello, Mummy,' said Bertie in a more or less normal tone of voice.

'You silly boy,' scolded Celeste, stroking him in obvious relief.

Wilf reviewed his hurried notes. 'Two men, Bob and Greg. Their boss must be Chaplain. Odd name. It could be a pseudonym,' he mused. 'These types love to give themselves exotic sounding titles like Tarquin Shagthrust or Zircon Studplugger.'

'Surely this changes everything.'

'Well, it's certainly one of the most unusual statements I've ever taken,' admitted Wilf.

'But you can use this, can't you? He's a witness.'

'Now just hold on a minute. Even if it came to trial, the only evidence is from a randy bird half-crazed from head butting the television. I can really see that standing up under cross-examination by the best briefs the Government can buy! Besides, he's a macaw. There's probably a law against animals giving evidence, although admittedly I haven't heard of one.'

Bertie still felt a little dizzy. Goodness knows what came over him. He knew he couldn't fly through the moving window but the sight of Millicent had caught him unawares. OK, so she wasn't the wittiest of raconteurs, but the chance of another jump could not be passed up, whatever her linguistic limitations. He shook himself vigorously and felt surprisingly lucid.

'I'm hungry,' he announced firmly.

'That's the Bertie I know,' said Wilf. 'Doesn't sound like he's too hurt.'

Bertie looked at Wilf with curious intensity. 'Detective Constable Thompson, I'm very pleased to see you again.'

There was a horrified silence. Wilf and Celeste stared at each other in shock. 'Something's wrong,' she gasped. 'He's never said anything like that before.' The sentence flowed from Bertie as it would have from any educated human adult. Far from scrambling his brains, the impact seemed to have produced the opposite effect and brought a moment of astonishing clarity.

'I don't think you should underestimate him. I think Bertie's a very clever boy indeed.'

Celeste turned to glare at the policeman. 'Well if he's that sodding bright, he can be a witness. Do what you have to, but I want those men arrested!'

Clifford Kelly threaded his way through crowds of his favourite people. The pub was full of them, the salt of the earth, the great British chattering classes. He liked their insatiable desire for salacious scandal, their collective curiosity and their cheerful gullibility, but for all that he'd learned long ago that they weren't stupid. They knew when they were being stiffed and displayed a ravenous appetite for anything causing discomfort to their elected leaders. An understanding of these qualities allowed Cliff to target his stories with incisive precision, providing him with a very handsome annual salary. In his job, if you were good, everyone came to you, and Cliff was one of the best. He was a freelance tabloid reporter, a gatherer of gossip, a collector of whispers, a shepherd of news – and these were members of his flock.

A wiry man with pronounced cheekbones, dark eyes, and a prominent hooked nose, it was no surprise he was known universally as Weasel. What was surprising, however, was that despite his seedy profession and indifferent physical attributes, women simply flocked to him like financial advisors to a confused lottery winner. Weasel's success with women had always been a source of great astonishment and exasperation to Wilf, whose love life, to be fair, could most kindly be described as quiet.

Weasel was how he was introduced to everyone, Weasel was how he liked to be addressed and Weasel was how he signed his pithy offerings. He revelled in his reputation, encouraged rumours he was hung like a donkey, swelled with pride whenever someone took a swing at him and thrived in the unprincipled world of celebrity journalism, laughing all the way to the bank each time one of his sensational exposés hit the front page.

Carrying two pints of Old Speckled Hen, he made for the corner snug. 'Here you go, Wilf. Cheers.' He sucked at the head on his beer and smacked his lips in appreciation.

Wilf took a deep sup. 'Thanks, Weasel. Got your machine?'

'No pleasant chit-chat tonight? Must be important.' Weasel rummaged in his coat pocket, produced an ultra-slimline digital voice recorder and set it on the table.

'That's a bit posh, isn't it?'

'A gift from Natasha.'

'Still with her, then?'

'Lovely girl, just got some new boobs as well, but enough of the pleasantries. What's up?'

Wilf considered. Weasel was as close a friend as he was ever likely to have. They met frequently over a pint to bounce their cynicism off each other and exchange such news as to be to their mutual benefit. This co-operation had led to some notable investigations and a satisfying number of arrests. Naturally, then, it was to Weasel that Wilf turned having been given the all clear from Celeste earlier in the day.

'Ever heard of a man called Chaplain? Hey, what's going on?' To Wilf's surprise, Weasel immediately switched off the recorder. The journalist took another sip of beer and carefully surveyed the crowded room over the rim of his glass. The pub was a busy place, solid, comforting and safe – and yet here was Weasel acting all squirrely. His eyes missed nothing. He turned his back on the room and adjusting his chair, leaned so far forward Wilf thought he was going to be Frenched. 'This man, Chaplain. Anything to do with the MoD, by chance?' he murmured.

'Might be.'

'This is strictly private and non-attributable, understand?'

Wilf grinned. 'I'm usually the one saying that.'

'I'm not fooling about, Wilf,' hissed Weasel coldly. 'This subject can result in serious damage to your career and I'm not going down for you, much as I like your sorry butt.'

'It may be dangerous to a lovable knob-head like you, but I'm a policeman.'

Weasel sneered. 'You think being a plod makes a difference to these people? Chaplain's one of life's dangerous characters. He's never seen, never heard, never quoted, but he's one of the elite. Even I can't get information, and when I ask, people clam up quicker than on a comfort stop in scorpion country. No one knows his first name, what he looks like, where he lives, what pets he owns, or whether he holidays at Butlins. Few wield such arbitrary power. We're talking higher than top Whitehall here, my boy, so you better be damn sure about yourself.'

Wilf whistled softly. 'Wow! That explains a lot.'

'He's a heartless predator, a fixer and a cunning, devious, thoroughly unpleasant bastard. I believe he's now one of the inner circle around the PM who smooths the way. A little pressure here, some adroit manipulation there, a fabricated criminal offence, and suddenly irritating problems seem to float away in the breeze. Officially, I have no idea what his position is, even though I've tried to find out, but Dom fell foul of him last year and I've been interested in Chaplain ever since. You remember Dominic Oxford?'

'Sure. Lovely chap. Balder than me, if that's possible. Works in the Home Office. Got a bright future.'

'Correction. We need to use the past tense now. "Worked" in the Home Office. Now carving out a new career as unemployed and with a very dodgy conviction for possession, all courtesy of Chaplain.'

'You're kidding!'

'That fate may befall you as well. Being plod won't make any difference so take my advice and leave well alone. He's a reptile.'

'Thanks for the warning, but I'm pretty sure he's orchestrated a burglary for political ends.'

'Good Lord!' snorted Weasel, 'they do that all the time. Discreetly, of course.'

'There was also an assault.'

'Whoopee. Pass the crisps.'

'You really don't care, do you?'

'Actually, you've got me very wrong there, Wilf. I do care. A lot. These people really rack me off, but caring won't produce jack, and even if it did, nobody will ever end up in court.'

'That's about to change,' ground out Wilf quietly.

Weasel lifted glass to lips again and took a long, leisurely sip, staring thoughtfully at his friend. He seemed to be weighing things in his mind. It was only right that high officials should be subject to the legislation they themselves make – but more importantly for Weasel, his instincts were twitching like crazy. He smelt a story. Despite the banter, he had absolute confidence in Wilf's abilities. He put his glass down, wiped his lips with the back of his sleeve and nodded slowly. 'OK, let's hear what you've got.' The recorder was switched back on again.

'A few days ago we were called to a burglary in Greenwich. The occupier, a woman, was quite seriously assaulted. It was a

164

nasty attack by two men who had no qualms about using telescopic truncheons.'

'I hate 'em already,' muttered Weasel.

'It was a professional job. Locks picked, proper burglar kit, the lot. Much too good for any of our local boys. Unfortunately for them, the house was the home of a highly intelligent macaw who has since supplied me with three names; Chaplain, Bob and Greg.'

'Really?' Weasel's brows shot up in amazement. It didn't happen often and Wilf felt pleased he'd actually managed to surprise the hack. Being jaded was a normal state of existence for Weasel. Probably why he and Wilf got on so well. 'How injudicious of them to name drop. The other two must be grunts under Chaplain's control.'

'Well blow me down, Kojak, I never thought of that,' observed Wilf with, it has to be said, crushing sarcasm.

'You're a really horrible old git,' sniggered Weasel. 'I think that's why I like you so much.'

'Thanks. I'll be expecting flowers. Now, knowing the reluctance to prosecute in such embarrassing cases, it strikes me the only way to pursue this is if the press makes such a fuss that something has to be done.'

'It could work.' Weasel seemed unconvinced. 'But it's a bit dry for the likes of me. Not enough –' He waved a hand negligently as he searched for the correct word.

'Sex!' offered Wilf.

'That's the word I was groping for.'

'What! Top Whitehall conspiracy and you consider it a bit dry!'

Weasel nodded over his shoulder. 'My readers. God bless 'em all, but do you really think they're interested in something like that?'

'What if I told you the macaw is clever enough to be called as a witness. I think I can get him to stand up in court and point the finger – or feather, or whatever it is they point.'

Weasel perked up considerably. 'Bloody hell, Wilf, that's an entirely different kettle of fish! Have you any idea what a stir that'll create; you'd be making legal history.'

'And if the path can be traced back, who knows what will happen.'

Weasel scanned the pub again and dropped his voice back to a conspiratorial whisper. 'I never took you as a man motivated by sedition! This is plotting on a major scale. Someone like Chaplain has to have the support of No. 10. He *has* to, otherwise what would be the point of his existence. We're talking possible fall of Government here, so why do you want to get so involved? Politics isn't normally your bag.'

'Why?' Wilf was suddenly angry. 'Because an innocent woman has been burgled and assaulted and it looks like she's not going to get the chance to see her attackers brought to book. The law can't touch these people and that really makes my blood boil.'

'Here we go again, forever allowing your sense of justice to inhibit your career as a policeman. It's no wonder you've never been promoted.'

'Thanks for the cutting analysis.'

'So what do you want me to do?'

'Root around. There's got to be other people who've encountered Chaplain in the past and suffered. Get something on the front page as soon as you can.'

'And get myself shafted? I thought you were my friend.'

'Then be careful while you do it – and in return I'll make sure you're there when I arrest these bozos. I'll keep you in the loop whatever happens and will protect you as much as I can.'

'I don't want to sound ungrateful but that doesn't exactly fill me with confidence. These people can out-think and out-rank you any day of the week.'

'Then make yourself high-profile. Being in the public eye stops you getting stabbed in the back.'

'Wilf, please don't talk about stabbing. You're making me nervous. Any leads?'

'I've got names, a vehicle and a witness. I'd be a pretty poor copper if I couldn't turn up something from that lot.'

'Vehicle?'

'Has to be a spooks van. These guys had all the tools, including skeleton keys. We got the plates.'

'Amateurs.'

'Yeah, they came up against one of my best narks.' Good old Daisy.

'I can't stand a sloppy job.'

'Now, listen carefully because here's a really big clue for you – the van is registered with the MoD.'

'Naughty, naughty! There's no chance they'll co-operate so we might as well scratch that one. Who's this woman, and why does she warrant the attention of our ever vigilant secret services?

'Her name is Celeste Gordon.' Wilf recounted details in concise sentences. Weasel grinned at the mention of James Timbrill. The reporter wasn't stupid. He switched off the recorder and stowed it away in his pocket again. 'So how do you want to play this, bearing in mind Chaplain will get you booted off the force if you annoy him? The man is virtually untouchable. If you fail to get him in cuffs first time then you've left a very dangerous adversary free to destroy your future and, more importantly, mine as well.'

'We'll start with the other two. They're the thugs I really want to nail.'

'And Chaplain?'

'We're going to have to box clever with that one. Let's keep him in reserve for the moment. If we come mysteriously unstuck then I'll know where to look. If we can trace any malign influence back to him then it's a charge of conspiracy to pervert the course of justice. Once charged, I imagine there'll be plenty of folk prepared to step forward and make him squirm, including your mate, Dom.'

'Never kick a tiger in the balls unless you have a plan to deal with his teeth!'

'What?'

'An old Basildon proverb. Rings true in this case. You better make damned sure you know what you're doing.'

Wilf considered for a moment, then a sly smile broke out on his lugubrious face. 'Don't you worry about him, I've got an idea. If we can arrest the foot soldiers then I know the way to defeat their boss.'

Weasel drained his Old Speckled Hen. 'Thanks, Wilf. I'll visit Dominic, see if he can help out in any way.'

'Keep me posted.'

'No problem. Look, if this takes off then they might start keeping tabs on you so better be careful about contacting me directly. Be subtle, but please, try not to make them think we're gay.'

Outside, Weasel buttoned his coat, thrust hands into pockets and strode around to the rear car park to pick up his Peugeot. A moving shadow caught his eye. Furtive steps closed in from behind. Weasel turned, suspicions already forming in his mind. 'Yes?' he snapped. Two figures loomed up, shadows in the dim light, their faces hidden. This was too much of a coincidence. Wilf was obviously a lot closer than he'd imagined. They probably picked him up after his visits to this woman's house. Weasel only needed a few seconds to make his preparations. He accepted his fate, but was damned if they were going to take his evidence. With one hand still in his pocket, he exchanged the voice recorder for another hidden in an undetectable inner pouch. This simple deceit had saved a good story on several occasions before. It was imperative these people remain ignorant of how much Wilf knew. He hoped they liked the poems of Pam Ayres.

They pounced. There were no formal introductions. Weasel screamed loudly to attract attention. His order of priority was to save the recorder then his testicles – he needed them to service Natasha. Everything else would just have to follow as circumstance allowed. It was a good plan which proved only half successful.

He saved the recorder.

Weasel's protestations were cut short by a heavy blow to the stomach that left him doubled over and gagging for air. 'Thanks Bob, or is it Greg?' he gasped, and was rewarded with a momentary hesitation that spoke volumes. 'Gotcha!' he whispered. A gloved fist slammed into his mouth, loosening teeth, followed by another to the gut. Unsurprisingly, his knees folded after this second body punch. He curled up into the traditional huddle on the tarmac but this proved no defence against a generous dollop of sadistic rage. A boot crunched into his happies. The pain was horrific. Wretched and sobbing, he just lay there and let them take the recorder, his mobile, wallet, and watch. Had to make it look like a common or garden mugging.

A welter of brutal kicks came his way for good measure before a shout sent the two sprinting off into the darkness. Someone ran to him, laid a hand on his shoulder. 'Cliff, it's me. You OK?' It said much for Weasel's distress that he couldn't even think of a scathing reply to Wilf's inane question. If he was OK he'd be on his feet. If he was OK he'd be hurling abuse after his assailants. If he was OK he'd be driving home to Natasha with her perky new boobs and sexy little skimpies.

Unfortunately, Weasel was not OK. He'd been beaten up over a story before. Twice. Each time, he'd ended up nailing the perpetrators, ruining both careers and bank balances in equal measure, and grovelling in agony amongst the cold puddles and discarded condoms of the car park, his cheek scraping the tarmac and blood streaming from a ruptured lip, he swore he'd do it again. His balls hurt so badly he was sick over Wilf's shoes.

How on earth was he going to explain this to poor Nats?

Chapter Twelve

Dressed in a flamboyant dressing gown, Hugo Chaplain polished off his late supper and mentally steeled himself for bed. It was a conscious action. The obligations of his marriage simply had to take a back seat as he found himself devoting more and more energy to his job. This increasingly demanding emotional expenditure was directly proportional to the ineptness of the Government. His recently successful colonic irrigation of the MoD had been a trifling affair when compared with some of the more complex problems requiring his unique talents.

A frown creased his impassive brow. The unexpected rebuff of Pritchard and Coberley perturbed him greatly. Such a simple operation should have been executed with aplomb yet they'd been put to flight by a common or garden pet. Perhaps he shouldn't have been so hard on them, especially after seeing their wounds at first hand, but whatever sympathy he felt was tempered by an exasperated anger at their bungling. It really shouldn't have happened and he was in two minds whether to drop the whole affair – after all, it was highly unlikely anyone as stupefyingly boring as Timbrill would have any succulence to his private life.

Unfortunately, the police were now becoming involved and that would require calling in one or two favours to ensure the investigation ended up foundering in a gelatinous ocean of bureaucratic indifference. Chaplain smiled. He was a world-class stonewaller. One of his core skills. He warmed in a smug glow of self-righteous appreciation of his own unique talents.

Retiring upstairs, Hugo padded softly into the bedroom looking every inch a corpulent Noel Coward. He hung his dressing gown on the back of the door and turned to face his wife, his pale lemon silk pyjamas shimmering in the soft light.

Maureen Chaplain was not asleep, as he fervently hoped she would be at such an advanced hour. She sat up in bed, bathed in the soft light of a table lamp, the covers drawn to just beneath her chin. Hugo's heart sank. She was watching him with a distinct gleam of expectation in her eyes.

He may have been the dynamic power behind Downing Street, but he hadn't had a thick one in two years!

Hugo loved his wife dearly. That he was capable of such emotion would have surprised those in Whitehall who only saw him as a cold and calculating manipulator who destroyed all who stood in his path. Hugo's was not a marriage devoid of passion – only a little firmness in the underpants department. It was as if the increasing demands on him had depleted his sexual drive, sucking him dry, so to speak, which, sadly, was more than Maureen had done in a very long time. She had tried to conceal her disappointment but his inability placed an increasing strain on their relationship and so, fuelled by the incessant problems at work, he spiralled down into penile lifelessness.

'Hello, big boy!' Maureen's greeting was just sufficiently mischievous to confirm his suspicions of her intent. Trouble of a flaccid nature loomed on the horizon. He sighed gently, aware that although he could shaft every member of the Cabinet, he couldn't extend the same courtesy to his long-suffering wife.

Maureen was a pretty woman, rather tall and elegant, with small breasts and, to Hugo's mind, comfortable hips. Her face wore an expression of hopeful optimism, a small smile playing on her lips. She flicked away the duvet and lay back in a nest of pillows, one arm flung behind her head.

'God's trousers!' exclaimed Hugo, profoundly shocked, his brows shooting up his expansive forehead like a pair of furry express elevators. She wriggled provocatively and patted the bed beside her, but Hugo remained rooted to the oatmeal Wilton, eyes bulging.

Unfortunately, they were the only part of him that did!

Always keen to try something new, tonight's theme was

172

Anatolian allure. Dressed as a Turkish belly dancer, Maureen was enveloped in the finest translucent pale blue silk shot through with sequins and silver thread. Harem pants lay low on her hips, sheathing her legs before gathering in at the ankles. A diaphanous blouse was cropped to just beneath her breasts, the short sleeves and plunging neckline trimmed with gold lace. Bangles clattered around her wrists, and numerous ankle chains glittered in the light. She had painted her finger and toe nails blood red, rouged her nipples, and trimmed her Epping Forest into a masterpiece of minimalistic pubic topiary. A large iridescent jewel surrounded by gold sun rays sat glued into her navel. The elusive scent of jasmine filled the air.

'Do you like it?' she husked in her best Greta Garbo voice. A golden tiara slipped over one eye.

'For heaven's sake, Maureen, what has got into you?' he complained.

She sensed his familiar response and took determined steps to avoid the inevitable consequences. 'Come here, my little Valentino, I want you tonight!'

Hugo edged closer with no little caution. He had to admit she looked divinely attractive. It seemed a cruel twist of fate that before his inconvenient problem the most alluring item in her tallboy had been sweet but shapeless cotton pyjamas. However, with the advent of their difficulties her wardrobe soon became stuffed with filmy scanties, sheer stockings with lacy frills, and delicate strappy things daringly cut at front, back, and other strategic places. The satin French maid's outfit once managed to raise more than a smile for an hour or so but was ultimately unsuccessful. The polished rubber frogman's suit still hung at the back of the wardrobe, unused, and the melted chocolate approach suggested by Cosmo merely resulted in a huge cleaning bill.

Still, perseverance was one of Maureen's great gifts. She grabbed his wrist and dragged him onto the bed. 'I want you to take me!' she murmured salaciously. Maureen was fifty-nine and to an outsider the scenario might have seemed comical, but to Hugo she was still the bright-eyed nineteen-year-old student he fell in love with back in the seventies. One by one, the pyjama buttons were plucked open, revealing the pudgy expanse of his grey-haired chest. 'Come on, Hugo, relax,' she urged gently, but try as he might he could not capture the mood. It was impossible. Too many worries crowded in to divert his attention. Hugo had lost the ability to divorce his mind from work and although he tried to concentrate on Maureen, all he could think of was that wretched parrot.

Desperate for at least some form of gratification, she decided to take the upper hand. 'What ...' spluttered Hugo as his pyjama trousers were ripped away, leaving him naked. His lack of rigidity became painfully visible to them both. Mister Stiffy was definitely not at home.

'Lie still!' It was an order. Maureen handed him a glass of water and an immediately identifiable blue pill. 'Here, take this.'

'But I haven't got a headache.'

'It's not for a headache, silly. You know very well it's to help you down there.' She nodded at his no-go area. Hugo swallowed the pill. She scrambled off the bed and swaying like a siren, danced on tip-toe, stroking herself as she spun around the room. He followed her slightly unsteady progress, thankful for the short respite. She became engrossed in her own sensual performance, hoping her arousal would reach out to him, but Hugo just lay there, genitally inactive, until she flopped onto the bed again, threw a wispy leg over his thigh and nipped at his neck with sharp teeth. Her manual dexterity should have produced the desired effect – it always had done so in the past, but success was far more elusive nowadays. She gripped, coaxed, stroked, kissed and sucked, all to no avail.

'It's no good,' sighed Hugo, slightly alarmed at his increasing soreness and chaffing. 'I suspect these pills are over-rated. Perhaps tomorrow night.'

But Maureen was now far too aroused to be so easily deflected. She wriggled up onto his shoulders and promptly sat on his face, determined to extract a little personal enjoyment from her efforts. Hugo struggled for air, his mouth full of clinging damp silk. Above him, Maureen rocked back and forth, raking herself over his features with eyes shut. She clutched his fringe of sparse hair with both hands and held him with an urgent, vice-like grip. Hugo flailed and flopped about on the bed like a landed grouper, gasping frantically for air before finally managing to dislodge her. Flushed and giddy, he surfaced, panting and perspiring, but this respite was short as powerful thighs clamped him back into position again. Hugo began to panic. Maureen mistook his stifled protestations for moans of pleasure and bore down harder, dropping her entire weight on his face. Sodden silk mashed over his nostrils. He couldn't breathe at all. A thin mist danced in front of his eyes as he fought for air. The prospect of imminent suffocation extinguished any last traces of ardour.

Pussied to death – just what he needed! He could imagine the titters echoing through the corridors of power and the headlines on the front page of the *London Evening Standard*.

Ministry Mandarin in Mysterious Muffing Mishap!

Great. Just dandy.

Desperate to avoid such an ignominious end, Hugo managed to dislodge Maureen with a final despairing wrench. His forehead raked up her belly and dislodged the sun disc in her navel. The paste gave out even as he took a huge, heaving breath and the jewel dropped into his open mouth.

Hugo felt something heavy rattle past his teeth and slide down his throat. Sharp metal raked his gullet and he swallowed convulsively, gagging, his face assuming the same delicate shade of blue as the silk adhering to his cheeks. Maureen's thrashing limbs and flushed features indicated her desperate desire for orgasm, whereas Hugo's thrashing limbs and flushed face indicated a desperate need for the Heimlich Manoeuvre. Sweat popped on his forehead. He gulped again, his throat spasming. An inarticulate gurgle escaped his lips as he choked, fish-eyed, swallowing convulsively until the obstruction slowly receded.

Downwards.

Maureen slumped sideways, only conscious of her failure to arouse Hugo and entirely unaware of his unexpected snack. She gathered herself with as much dignity as she could summon and quietly fled the room without a backward glance, tears starting in her eyes.

It broke Hugo's heart to see her so distressed, but what could he do? Resignation was the only course of action which would reverse the permanent dormancy in his joy department, yet that was not an option. Hugo was hopelessly addicted to the narcotic influence of power. To willingly walk away from such power was unthinkable. There was nothing he could do to comfort her and a few minutes later the front door slammed. Off to her sister's again, that ultimate refuge from the unpleasantness of reality.

He sighed and belched uncomfortably. The gas tasted sour and metallic. His abused throat burned from the scraping passage of the jewel and he knew his meal had only just begun its long and convoluted journey. He clambered off the bed, slipped into his dressing gown and picked up the phone.

Adrian Brighouse, unlike his colleagues, rather enjoyed being on call after-hours. Night problems were usually serious and those were the cases he liked the best; one can only stand so many fungoid feet, thrush infections and snivelling noses. He picked up the receiver before the second ring. 'Chatham Crescent Surgery, Doctor Brighouse.'

'Hello, Adrian. This is Hugo.'

Brighouse groaned mentally. At this time of night Chaplain could only be calling about his chronic impotence again. The attitude of the man exasperated him. It was almost as if he personally blamed Brighouse for his condition. The GP had investigated thoroughly, diagnosed a psychological problem and advised the services of a counsellor. 'Yes, Hugo?'

'It's a little embarrassing.'

'For God's sake, Hugo, I'm your doctor.' Annoyance at being disturbed over such a trifling matter made Brighouse a little short. He had a reputation for being notoriously rude to patients who abused the emergency out-of-hours service provided by his practice. 'I've probed and prodded my way around your body for the last ten years. There isn't a crevice of you or Maureen I wouldn't recognise with my eyes blindfolded. What could possibly embarrass me now?'

'I've swallowed something.'

Hello, that was a new one. Brighouse bit his lip against the scathing retort he was about to launch down the phone line. 'Poisonous?'

'No. A jewel of some kind with pointed edges. Bloody well nearly choked me on the way down.' Hugo's voice still shook a little. 'What shall I do?'

'Will it flush though, do you think?' A jewel! What the hell had the old porker been up to now?

'You're the doctor – you tell me.'

'If it's big and has spikes it'll lacerate your gut and get stuck going around a corner. I don't want to worry you but that means emergency surgery. You'll have to go to A&E.'

'Can't you help?' pleaded Hugo, unwilling to involve any strangers.

'Not a chance. You'll need an X-ray whatever happens, and that crappy little private hospital you're so keen on won't be interested in this one, believe me.'

'But Adrian, I –'

'No, Hugo. It's too big for me to do here. I could attempt to pump you out if it was a dire emergency to save your life, but you'll be OK for an hour or two so let the experts take care of it. They've had plenty of experience removing all manner of foreign objects. Shouldn't be too busy at this time of night,' lied Brighouse. He replaced the receiver before Hugo could reply and stared at the phone. 'Bloody druids!' he muttered angrily.

Hugo took a taxi to King's College Hospital. King's was a little removed from the city centre and so he figured there was less chance of being recognised there than at any of more well-known establishments closer to Whitehall – places regularly frequented by the more clumsy of Her Majesty's Members of Parliament. He made his way into the Accident and Emergency Department and groaned at the sight that met him. The place heaved, even though it was now the early hours of the morning. He cursed Brighouse roundly and barged his way through aimless, milling crowds to the reception desk. A woman dealt with the steady stream of arrivals, demonstrating a peerless competence in coping with the pressures of her position whilst still maintaining a sunny smile of welcome. How wonderful, it seemed to Hugo in a fleeting moment of abstraction, that English social etiquette still required a courteous welcome, even to an A & E department! She addressed Hugo in a business-like but kindly manner.

'Good evening, sir. How can we help?'

Hugo hesitated – but already the beginnings of a queue were forming behind him. 'I've swallowed a metallic object.' Might as well get on with it as quickly as possible. This was a place, he decided, where it was probably best to put delicacies to one side.

'Have you, now. Dear me. Name?' She did not seem at all surprised at Hugo's discomfiture. Probably seen a lot weirder in her time.

'Chaplain. Hugo Anthony Chaplain.'

'National Insurance number?'

'Haven't the foggiest.'

'OK. We have more than one Chaplain here.' She peered at her screen.

'I live in Carsington Mews.'

'Got you. Right. What is it you've swallowed?'

'A jewel. It lacerated my throat on the way down. I'm not coughing up blood, nor do I have stomach cramps.'

'Is it large?'

'Large enough. It has spikes around it to represent the rays of the sun.'

'Ah, another druid.'

'Certainly not, madam. I'm Church of England,' he replied with no small amount of ruffled indignation.

The receptionist curled a lip at him knowingly. 'Sure you are,' she said in a tone which expressed total disbelief in his statement. 'Well now, Mr Chaplain, please take a seat. You're in no immediate danger of choking so you'll be a little while, but hopefully not too long. Fortunately, we're having a quiet evening.'

Hugo could not tell if she was being sarcastic or simply stating the truth. Having never visited such a place before he had no previous experience upon which to judge her assessment, but it seemed to him the reception area closely resembled a war zone. Seats were filled with subdued and anxious-looking people who either appeared externally intact, but very worried, or who were obviously injured – and extremely worried. Everyone kept glancing surreptitiously in wide-eyed concern at a man sitting quietly reading a magazine with a hatchet wedged in the top of his skull. The sight was horrifying but he appeared to be in no discomfort and thumbed the pages casually, a great wad of gauze wrapped around the protruding blade.

Hugo loitered, trying not to show his dismay. He made a promise to vastly increase the cover of his private medical insurance. Exposure to ordinary people always made him feel uncomfortable and, as for the humiliation of actually having to stand there amongst them, well, it was simply too much to bear. In addition, to his intense mortification, he felt an entirely unsolicited turgidity begin to fret against his trousers.

Maureen's pesky little pill had kicked in at last!

Hugo tried to adjust himself with discretion but all the wriggling in the world wasn't going to make him comfortable. His chemically induced and entirely unwanted erection continued to grow, tenting outwards. A woman cradling a sick child in her arms glared at him disapprovingly and moved away, her unspoken accusation making Hugo cringe. All he could do was stand there and force himself to think of dirty frying pans and smelly socks and Queen Victoria and rancid drains and Birmingham and every other image of a sexually inhibiting nature.

Slowly, the gallantly cheerful but hopelessly overworked staff made gradual inroads into their distressed flock. Those honoured with selection shuffled off through a doorway to clinical Nirvana beyond. Hugo watched them go, desperately hoping he would be next. Axe Man finally got the call and made towards the inner sanctum, ducking to ensure the hatchet handle did not hit the door lintel. Eventually, Hugo was summoned. He left his corner with alacrity and fairly sped through, following a nurse to the X-ray suite and then an inner waiting room. His shoulders slumped at the thought of further delays, but at least this one had a seat.

'What's up with you?' asked his neighbour to the left, a huge man sitting very gingerly and wincing with pain. Hugo's own generous girth and the size of the ridiculously inadequate chairs meant the two were cosying up rather more than he would have liked. This seemed particularly perilous considering the highly noticeable activity in his happy regions.

'I'd rather not talk about it,' muttered Hugo, hoping his lack of interest would discourage further conversation. An overwhelming aroma of stale beer hung around the man like a dank miasma.

'Suit yourself. Only trying to be polite.'

The conversation faltered, much to Hugo's relief. The man was obviously much the worse for drink. There was something so, so – well, common about getting drunk on beer. It was a pastime the working class engaged in because they were too stupid to appreciate fine wines or a really good liqueur. Beer, in Hugo's opinion, produced an offensive drunk, a violent drunk, an anti-social drunk. Unfortunately, it also produced a garrulous drunk.

'So, I'm Brendan,' the inebriate announced suddenly, determined to return to their conversation and blissfully oblivious to Hugo's cross-armed, blank-eyed apathy. 'Want to know what I'm here for?' he slurred conspiratorially.

'Not really.' Hugo's incuriosity made no impact.

'Went out with the lads on a bender. Went pole dancin', we did.'

'You, in hot pants?'

'Not us, yer prat. We went to a club. Me an' Four Balls an' Morocco Joe.'

'Four Balls!'

'Thassright. Had to have two vastec – vastretch – snips. Firss one didn't work.'

'Lovely image.'

'Speckt they're still at the club shoving tenners down gussets. I'd be there too but ...' and here he dissolved into a fit of the giggles.

Hugo sighed. He was going to get the story whether he liked it or not. 'But what?' he asked dutifully.

'But I was 'aving a dump when I dropped me brandy an' me ciggy. I've burnt me chuckles something wicked!'

'Oh, sweet mother of Moses, please rescue me.'

Hugo's prayers were answered. A doctor appeared. The man wore his white coat casually unbuttoned at the front with a stethoscope draped around his neck and a reflex hammer jutting from his breast pocket. His badges of office. He peered down the line of expectant patients over a pair of tinted John Lennon glasses perched on the end of his nose.

'Hands up which one of you has swallowed something nasty!' he called out. Hugo promptly stuck up his arm, desperate to get away from his pyrotechnically inept acquaintance. Everyone stared, much to Hugo's embarrassment. Necks craned, and there was a subdued, 'Oooh!' of interest from the walking wounded. This was obviously part of the doctor's intent – it seemed ritual humiliation was an important element in the prevention of further mishaps.

'Ah, yes, you must be the druid.'

'Are you people fixated on paganism?' Hugo snapped acidly. He had the feeling he was getting caught up in something surreally bizarre. The other waiting patients merely nodded sagely.

'Definitely,' murmured one.

'Always so keen to deny it,' whispered another.

'Yer didn't tell me you was a bleedin' druid. No wonder you're 'ere,' observed Brendan, nudging Hugo in the ribs and grinning slyly.

'Is there something going on around here I don't know about?'

'Of course not, sir,' replied the doctor, using an identical tone of voice as that employed by the receptionist outside. 'We're not here to judge. Please follow me.' At last Hugo experienced a little privacy, even if it was just an alcove to one side of the bustling treatment room. The doctor indicated a chair. 'Please sit down, Mr – ah, Chaplain. I'm Doctor Linden. So it's a jewel this time.'

181

'What do you mean, "this time?" There hasn't been a previous time. Ever! And there won't be a time after this, either,' said Hugo with some heat. He wriggled in his seat as if he had ants in his pants and a hand strayed towards his bulging crotch, only to be snatched back. The doctor glanced down for a moment, then stared at Hugo over his glasses, regarding him with droll, professional coolness, his only reaction a slight sardonic raising of an eyebrow. 'Don't even think about it,' ground out Hugo, reddening badly.

The doctor was completely impervious to his protestations. 'How many times have I told you guys, Christianity is a much safer non-contact religion.'

'Just get on with it. I want to be out of here as soon as possible.'

'You're not going anywhere, my sword-swallowing friend, except upstairs to an operating theatre.'

'What!' exploded Hugo.

The doctor rammed an X-ray film upwards into the clips of a viewing box. Hugo's innards stared out at them, all faint and tubular. In the centre of the film was a stark black silhouette, circular and rayed. To Hugo's anxious eyes the spikes took on the proportions of daggers. The jewel was enormous. 'That's not going to come out easily,' murmured the doctor, peering closely at the film. 'From either end,' he added pointedly. 'Frankly, it's a bit of a miracle you didn't choke. Biggest I've ever seen, and I've seen a few, believe me!"

'You can't pump it out or something?'

'No. Can't risk lacerating your oesophagus. Besides, it might get stuck. Too dangerous. I've called one of our general surgeons and they're prepping the theatre now. A porter will be here shortly to take you up. Emergency keyhole surgery and a small scar. It's your lucky night!'

'You call this luck? Let me tell you about luck …' spat Hugo, stabbing a plump finger at the doctor, but he never completed his sentence. A bell suddenly rang. It had that particular note of urgency which stops every conversation in mid-sentence and compels all within earshot to stare around in confusion. Hugo became aware of a commotion out in the waiting room. The doctor didn't bat an eyelid. 'Excuse me for a moment,' he said pleasantly, stood up and strode away. Nurses congregated, worried expressions on their faces. Hugo wondered just how bad it had to be to worry these nurses. He didn't have long to find out.

An elderly man stood in the centre of the room, tall, dignified, well-dressed in a blue blazer and grey trousers. His bouffant hair was silver, his moustache clipped neatly, his complexion florid. He faced the doctor with the upright bearing of an old soldier. Hugo was close enough to bear witness to their conversation.

'So, Squadron Leader Dandridge, can you please tell me again precisely what you've done,' asked the doctor, hands in pockets. Hugo suspected the man's nonchalance was for the benefit of his agitated staff – and to make himself look pretty damned cool. Some of the nurses stared at him with drooling adoration.

'Certainly, old chap,' replied the officer in a clipped ex-RAF kind of fashion. 'Nothing to tell really. Had piles for years. You know – haemorrhoids.'

'I'm aware of the condition, yes.'

'Damned nuisance, they are, always itching and getting in the way.'

'That's frequently the nature of the complaint.'

'Well, when they get really irksome, I grease up an old cannon shell and use it to poke the blighters back inside!'

'A cannon shell!'

'That's right. Can't use a bullet. Too small. Not enough pushing power. I know, I've tried. That's why I prefer the shell. It's got a much nicer taper on the nose. Just the ticket.'

'This – er, utensil, is it by any chance a live round?'

'Of course it is, old chap – what's the point in using a dud? Genuine World War Two RAF cannon shell. Used plenty in my Mosquito. That had four barrels. Pinky Moreton and I used to go hunting Messerschmitts. Jerries hated 'em.'

'And where is it now?'

This was a bit of a stupid question really. Everybody knew where it was. The hospital alarm bell should have been clue

183

enough. Even Hugo, thoroughly untrained in the subtleties of gastro-intestinal medicine, even he knew where it was.

'Ah, rather embarrassing actually. It's slipped inside.'

'So you're walking around with a piece of live ammunition in your rectum.'

'Er, quite.'

'And this doesn't bother you?'

'Not at all, dear boy, not at all,' beamed the old flyer. 'It's quite safe.'

'So why have you come here?'

'The damned thing's been stuck fast for two days and I'm beginning to feel bloated. Thought you chaps would be able to help out. It's the least you youngsters can do for a chap who won the Distinguished Flying Cross beating up the Luftwaffe.' He proudly tapped at a medal pinned to his chest.

'So you want us to rummage around inside your bottom with a pair of forceps and extract a live – and by now quite possibly unstable – piece of high explosive ordnance.'

'If you'd be so kind.' There was no mistake, Squadron Leader Dandridge possessed two remarkable qualities, thought Hugo. The first was that he was impeccably polite, the second was a very distinct possibility not all his parsnips were evenly buttered. It seemed Linden had also come to the same conclusions.

'Well, I'm sorry to disappoint you, but this is a just a tad beyond my remit. We'll need some expert advice on how to deal with your – um, your condition.'

'I should say so. You seem a pleasant enough fellow and I say this with all respect, but you're a bit of a whipper-snapper – too young by far to know anything decent about handling aircraft ammunition.'

'No offence taken, Squadron Leader.' Linden frowned in sudden irritation at the alarm. 'Nurse Koliasnikoff, can you please turn off that noise and call the police.'

'They are already on their way. With the bomb squad.' There were no flies on Tatiana Koliasnikoff. Not where explosives were concerned. She was from Russia. To the relief of all, the alarm subsided into a blessed silence.

'Thank you. In the meantime, Squadron Leader, I think it would be best for all here if you just go outside and stand as far as possible from any people. And cars. And buildings. Actually, just stand as far away as possible from anything. Saves us having to evacuate the entire department.'

'Certainly. Happy to oblige, old boy.' Dandridge reeled off a snappy salute, spun on his heel and marched outside. Now there was a military man who knew how to shock and awe!

'Back to work, everyone,' called the doctor cheerfully. 'Let's at least try and keep on top of it tonight.' He spoke briefly to the nurses in reassuring tones, got a laugh out of them and then rejoined Hugo. 'Now, where were we? Oh, yes, your unusual diet.'

'Do you get a lot of that?' asked Hugo querulously.

'UTB incidents? Yes, we do, a surprising number.'

'UTB?'

'Up The Bottom. Our nickname. Got to say, though, it's the first time I've ever seen anyone use ammunition. That's a new one even for me, but you'd be amazed what some people manage to lose inside themselves.' Linden favoured Hugo with a knowing look. A cheerful, dreadlocked, and eyebrow-ringed porter breezed in with a wheelchair. 'Hi, doc. Hear you've had some excitement.'

'Hello, Gordon. Yes, I'll be able to dine out on this one for months. You here for Mr Chaplain?'

'Uh-huh. The druid.'

'I am not a druid!' shrieked Hugo, suddenly very much overwhelmed by the events of the evening. 'I never have been and never will be a druid, do you all understand?'

'Well, OK,' said Gordon slowly and carefully, clearly taken aback by Hugo's splenetic outburst. 'Anything you say. Wanna get in the chair. We're going straight to theatre.' He slapped an envelope of notes and X-rays against Hugo's chest. 'Hold these.' Hugo did as he was told and was wheeled away. Gordon looked back over his shoulder at the doctor and mouthed 'Druid' silently, at which Linden nodded in agreement.

Morosely, Hugo stared ahead along the corridor. It was so humiliating to be treated like an invalid. They passed a window and Gordon jerked the chair to a halt. 'Whoa there, Trigger, let's see what's going on outside. Surgery can wait for a minute.'

The front of King's was a sea of flashing blue lights. The police had shepherded a few sparse bystanders back behind their cordon and Hugo could see an army truck parked on its own inside the tapes. Several squaddies were just finishing off the construction of a waist-high circular wall of sandbags. Protruding skywards from the centre of this temporary structure was the unmistakable silhouette of an up-ended bottom.

Naked. Pallid. Dandridge's.

An officer was physically pushed forward by some soldiers, his reluctance plain for all to see. Dressed in full bomb-disposal body armour, he looked for all the world like a chunky samurai warrior. He carried himself with the stolid unwillingness of a professional man who knew there was an unpleasant duty ahead and approached the bottom warily, as if unsure as to how to proceed. After examining it from every angle, he picked up a pair of formidable forceps in gloved hands, snapped them open and shut a few times, then leaned forward.

'Time to go,' announced Gordon smartly. 'That's a sight no man should ever have to see.'

'I agree,' replied Hugo with equal feeling. 'Lead on, MacDuff!' Gordon deposited Hugo and departed. He was stripped, washed and prepared before being whisked into the theatre ante-room, his stoutness tenting the green gown covering his body, but by now Hugo did not care any more. He just wanted this dreadful ordeal to be over as quickly as possible. A sniggering anaesthetist administered an injection and almost immediately Hugo began to drift away, smothered in a comforting warmth as if wrapped in cotton wool. 'Got another druid for you, Jeremy,' he called over his shoulder to the surgeon.

'For God's sake,' mumbled Hugo, 'Can't you people understand I'm not a ...'

When he woke up, the jewel had gone – and mercifully, so had his unwanted turkey neck!

Chapter Thirteen

Hospitalisation didn't present much of an obstacle to a man of Weasel's gritty disposition. A day after his emergency admission to King's and still considerably mellowed by a cocktail of delightfully hallucinogenic pain medication, he downloaded his article to an editor already holding the front page. The press were never very sympathetic to any government at the best of times, but here was a corker of a story. Wilf stared in disbelief at the banner headlines and vowed never to cross the journalist.

It was all there, written in the inimitable sensationalist style Wilf had long associated with his incapacitated friend; the unusual nature of the burglary and brutal assault on Celeste, Bertie's stout defence of his home, Celeste's association with James Timbrill, speculation over the PM's motives for the stabbing and an appeal by the police for information on two men called Bob and Greg, all wrapped up in one plump, juicy, lurid account. Throw into the mix a description of the horrifying attack on Weasel, the suspicious nature of its timing, and the foundations of a top-quality conspiracy theory were laid before the British public, and if all that wasn't enough, it was announced the police were pursuing their investigation with the aid of an eye witness who could identify the culprits, a witness who, if called, would create legal history. Bertie! The story was a guaranteed sensation. It had everything the tabloids dreamed of; intrigue, corruption, the discomfiture of those in high public office as well as a liberal sprinkling of laughably inept spying.

And a large blue macaw!

Wilf scanned the paper again. It was almost as if he couldn't bear to put it down. 'Satisfied?' asked Weasel weakly. He lay covered in dressings and attached to drip bottles. Wilf had to admit his friend didn't look his best.

'They can't hush this one up, that's for sure. Was the headline your idea?'

'"Pollygate!" Sure. Why break with journalistic tradition.' Weasel chuckled, then winced in agony. Sweat sheened his forehead. His features were grey with pain, his lips thin, his cheekbones disturbingly prominent. He looked truly dreadful.

'Dare I ask?'

'Big, black, and swollen!'

'A virgin's dream.'

'Not this week,' he whispered.

'Remember any more from the other night?'

Weasel shook his head and closed his eyes. Wilf thought he was doing pretty well, considering. The unplanned rearrangement of his internal organs had worried the doctors for a few hours before all his vital bits sorted themselves out and more or less settled back down into their original positions.

'You know it's the same two who burgled Celeste's,' he observed thoughtfully.

'Figured that out myself, Ironside. Too much of a coincidence. Besides, they weren't very good actors – there was a definite flinch when I mentioned their names. Must have come as a bit of a shock – if you're in that line of work the very worst person to know your name has got to be some vindictive blabbermouth like me. Still, they missed the recorder.'

'That was sharp work, Cliff. I guess you've used that trick before.'

'Yeah. Gotta protect my sources.'

'Thanks, Weasel. Much appreciated. Still, look on the bright side – you'd never have met all these dedicated nurses if it wasn't for me.'

'Thanks for being so concerned about my welfare.' A spasm made Weasel gasp, sobering him instantly. 'I looked for One-Ear, but it was too dark and they were wearing balaclavas, then my attention was diverted by a hefty fist in the chops. Sorry, Wilf, I wish I could help, I really do.'

'Just take it easy. How much longer before you get out of here?'

Weasel's bruised and battered face looked like a cross between a burnt pizza and a relief map of the Appalachians. Add to that a ruptured spleen, two broken fingers, a sprained wrist, seven broken ribs, a cracked collar bone, dislocated jaw, numerous cuts, bruises, contusions and scrapes, as well as concussion and the extensive damage to his legendary endowment, he was in what the doctors laughingly described as a "comfortable" condition.

'Dunno. A couple of weeks, maybe – if the nurses let me go.'

'How can you even think of shagging with your nuts in the state they are?'

'I can't help it – it's those sexy little costumes they wear. Besides, I can't really hide the size of my balls in here. Now they fight over changing my dressings!'

'You sad, sad man. How long have you been out of touch with reality?'

Weasel smiled wanly. 'So how's it going?'

'Nothing yet.'

'There's the van.'

'The van's disappeared. The DVLA records were changed early this morning. Someone hacked in and cleaned out the lot, including all the back-up and archive records. Officially, that vehicle never existed. Physically, I expect it's already had an identification make over and reappeared back on the streets with different plates.'

'Bugger!'

'My sentiments exactly. Even the speccy geeks at Swansea don't know how it was done. Some kind of cognitive Trojan worm apparently, whatever that is. They're checking again but I know they won't find anything. Better keep that news to yourself for the moment.'

'All the other hard evidence might disappear as well. Better move the ear somewhere safe.'

'It should be OK at the station.'

'Are you sure?'

Wilf pondered on that. Only another police officer could possibly have access to the Evidence Room and all visitors needed to sign in and out, but a breach of security at the station was unlikely. Weasel guessed his train of thought. 'This isn't an ordinary case. You could be ordered to hand it over.'

A nurse arrived at the foot of the bed, serious, professional and quietly gorgeous. She consulted Weasel's chart for a moment, then smiled at her patient in a peculiar way before moving on to the next bed. 'What was that all about?' asked Wilf quietly.

'It'll be another bed bath. I've already had two this morning. They're hot on hygiene in this ward.' Weasel's expression indicated he wasn't at all unhappy with the situation.

'Let's leave your sexual adventures for another time, shall we?'

'Jealous!'

'You bet your soft-sprung arse I am,' retorted Wilf with some considerable feeling. Nurses gathered at the end of the ward like a pack of starched succubi out on a hen night.

'Just watch you don't lose any more evidence. It's a shaky enough case as it stands. Still, they're finished, whether it comes to court or not. How can you be an undercover agent if everyone knows who you are? All you need to do is arrest them and they're history, even if you can't get a charge to stick. I'll make sure there's such a stink in the press they won't even be able to get a job stacking shelves at Tesco. Hey up, here they come!'

The squadron of nurses was on the move. They approached in formation with a predatory air Wilf found unnerving. 'OK, Clifford, time for your bath.' They bustled around the bed, pulling the curtains shut.

Weasel winked at Wilf. 'But I've only just had one.'

'Since when have you been a medical expert? Excuse me, sir, but you'll have to leave.'

Wilf was shooed away and Weasel disappeared behind a swishing curtain. There was a moment's silence, then a collective gasp of astonishment followed by much suppressed girlish giggling.

Wilf sighed in disbelief and headed down to the foyer. The sight of a newsagents-cum-florists just inside the main entrance reminded him he'd left his paper with Weasel. It wasn't worth a trip back up the stairs, not that he'd be allowed access by Weasel's coterie. The screaming headline lured him over. He waited patiently in a short queue at the checkout staring at nothing in particular and thinking about Celeste and Bertie. Outside, through the glass wall, people milled around, some happy, some sad. Hospitals always induced extremes of emotion.

Two burly men strode past his field of view and headed for the lifts, their faces striped by plasters. One had a dressing over his ear.

Wilf experienced a quiet surge of interest but was far too experienced an officer to jump to conclusions. He watched the men hurry across the crowded foyer, paid for his newspaper and drifted in leisurely pursuit. It was probably nothing, in fact, it was almost certainly nothing, nevertheless, he still followed, intrigued by the appearance of two men who fitted the description of Celeste's assailants. They entered a lift and Wilf watched the indicator move up to the sixth floor. He ignored the other lifts and strolled up the stairs, turning his paper over as he read Weasel's article again.

The nursing station was manned by a sister who exuded that comforting air of supreme confidence which came from years of experience in dealing with the infirm. Wilf flashed his ID. She peered at it closely, then at Wilf. 'What's the problem, officer?'

'No problem at all. Just let me have a look at your passenger list and I'll be on my way. Official police business,' he added conspiratorially, tapping the side of his nose and winking in a grandfatherly manner.

'Well, OK, but you're not going to make a scene, are you? This is a surgical ward and I've got some critical patients in here.'

'Sadly, I'm far too arthritic for kung fu.' She handed him a clipboard. There were about twenty names in all, but one immediately caught his eye. 'Mr Hugo Chaplain?'

'Third door on the left,' informed the sister, 'but he already has visitors.'

'I won't bother, then.' He turned to go, then looked back. 'He's not in any real trouble, is he?'

'Not really. He's recovering from stomach surgery. Something he ate disagreed with him. We'd have discharged him already but an infection set in post-op and we're keeping an eye on him for a few days while the antibiotics clear it up.'

'Ate something?'

'Yeah, these damned druids are always experimenting, but he'll pull through.'

'I'm glad it's not serious. Best not to tell him I've been here, OK?' So Chaplain was a druid. Interesting.

Wilf returned to the foyer, sat in a distant corner and hid behind his paper. Chaplain! Bertie had uttered the name. Weasel had warned him. Now he'd spotted, in one of those fortuitous accidents, two men, one with an ear injury, visiting a Hugo Chaplain. The odds were too phenomenal to calculate and he was convinced that by sheer good fortune he'd stumbled across some of the men involved in the conspiracy against Celeste. Seasoned, cynical and weathered though he was, he'd always believed in luck and coincidence. If only those guys had just pushed Weasel about a bit and nicked his recorder, but they hadn't, and as a result of their own viciousness Cliff had ended up in the same hospital as Chaplain. Now how about that for divine intervention.

Twenty minutes later the men strode back across the foyer and disappeared through the main entrance doors. Wilf tucked his newspaper under one arm, wandered outside and stood examining a map of the hospital layout as the pair conversed together briefly before heading off to their individual vehicles. One turned left, the other right, and as both disappeared into the traffic he glanced at the receding registration numbers.

It was all he needed.

'We've been hit!

'What are you blathering on about, Ian,' muttered Wilf, hanging up his disreputable mac and keen to get to his desk to access the DVLA database.

'Everything on the Gordon case is gone.'

'What!' Wilf's fury attracted attention around the office.

'Yates is hopping mad. Two guys impersonating CTC officers distracted our attention while a third slipped into the Evidence Room and took the lot. Our computers have been wiped as well. There's nothing left. The ear and surplus blood samples, Debbie's forensic evidence, the telescopic truncheon, all gone.'

Ian thought Wilf was about to explode. His shining dome darkened like a chameleon strolling over a coal seam, his face cold with fury. Drewing had never seen anything like it before. Wilf was well known around the station for his carefully cultured unflappability. 'You having a heart attack?' he asked, but got grabbed by the lapels and thrust down onto a desk for his flippancy. 'That's it, Wilf, you take it out on me. Then when you've calmed down we'll think about how we can nail these bastards.' Christ, the old sod was as strong as an ox!

There was a tense few seconds before Wilf relaxed, released his grip and pulled his friend to his feet. 'Sorry, Ian. Bit of a moment there.'

'No problem. Nice to know there's still some passion in there under all that 'orrible gittiness.'

Yates beckoned Wilf into his office. 'Glad you've taken the news so calmly. OK, tell me everything you've got on the Gordon case.' Yates sat behind his unfeasibly tidy desk and listened. Even his ears appeared scrubbed to a surgical cleanliness. When Wilf finished, the two sat in silence for a moment. 'Clever move, masquerading as CTC officers. Good use of intimidation,' observed Yates. Counter Terrorism Command, known as SO15, were charged with dealing with crimes against the state. Wilf remembered them more fondly as Special Branch. They're a pretty fearsome bunch.

'Well it certainly allayed your suspicions, Tris. What did they look like?

'One was stocky, pale, and extremely hirsute, with a full black beard. Never actually saw his lips, just a nose and pair of blue eyes. His companion was taller and more powerfully built, muscular shoulders. Looked like an extra from a George Raft movie. Why?'

'Thought it might strike a memory. What about the Evidence Room log?'

'All our own boys except for an officer from Paddington Green about an hour ago. I've just called their Superintendent and guess what – no such person. The forensics lab got a visit as well. All gone.'

'Did you get their names?'

'Already been on to the Yard. No such officers exist. Their ID was spot on.'

'Good forgeries need resources. There's a lot at stake here for someone very high up the food chain, so now what do we do?' Wilf eyed his boss. There was no doubt Yates was in a state of shock. He may have been a first-class pillock but this was a direct attack on his ability to run his own police station and that was likely to put a serious spanner in his career plans.

'Matters have suddenly got way beyond your usual stuff so I'm going to hand it on to someone with more experience in this kind of enquiry.'

'What?' snapped Wilf. 'Don't you dare. It's mine. I'll handle it. I'll make any arrests. I'll get this to court. Is that clear?'

Yates had every right to pass the investigation on to a more competent team of officers and in view of the potential consequences was strongly tempted to do so, but something in his heart told him no one was more capable than Wilf in cracking the case. Besides, another thought crossed his sly mind; if Wilf did upset some high-flying Whitehall types then any retribution could be smoothly diverted back on to the officer running the enquiry, neatly missing his own Teflon-coated hide. He considered for a moment, eyeing Wilf thoughtfully. 'All right, you carry on. Listen, Wilf, I know we haven't exactly seen eye to eye in the past, but this is personal. Whoever's behind this has made us look like fools and I'll not abide that. You get stuck in and if anything turns up you'll have my full support.'

'But without any evidence?'

'Then you'll have to do it the old-fashioned way, Wilf, and there's no one better in this station, though it galls me to say so,' he added wryly.

'Thanks, Tris. I'm not entirely out of leads.' For the first time he could remember, he left Yates's office with a smile on his face.

'OK, my boy, let's get back to work.'

'You got something?' asked Ian, rolling over on his chair to join Wilf at his desk.

'Surely have. I visited the author of that fine piece this morning,' he said, nodding at the newspaper sitting atop his in-tray. 'And guess what happened while I was there.'

'No idea.'

'Opportunity and coincidence. Never underestimate their importance.' Wilf accessed the DVLA database and typed in the registration numbers of the two cars he'd seen leaving the hospital. Details of Gregory Alan Peter Coberley and Robert John Pritchard appeared. 'Excellent,' he murmured, and changing the menu slightly, typed in another name. He was rewarded with the driving record of Hugo Anthony Chaplain. Wilf worked at the keyboard again to access more personal details held on a variety of official databases, then printed and carefully examined all three files.

'Those two are big lads,' observed Drewing. 'I think we'll be needing body armour and dogs.'

'Good idea. The third is my target and he's another kettle of fish altogether. Dangerous, yes, but in an entirely different way, but we're going to have to work quickly. I know where he is at the moment and I know he'll be feeling vulnerable because he's not in a familiar environment. We can use that. Come on, let's get a team together to collar the other two thugs and then, Constable Drewing, I feel like a house call coming on,' he said with a grim smile. 'Fancy joining me on a trip to hospital?'

Early evening found Hugo propped up in bed, increasingly listless. All he wanted now was to go home, to get away from all these sick people. These sick *ordinary* people. He desperately needed to get back to work, despite the dull pain throbbing persistently in his ample midriff. Maureen had just left after her daily visit and he'd been genuinely pleased to see her, but she'd informed him she intended to talk seriously about their marital problems the moment she got him home again. It appeared she was proposing to keep him housebound for at least a fortnight, a length of time Hugo knew was just far too long.

He picked up the newspaper brought earlier by Pritchard and Coberley. "Pollygate!" screamed at him. The two had been nervous, despite his reassurances the steps he'd already taken would irreparably damage any case the police cared to bring. Bloxham and Petronelli had played their parts well, diverting attention to allow Adam Sangster to sneak in to clear out the Evidence Room at Greenwich, and Coberley himself had done a masterful job online, using that Chinese worm they'd pinched from GCHQ to hack the police and DVLA. There were still a few loose ends to tidy up, but Hugo was confident JSON had escaped to fight once again.

He looked up. A man stood in the doorway of his room, bald, hangdog of expression, wearing an ill-fitting and somewhat rumpled suit under a faded grey mac, the pockets of which currently housed his hands. Hugo frowned his most unfriendly frown, hoping his hostility would discourage his visitor. He flicked up his newspaper dismissively and buried himself behind the pages. Not a sound was heard in the room. He counted to twenty in his head and then lowered the paper. The man was now standing at the foot of his bed. Really, this was quite insufferable and once more he vowed never to grace an NHS hospital again – the lack of privacy was simply appalling.

'Yes?' he snapped. 'Can't you see I'm busy being ill?'

The man merely smiled. 'Hello, Hugo,' he said softly.

Hugo started so violently the paper slipped from his inert fingers and fell to the floor. His identity was a closely guarded secret known to only a very few, yet here was this shabby interloper casually standing in his room – and he knew his name.

The man stooped to pick up the paper. He shuffled it back

together, perused the strident cover and tossed it on the bed again. 'Your reaction is not entirely unexpected, yet instructive,' he said quietly. To Hugo's extreme consternation, he placed a chair next to the bed and sat. He seemed in no rush to depart.

'Who are you?' demanded Hugo peevishly.

'Detective Constable Wilfred Thompson,' said the man, flashing his ID. 'Nice to meet you at long last.'

Now that was extremely disturbing. It implied the man had been searching him out. Impossible! Even MI5 had difficulty keeping tabs on his activities, and they were pretty damned good at sneaking around after people.

Hugo adopted a familiar tone, one he'd had occasion to use before when dealing with the lower and denser echelons of authority. 'I do not know you. I have no wish to speak to you and I can assure you that, unless you don't value your career, you should leave immediately. You have no idea how easily I can make you wish you'd never been born.'

'*We're* not going anywhere.' This, delivered in a tone normally reserved for recalcitrant children, further alarmed Hugo.

'We?' he snapped. 'We?'

'That's right. Me and my pal here.' Drewing appeared in the doorway, arms folded across chest in his best hard-man pose, impressively caparisoned with all the tools of his trade; stylish Kevlar stab vest in fetching black, clip-on anti-strangle tie, shoulder radio and ear-piece, Bat Utility Belt hung with all manner of pouches, weapons of defence, handcuffs, pepper spray and other essential law-enforcing bibs and bobs.

Hugo gaped. 'This is outrageous,' he stammered. 'Don't think you can threaten me. I demand to know what's going on.' He pulled the sheets up a little as if the policemen were ogres escaped from a fairy tale.

'And I'll be happy to oblige.' Wilf settled himself, flicked a speck of lint from his lapel and addressed Hugo with a winning smile. Ian was seriously impressed. He never failed to enjoy watching how effortlessly Wilf controlled a situation. It was a travesty he'd been overlooked for promotion for so long – Wilf was by far the best copper he'd ever seen. 'It all started in Brazil a long time ago.'

'Brazil? Never been to the country,' sniffed Hugo.

'Neither have I, but Celeste Gordon has.'

Score one for Wilf. Hugo's eyes widened momentarily before the shutters came down. 'I have no idea who you're talking about.'

'Come off it, Hugo, we all know that's a lie.'

'I'm calling my solicitor.'

'Why? All I'm doing is telling you a story. We're here to – ah, clarify a few points. No need for a brief, unless you've got something to hide, of course, in which case I'd be very interested in what you have to say and then our relationship will become considerably more formal. Not to your advantage, I would've thought, to swap that nice comfy bed for an interview room back at the station, so let's just keep things pleasantly casual, shall we? Anyway, as I was saying, the very attractive Miss Gordon, formerly resident of Brazil, now lives in Greenwich, but although a spinster, she doesn't live alone, does she, Hugo?'

Silence.

'No, there's another who shares her house, but he's not quite what you'd expect to see in London. He's definitely a native of Brazil and he certainly surprised Greg and Bob, who, even as we speak, are being taken into custody on suspicion of committing aggravated burglary and actual bodily harm. What's up, Hugo, nothing to say? No further threats to my career?'

Hugo's mind stalled in a whirlwind of conflicting emotions. The blood drained from his face, the change in skin tone not unobserved by Wilf. This was fatal news and he recognised it as such, absolutely catastrophic coming on the back of the revelations in the gutter press. The survival of JSON – and his very freedom – suddenly hung in the balance. There was something implacable and unrelenting in the detective's manner which displayed an unshakable resolve and Hugo knew the man could not be intimidated, bribed or bullied. How had it come to this?

'I've been to Miss Gordon's house. I've spoken to her – and

198

to Bertie, the little scamp. He's quite the chatterbox – and he's the one who's fingered you and your two buddies. That was a big mistake, Hugo. Breaking into a lady's home to steal her diary. Very ungentlemanly, wouldn't you say? Checking to see if James Timbrill had anything juicy you could use as leverage? All these questions, Hugo. Any chance you'd like to answer? Better here and now. You're in that cosy bed, you're not under caution and I'm not taping our little chat.'

'I have nothing to say to you,' mumbled Hugo, overwhelmed that this nondescript-looking man, so lugubrious and dreary and, and – *common*, could have such concise knowledge of events. For the first time in his life he knew he'd met his equal.

'Fair enough, we'll leave you to your mags and hospital radio.' Wilf leaned forward and stared unwaveringly at Hugo. All bonhomie bled from his voice and his eyes were hard. 'But before we leave I want to make one or two things plain to you, old chum. I'm not arresting you, even though I could. I've nosed around your life a bit and discovered you're a repellent person. All agree on that, although I guess the danger is intellectual rather than physical.' Wilf swept a dismissive gaze over Hugo's blubbery bulk. 'You've done enough to answer a charge of perverting the course of justice and conspiracy to commit burglary. Now that's a winning hand for me. I think you'll find the boot is now on the other foot. Not very nice, is it, having someone who's got the drop on you for a change, so I think I'll bank my advantage for the moment. However, there are a few things you really need to do urgently to prevent my immediate reappearance with an arrest warrant.

'Firstly, there's a man called Dominic Oxford. Make sure new evidence comes to light exonerating him of all charges. Then there's my friend, the reporter, currently languishing in more pain than you'll ever experience in your lifetime. I know your two psychos worked him over. He's to be left alone. Completely! Or else!'

'Or else what!' sneered Hugo, trying desperately to counter the patient assault on his world by this morose, polyester-clad man.

'I imagine there are a few individuals who've suffered as a result of their contact with you. People with influence. People with a grudge to settle, who would be only too happy to step into a witness box. I guess there are enough wronged souls littering your past to charter a fleet of taxis to bring them to court.'

Now there was an uncomfortable thought for Hugo.

'But, as a master of manipulation yourself, you know there are ways to avoid such unpleasantness. Don't get your hopes up, matey boy, I'm not striking a deal with you. A deal implies you have something I want. You do not. Don't imagine you can encourage any reluctance to prosecute on the part of the CPS or bring pressure to bear on me personally because if I get one whiff of your diseased interference in my professional life or in the execution of this case then expect a knock on the door in the middle of the night. Next time I won't be so chatty. In fact I'll be certain to bring my favourite pair of handcuffs and my friend, the reporter, will make damned sure you'll be on the front page of this fine journal the following morning.' Wilf nodded at the paper draped over Hugo's knees.

'Finally, if I ever catch you or your boys in sniffing distance of Miss Gordon again then there'll be hell to pay. You leave her and her talented boyfriend alone. That's a message you'd better take back to your master. I'd deliver it myself but I figure you've got his ear. I know exactly where this leads, Chaplain, and it's only the very narrowest lack of evidence that's preventing me from taking further action. I might not be able to get right up to the top of this particularly unpleasant pile of poo, but I'll make damned sure there'll be a resigning type of fuss over in Westminster. I don't think he'd want that, do you?

'You're lucky. You're getting off lightly, although I guess you think otherwise. All this high-profile attention must be bad for business. I imagine you've suddenly become a liability. I think your career path has just taken a turn for the worse, but believe me when I say there's a lot more to lose than your job and status. You can skulk away a free man because in exchange for my generous co-operation you're going to give me Pritchard and Coberley. They're the ones who committed the burglary and assaulted Miss Gordon. They're the ones who are about to discover their boss is throwing them to the wolves. They're the ones who'll be facing trial and they're the ones who are going to pay.

'Naturally they will be compelled to stay silent in court for reasons of national security, but I can tell you now that really hacks off the judge and jury. It seems ironic to me the only viable defence they can use to protect you and your master will be the one which ensures their own conviction, especially when Bertie fingers them in court. Did I mention that, Hugo? How do you think the press are going to react when they discover a macaw will be giving evidence in a trial for burglary, that the victim is the partner of the Minister for Defence and that the offence was committed by two espionage officers employed by the MoD, men who were quite happy to offer violence in the course of their duties? Do you think there could possibly be some media interest, Hugo? I do. Miss Gordon is an innocent and I'm going to make damned sure she gets the chance to see your grunts squirm in court.

'Attacking a woman? Can't have that, now, can we?'

Wilf stood and put a hand in his pocket. 'Oh yes, here's one last thing. I almost forgot.' He pulled out a banana and placed it on the bedside table. 'Doesn't look much, does it. A nice piece of fresh fruit. Traditionally found in hospitals and jails. Old lags will tell you – no matter where you're locked up, HM Prison Service can guarantee you three things,' he smiled. 'Bars, buggery, and bananas!'

Wilf turned on his heel and strode from the room with Ian at his side. 'Jesus,' he muttered. 'You frightened every shadow of hell out of me so God knows how Fat Boy felt. If what you think is true then that bloke's just about the most powerful man in the country.'

'Bullies come in all shapes and sizes. I hate 'em all.'

They stood alone as the lift descended in stately silence. Sequestered inside the anonymous metal cube seemed to remove them from reality – apart from a poster warning of the dangers of contracting gonorrhoea. 'So who's his master?' asked Drewing casually.

'See if you can figure it out before we reach the ground floor. Don't worry, you've got plenty of time.' The floor indicator continued to count down with all the speed of a rheumatic tortoise. National Health Service lifts were without doubt the slowest on the planet. An infection on the top floor could easily sprout into full-blown gangrene in the time it took to reach the lobby. To step into an NHS lift is to step out of time itself. Wilf glanced sideways at Drewing and his puzzled expression. 'Think about it. Who's the only person to whom Chaplain could have possibly answered?'

The lift doors finally opened and the two officers emerged back into a universe where time bounced along at its usual lively pace. They were halfway across the foyer when it finally struck Ian. The knowledge stopped him dead in his tracks.

'Holy crap on a cream cracker!' he gasped, eyes widened in disbelief. Several people stared at him disapprovingly, tutting at such inappropriate language from a police constable. He stood for a moment in complete shock, then sprinted after Wilf. 'You mean to tell me it's –'

Chapter Fourteen

'Call Bertie Gordon!'

A collective shiver of anticipation stirred every journalist in the court. Not a seat was spare in the public gallery, not an inch of floor but covered by the packed ranks of the world's media – and they were all there for one thing. A non-human was about to be put on the stand as a witness for the first time ever.

Ever!

This was *the* story of the decade. From the most sophisticated Western democracy to the poorest Third World state, from frigid Spitzbergen to sun-drenched Polynesia, from the Olympian heights of Tibet to the sunken shores of the Dead Sea, all were truly united in their avid interest. For the only time since Neil Armstrong kitted up and went for a stroll on the moon, mankind was as one, all waiting with lively anticipation for this extraordinary moment. Events from this courtroom would be sent by fibre optic and microwave and shiny expensive satellite to every nation on the planet.

Even France.

Reporters shifted in their seats and leaned forward. Pens were poised in readiness above the pages of a hundred notebooks. Artists busily sketched the scene for immediate release to the TV news channels; unlike the US and other liberally inclined countries, cameras were still banned from British courts, and these hurried caricatures would be flashed across the globe to satisfy an expectant audience. They were as prepared as they could be, all had made damned sure there were plenty of blue and violet pastels in their palettes – and not one of them would ever forget the dramas of that day.

Celeste brought in Bertie accompanied by the usher, her arm protected from his needle-tipped claws by her leather falconry gauntlet. A perch had been placed in the witness box and Bertie stepped on to it with an effortless flutter, a little disappointed at the lack of a food tray. She stroked him for a few moments, whispered soothing words in his ear and turning away, left the courtroom. Defence counsel argued she could have influenced him by remaining in court so she'd agreed to wait outside, promising Bertie would behave himself if treated with respect. In turn, the judge had assured her there would be no upsetting legal histrionics.

Bertie watched his mummy leave, then seeing a large number of people gazing at him, displayed majestically, spreading his wings to their full stretch and twitching his long tail feathers. He turned this way and that to ensure everyone got a good look. It was always best to let them know who was in charge. The magnificent sight brought soft coos of admiration from the public gallery, his plumage bringing an exotic splash of azure to the sober room. It was doubtful such vibrant colours had ever been seen before in the grave atmosphere of the Old Bailey. Bertie carefully folded his wings and looked around with great interest.

The room was pleasantly large, with a high arched ceiling from which a goodly amount of light flooded down, warming panelled walls. The place was crowded with banked benches, a high gallery at one side filled to capacity and before him, sitting at desks, a number of oddly dressed men with long dark cloaks and strange grey hairy hats perched upon their heads. These did not seem to fit at all well and looked uncomfortable. Bertie guessed they were wearing them as some kind of punishment.

Nearby, twelve more people sat inside a rectangular wooden box, separated as if they were somehow important. Or possibly they smelt bad. Another smaller box across the room contained a pair of men with a third in uniform sitting just behind, but he didn't give any of them too much attention. Instead, his eye was drawn to the only other colourful figure in the room. This silent man sat alone in a high-backed chair overlooking the room. The panelling behind him rose up into a grand canopy overhead, as if to emphasize his importance. He wore a scarlet robe with white cuffs and collar, and his coarse hat was just that little bit bigger and more luxuriant than the others – it almost looked as if Sebastian was draped over his head, a notion Bertie found amusing. A few other personages were dotted around, standing in discreet corners keeping an eye on things. Bertie had rarely seen so many humans together in one room and settled himself, curiosity piqued. Now what?

A hushed silence fell. There was an awkward hiatus, as if nobody was quite sure what to do next. The court usher, having escorted Celeste outside and returned to his position, looked at the judge and shrugged helplessly. Mister Justice Alistair Cruikshank cleared his throat and there was instant silence. Bertie was impressed.

'Ladies, gentlemen, I want it made quite clear that I will not tolerate frivolity of any description,' he announced in a rumbling Western Isles accent. An avid fan of opera, he possessed a fine baritone voice and in addition to his numerous judicial duties sang with the Lincoln's Inn Operatic Society, a pastime giving him as much pleasure as sentencing the guilty. Consequently, he was able to project his words without effort. 'The unusual nature of this case makes no difference to procedure, although certain allowances will have to be made to accommodate this – ah, witness.' He paused for a moment, then looked over his half-moon reading spectacles at the reporters packed into the press bench and up in the public gallery above. 'Decorum will be maintained or I will have no hesitation in clearing the court,' he concluded firmly. 'I trust that is quite understood.'

'Nuts!' said Bertie, quite distinctly. There was a suppressed giggle somewhere, instantly stifled under a flash of Cruikshank's iron gaze. It was well known he rigorously applied the law of contempt. Scores of pencils recorded Bertie's no-nonsense request for a little light refreshment. The judge regarded him with a shrewd glance, undecided if this was a simple overture for comestibles or an irreverent observation on his last statement. He waited, but it appeared the macaw had no further immediate comment and so he turned back to the usher.

'Mr Hall, you may proceed.'

'With respect, My Lord, how?'

'These are uncharted waters, Mr Hall. I suggest we carry on as normal unless obvious difficulties are encountered.'

'Yes, My Lord.' Duncan Hall approached Bertie with a great deal of trepidation. He was a slight man and somewhat height-challenged, an unfortunate combination of physical disappointments which had led to much bullying at school until he'd set about his tormentors with a cricket bat. Well, honestly, what's a guy to do? Small, yes, but tough in a surprisingly inventive way – and he loathed bullies in all their forms. To Duncan, the strapping macaw loomed very large indeed. He moved in cautiously and held up a Bible and the oath card. Bloody hell, the bird was huge! 'Bertie Gordon, repeat after me: "I swear by Almighty God that the evidence I shall give is the truth, the whole truth, and nothing but the truth".'

Pause. Followed by a rather longer silence.

Bertie preened a flight feather with casual nonchalance, cocked his head to one side and stared at the usher. Obviously he was being spoken to, but what the tiny man was saying was quite beyond him. Duncan looked expectant, Bertie looked blank, the jury looked puzzled, the press looked on and the judge pondered on the wisdom of proceeding any further.

Bertie's response to the oath was absolutely crucial. Legal experts had argued for weeks beforehand that his understanding of the need for truth was vital to the case. The debate had swung back and forth until finally the Lord Chancellor quietly observed that as far as he was concerned, any witness, feathered or not, could only testify under oath, and that the oath was not only an acknowledgement of the requirement for truth but also an indication of minimal understanding and intelligence.

No oath, no witness. Case dismissed. So far, the trial had gone in favour of the defendants. Pritchard and Coberley were answering charges of Actual Bodily Harm and Aggravated Burglary, both indictable offences that the magistrates had duly passed on to Crown Court. Several months had passed since the original burglary and now the case was being heard at the Old Bailey. Although normally reserved for far more serious trials, the famous courts also had a reputation for hosting high-profile cases – and they didn't get more high profile than this. In addition, because the case set a unique precedent, matters were under the control of a High Court judge.

The trial had proceeded with the usual gravity for which English courts were noted. Prosecuting counsel outlined the case and began calling witnesses. Daisy gave evidence in her usual shambolic way and even managed to get in a quick character assassination of Alice Henry before being coaxed back into line by the judge with gentle firmness. However, his compassion was not shared by the defence counsel who cut poor Daisy to shreds, although it was clear his hectoring did not impress the jury. As a result, it was determined Daisy was able to provide details of the surveillance van, but she could not identify the two defendants as being the occupants.

Wilf, in turn, had been thoroughly professional and came through unscathed, answering his questions efficiently, but at no time or in any way did he allude to the part played by Hugo Chaplain. Neither did Pritchard and Coberley. Their mouths remained firmly shut. From the moment of their arrest they denied all knowledge of the burglary. Both admitted that on the night in question they'd been engaged in an operation for the MoD, but the details of this investigation, for reasons of national security, would always remain completely confidential. Hugo had informed them in no uncertain terms that if they didn't assume full responsibility then it would be made known to the police that much darker crimes could be laid at their feet.

When Hugo hung someone out to dry, he didn't mess about.

Then it was Celeste's turn. She'd dazzled the court with her halo of brilliant copper hair but admitted she was unable to recognise either Pritchard or Coberley as her assailants. The question of Coberley's severed ear was explained away by an unfortunate encounter with a wilful grass strimmer, a surprisingly common source of injury, by all accounts. Mr Cedric Penry-Williams, acting on behalf of the defence, then implied police incompetence was responsible for the loss of all evidence, and so the trial had wended its stately way to this moment.

Duncan Hall looked at the judge for guidance. Cruikshank nodded. 'Again, Mr Hall, if you please.' Duncan repeated the oath to Bertie in a more distinct voice. Up in the gallery, Weasel bit his lip. 'C'mon, Bertie,' he muttered under his breath, sensing the judge's growing impatience. There was no doubt Cruikshank would dismiss Bertie if he didn't reply soon.

When the repetition again produced no response, Cruikshank stroked his chin thoughtfully. He was prepared to be reasonably patient with Bertie but there were limits. He pondered for a moment and suggested a new tack. 'Mr Hall, under the circumstances I think a simpler definition of the oath would be acceptable, one the witness might stand a greater chance of comprehending. Perhaps you could endeavour to improvise.'

'Thank you, My Lord, I shall try,' replied Duncan. He always enjoyed working with Cruikshank. The man was scrupulously fair to all who graced his court and did not suffer from pomposity like a goodly number of the other judges. Right bloody curmudgeons, some of them, real grumpy old sods. No one liked to be on the receiving end of an acid tongue in court, especially when every sarcastic comment was duly noted by the stenographer. Duncan thought for a moment before carefully easing the Bible onto Bertie's perch. The blue macaw automatically reached out to touch it with his barbed claw, bending to investigate the old leather cover curiously. 'Do you promise to tell the truth?' he asked slowly. Bertie cocked his head from side to side, peering intently at the man.

'Well? Do you?' asked Duncan in a soft, persuasive voice, trying his very best to encourage the bird. Aha! At last, here was a phrase Bertie recognised immediately. Admittedly, this little man with the kindly face showed no signs of producing any food, but Bertie was ever the optimist.

'Yes,' he replied promptly in perfect English. 'I do.'

There was what could only be described as a collective gasp of profound shock from around the court. Journalists scribbled furiously, chortling to themselves. The blood drained from Coberley's face and he swayed slightly in his chair. Even Pritchard, who was proving to be made of much sterner stuff, paled noticeably. Duncan withdrew the Bible cautiously from under Bertie's clawed foot, glanced discreetly at the judge and let an eyebrow ascend in a way that conveyed his bubbling amusement. Cruikshank, in response, and to his great surprise, had to cover a broad smile with his hand. This was quite extraordinary and would certainly entail an entire chapter in his memoirs. He nodded thanks to Duncan, let the court subside again and motioned to the prosecuting council.

Geoffrey Barrington, QC, stood and shuffled his notes. Bertie moved his attention to this new face since the small man had now sat down. It seemed he wasn't going to hand over any nuts after all, which was a little disappointing. 'Is your name Bertie Gordon?'

Bertie knew the answer to that one. 'Yes. Oh, yes. My name is Bertie. I'm very pleased to meet you. Who are you?' Barrington seemed most taken aback by this unexpectedly eloquent rejoinder. Quite discombobulated, in fact. It didn't happen often, especially in court, but then he'd never had a conversation with a parrot before so felt his momentary hesitation justifiable.

'That's, ah, that's of little importance. Tell me, Mr – er, Gordon, can you please describe to the court clearly and in exact detail your precise movements on the night in question?'

A bewildering blankness seemed to descend on Bertie. Completely at a loss, he merely repeated his own last sentence. Judge Cruikshank removed his spectacles in a rare display of minor irritation. 'Really, Mr Barrington, do we have to be so formal?' he chided, his mellifluous accent momentarily thickening. 'Reports have suggested Mr Gordon has an intelligence quotient in the low sixties which equates, I believe, to that of a four or five-year-old child. Would you really ask a child so abstract a question? I think not. May I remind both you and the defence counsel that as far as I'm concerned the sole purpose of this part of these proceedings is to determine two matters. The first is that Bertie – perhaps it would be better for all concerned to refer to him by the name with which he is most familiar – that Bertie understands the necessity for truth. I think that has already been satisfactorily established. The second is that he identifies beyond all reasonable doubt the defendants as the men responsible for the charges. Having taken, I have to say, a wearying amount of advice from the Lord Chancellor's Office and from my fellow judges, I have decided this is the only requirement to satisfy me, and so I ask that, please, for the sakes of the witness and for the sobriety of my court, you direct any questions to that end and that end alone.'

'Thank you, My Lord, I shall endeavour to do so.' Barrington fought hard to conceal a moment of elation. His seemingly innocuous but complex opening question had just achieved exactly what he wanted – and Cruikshank had fallen into the subtle trap, bless his tartan socks. All Bertie had to do was identify the accused, a relatively simple act, and now Cruikshank's directive meant the bird could not be cross-examined on that crucial point.

He duly discarded his notes and sighed, as if reluctant to abandon a carefully planned line of examination, but felt a growing conviction things might just work out after all. There was no need to ask any further questions. He glanced at the defending counsel and saw only frowns on the forehead of his learned friend. Cedric Penry-Williams, also QC, was a superb barrister and knew he'd just been thoroughly rogered. Thank God for Shankie – the old badger had just scuppered any chance of Ceds bamboozling Bertie. He'd dealt a killing blow to the defence team about which they could not even object. Everything else was suddenly irrelevant. It was now up to the bird's memory – and who knew which way that would go?

The last interchange left Bertie totally confused. He looked around to see if Celeste was nearby but only strange faces peered back at him, so he detached himself from his surroundings and allowed his thoughts to turn, as they invariably did in these moments of contemplative idleness, to food and sex.

Perhaps there wasn't such a gulf between the males of different species after all.

'Bertie?' He looked up again at the sound of his name. The tall man in the long cloak and funny little hat was speaking once more. 'Bertie, can you –'

'I like apples,' Bertie confided firmly, his mind now set on a

210

campaign to extort some kind of nutritious dainty out of these people.

Barrington seemed a little flustered. Bertie's statement was entirely unexpected, but at least the macaw was now talking. 'Good, I'm glad.' He tried to deflect Bertie's intent and opened his mouth to speak, but Bertie got a quick one in first.

'Granny Smiths. Very nice.'

'I'm sure they are, however –'

'And pears. Oh, yes. Big pears, lovely pears.' Bertie's head bobbed happily. He absolutely adored pears, but they had a loosening effect on his digestive solidity. Unfortunately for Pritchard and Coberley, he'd feasted on a succulent, over-ripe pear on the morning of the burglary. It was one of those delicious twists of fate which really does make you believe there is a God.

'Splendid,' said Barrington. Actually, thinking about it, he was rather fond of pears himself. There was a pause as he found himself lost in wonderful childhood memories of pears in chocolate sauce and summer days fruit-picking with his parents.

'Have you finished already?' enquired Judge Cruikshank mildly. 'I didn't expect you to take my advice so literally as to not ask any questions at all! May I point out it is traditional to sit upon finishing the examination of a witness. I recommend you to that course.'

'Forgive me, My Lord, I was elsewhere for a few moments.'

'Then I'm sure I speak for all here when I offer my congratulations on your safe return. The continuation of these proceedings does rather depend on you, Mr Barrington.' There was just enough gentle humour in the judge's voice to raise a smile around the court. Even Barrington had to admit the censure was delivered with avuncular Highland charm and his lips twitched in amusement. Bertie flexed one wing and looked vacant.

Geoffrey Bentley Barrington, a man who fully appreciated the implications of this case and who certainly planned to improve his status accordingly, made a minor adjustment to his wig, gathered his thoughts and spoke in a firm and clear voice. 'Bertie.' He was rewarded with a steady gaze of interest from those disturbingly perceptive brown eyes. 'Do you know these men?' Barrington pointed and Bertie's gaze automatically followed the direction of his outstretched arm towards the dock.

'Will the defendants please stand.' At the judge's signal, Pritchard and Coberley rose to their feet, both waxen-faced and perspiring visibly. Behind them, the dock custody officer also stood, on hand just in case there was any unseemly disturbance. Mr Penry-Williams, having consulted a number of experts in bird behaviour, had assured them the delay in bringing the case was of ample length for Bertie to forget the burglary, but even so, the whole affair stood or fell on this point. Bertie regarded them briefly before looking back at Barrington. The QC pointed again. 'Over there, Bertie,' he said. 'Do you know these men?'

Several members of the jury wriggled in their seats, leaning forward in rapt attention. Here we go. This was it. This was the moment.

Cruikshank gestured the two men out of the dock and they shuffled across the court to stand directly in front of the witness box. Coberley stared at his feet while Pritchard continually swept back his hair with one hand, also reluctant to look at Bertie. To Barrington's eye both appeared miserable and tense. He had absolutely no doubt they were as guilty as sin and knew Shankie did as well, but this was trial by jury and without Bertie's help he doubted if he could make the charges stick.

'Gentlemen,' said Judge Cruikshank, 'please look directly at the witness.' Reluctantly, they did so. Bertie sat impassively, peering down at them from his elevated position. Nothing happened for a long time. There was absolute silence in the court. Even Sally Bingle, the superbly competent court stenographer, stole a quick glance at Bertie, her nimble fingers poised over the keys of her machine. The atmosphere tightened palpably. Duncan carefully stood up from his table in front of the judge. Some indefinable sixth sense of impending trouble produced a frown on his face. He exchanged a look with Cruikshank, who nodded fractionally, freeing Duncan to drift slowly and unobtrusively in the direction of the witness box.

Defence council began to fidget, but the judge was prepared to let Bertie take his time and stayed Penry-Williams with a

212

placating gesture. With Celeste unable to identify the accused and all other evidence now lost, Bertie had to give some signal to the court that these were his assailants or the two defendants would undoubtedly walk free.

Sweat trickled uncomfortably down Pritchard's spine. He looked at Bertie without any expression, trying to assess the macaw, but it was impossible to tell what was going on in that strange and complex mind. A full minute passed and Pritchard was suddenly seized with the certainty that, after all, Bertie did not recognise him, and allowed a smug smile of satisfaction to twitch on his lips. For some reason, the pale scars on his cheek began to itch and he absently raised his hand to scratch at the irritation.

Bertie's gaze followed the movement. Those marks looked strangely familiar, even though they were difficult to see. He turned his attention to the other man. Now that was odd. His cheek was also faintly marked and there was something very wrong with one of his ears, giving his countenance a distinctly lopsided appearance. Bertie dipped his head slightly to stare with unflinching intensity at the two battered faces. Memories tumbled in and out of his consciousness. His claws had once made marks like that all over Sebastian's back. The cat was a menial, conceited creature, always sneaking around the salon. The salon. A familiar place. His home, his favourite perch. And Mummy! Mummy crying out in pain and falling. Falling? Something suddenly stirred deep inside; a vague resentment, a faint and woolly recollection of blood and fighting and screaming and extreme violence.

"'It's the sodding parrot!'"

The court froze. There was not a sound. Pencils skidded to a halt. Jaws dropped open in shock. Bertie's perfect imitation stopped everyone absolutely dead in their tracks. There was no question that the voice was Coberley's.

The feathers on the back of Bertie's head stood up. He spread his wings, crouched down low and hissed venomously at the pair like an enraged cobra, his impressive bulk almost doubling in size. Coberley recoiled, entirely aware of how dangerous Bertie could be, but Pritchard stood his ground and glared pugnacious defiance. 'Come on, then!' he ground out in fury. Bertie took this as a challenge and launched himself like a bolt of blue thunder. He remembered now. Oh, yes, he remembered. These men had hurt his mum.

Instantly, in a split second, utter pandemonium erupted in the court. 'Not again!' moaned Coberley, the significance of this unwise whisper not lost on either Barrington or Judge Cruikshank – or the jury. Since that awful night of the disastrous burglary and Ellen's violent misinterpretation of events, he'd been compelled to endure another long period of humiliating sexual denial. These frustrations and the pressures of the impending trial culminated in this one fatal error, caught for the record by the ever-vigilant Sally and her dancing fingers, but before anything could be done to capitalise on his mistake, calm had to be restored.

It was going to take more than a few dignified cries of *Order!* to quell this particular altercation!

Wisely motivated by his previous encounter with the macaw, Coberley dived for cover beneath a nearby table, a look of utter horror on his ashen face. He was joined by the instructing solicitors and Penry-Williams, who only needed to take one look at Bertie's impressive arsenal before deciding to beat an immediate retreat to safety. The prudence of such an action was also not entirely lost on Barrington, who crouched under his own table, wig clutched in hand. Sally ripped her Stenotype machine off its mount and cradling it under one arm, scrambled down behind her chair. Displaying the unflustered professionalism for which court stenographers were renowned, she then continued recording the varied collection of onomatopoeic grunts, shrieks of pain and snarling vulgarities peppering the uproar, holding her handbag above her head as a shield whenever Bertie swooped in her direction.

Mr Justice Alistair Cruikshank was made of much sterner stuff and barked at the police and court security officers to restore order. He refused to panic, assuming that in the scene of chaos unfolding before him at least one person should remain calm and collected. He didn't even duck when Bertie skimmed low overhead before turning to dive on Pritchard, the chamber spacious enough to allow a comprehensive aerial assault. The court floor was a complete shambles of writhing bodies and crashing furniture, the gallery seethed in uproar. The dock custody officer made to grab Pritchard around the chest but inadvertently caught an elbow hard in the face and staggered back, stunned and bleeding, only to collide with a solicitor, the heavy impact toppling both men. Reporters watched in shock as Bertie plunged in to buffet Pritchard, whistling like a banshee, his lethal claws hacking and scything at the man's face.

'Go on, Bertie!' screamed Weasel. His certain knowledge that Pritchard and Coberley were responsible for his genital discomfiture had never been proven, but that didn't prevent him from encouraging Bertie to tear the bastards limb from limb.

In a superb manoeuvre which would have brought a hearty nod of approval from Squadron Leader Dandridge, Bertie banked in a tight turn over the witness box, one wing dipped and the other lofted high, and descended on Pritchard again like an avenging violet titan. Evading the sweeping fists with a lightning twist of the body, his left claw struck. It was a good hit, starting just above the ear and opening the man's scalp for several inches. Blood spurted horrifically, spraying across the floor and those who cowered there. The man's scream of pain was music to Bertie's ears and he turned again to savage his target, but by this time Pritchard had been taken down by Duncan with a brutal flying rugby tackle to the knees. The two men sprawled among the upturned chairs even as Bertie swept overhead, his talons missing Pritchard's crown by a fraction as he pitched to the floor in an unceremonious heap, fists still flailing at his adversary. He did not seem at all appreciative of the fact that Hall's action certainly saved him from another catastrophic head wound. With arms wound tight around Pritchard's shins, Duncan grabbed a mouthful of trouser leg and worried at the cloth like a terrier, a look of flinty determination on his normally placid face which Mr Justice Cruikshank had never seen before.

With Pritchard otherwise engaged, Bertie turned his attention to Coberley, cowering under a table. Unable to reach him, he simply let fly with his other favourite weapon. Coberley saw the squirting mayonnaise cascade down and ducked, exposing Penry-Williams to the full force of spraying poo. Creamy crap spotted his face and shoulders, splattering wetly. He was not at all impressed, his interest in securing a not guilty verdict evaporating instantly.

Pritchard tried to shake off Duncan, but the smaller man made up for his physical shortcomings with a mixture of sheer grit and astonishing persistence. God, he loathed men like Pritchard and sincerely wished for a good solid cricket bat, his favoured weapon of choice! His iron grip never slackened for a moment as his teeth tore holes in Pritchard's trousers. Pritchard lashed out at Duncan's head and caught him a glancing blow across the brow. Duncan merely growled and countered with a winning move. Wriggling like a monkey, he managed to clamp his legs around Pritchard's waist in a brutal body scissors, ankles locked together in the small of Pritchard's back. Using a table to lever himself back to his feet, Pritchard tried to attack Bertie again but could not shake off an upside-down Duncan, still wrapped tight around his belly and legs like a drunkard hugging his favourite lamp post!

With a thunderous crash, the entrance doors burst open and a charging mass of uniformed policemen piled into the court, closely followed by Celeste and Wilf. She stopped short, aghast at the sight of utter carnage, of blood and wrestling men, wild cries and muffled snorts. She immediately guessed Bertie had been the cause of the tumult and called to him, but her voice was drowned by the sounds of splintering furniture and wildly desperate shouting. She tried to run into the body of the court only to be jerked back by Wilf, yelling in her ear and pushing her forcefully against a wall to shield her from any danger.

The swarming policemen launched themselves into the fray with commendable gusto. Pritchard went down under a flight of burly bobbies, burying him instantly, so Bertie aborted his assault, soared over the public gallery screeching in triumph before gliding down to land with a majestic sweep of his wings on the top of Cruikshank's high-backed chair, arriving in a swishing flurry of deep blue. His bloodstained claws gripped the polished oak not twelve inches from the judge's right ear, steel-coloured tips indenting the hard wood. He folded his wings and composed himself with a shake.

He and the judge, violet and red sitting side-by-side, watched the scrambling, undignified imbroglio slowly subside. Gradually, some semblance of normality returned to the chaotic court. Members of the jury, who found their box had ably doubled up as a temporary air raid shelter, popped up to check the coast was clear before retaking their seats. Roaring with rage, Pritchard still fought hard beneath four enormous police officers who were attempting to handcuff him. Duncan continued to cling to his legs like an Ilfracombe limpet clamped to a north Devon rock, chewing at the man's trousers with bared teeth, and only released his grasp when the officers finally subdued their captive. He bounced back to his feet nimbly and adjusting his tie, grinned broadly and winked at Cruikshank before going to help the other ushers right upturned chairs and gather spilled papers.People began to reappear from cover like refugees emerging after an artillery barrage, glancing with understandable nervousness at the silent blue gargoyle perched beside the judge. One by one, the press returned to their benches up in the public gallery. Penry-Williams and Coberley surfaced from under their table. The custody officer, now suffering from a substantial nosebleed caused by Pritchard's elbow, took Coberley's unresisting arm and led him back to the dock while squeezing a wadded tissue to his nostrils. Barrington replaced his wig rather self-consciously and dusted himself down. Sally resumed her position behind the reassembled Stenotype machine, checked her make-up in a compact mirror and wriggled her bra straps back into position with a demure shake of the shoulders.

Mr Justice Cruikshank just sat in his chair like a resplendent, red-robed Bela Lugosi and waited patiently for the hubbub to die down. It had been an altogether extraordinary and memorable five minutes. Eventually, an abashed silence fell, broken only, for some inexplicable reason, by the sound of loud purring. Now what? People cast around quizzically. A cat? In the Old Bailey?

'Thank you, gentlemen,' said Judge Cruikshank in a
217

perfectly normal tone of voice. 'Mr Hall?'

'Yes, My Lord.'

'May I compliment you on an admirable tackle. You displayed the spirit of courage and tenacity one would normally expect from a person of considerably greater physical presence.'

'Thank you, My Lord.' Duncan beamed happily at the praise while Barrington, a good six stone heavier and twelve inches broader and taller, looked abjectly sheepish after his own abrupt and undignified scramble for shelter. Shankie hadn't even moved a muscle during the entire fracas – the old goat was as cool as a cucumber.

'Mr Barrington, I think we can take that as a positive identification by the witness, don't you?'

'Yes, Your Honour,' replied the barrister, bowing fractionally. The jurors looked entirely satisfied, smiling slightly to each other.

'Any further comments, Mr Penry-Williams?'

'None, My Lord.'

'Then in view of what has just happened, I believe a short recess is in order for nerves to calm. Miss Gordon, would you be so good as to take charge of Bertie? Thank you. Mr Penry-Williams, please be so good as to wash and change into fresh robes. I also require my court – and the defendant – to be cleaned.' Judge Cruikshank nodded sourly at the spattering of blood on the floor and table. Pritchard himself, now held firmly between two constables, was bruised, battered, and bloodstained, his formerly crisp white shirt torn and missing several buttons. He looked like he'd just been sprayed by an exploding ketchup bottle.

The judge surveyed his court calmly, then noticed the stares. Everyone gaped at him with some considerable concern. Duncan's eyes widened and he pointed anxiously. It all went very, very quiet. Cruikshank felt a sudden coldness wash through his stomach and slowly turned his head to find Bertie edging closer, claws clicking as he sidled along the back of the chair. Bizarrely, the bird was purring like a Cheshire cat – Cruikshank could clearly feel the rumbling vibrations through

218

his seat. He glanced up to see the macaw towering over him. 'We will reconvene in an hour,' he said in as even a voice as was possible.

'Nice hat,' said Bertie affably, bending to stare at the judge's florid wig. 'Very nice hat!'

Chapter Fifteen

To say the media had a field day would have been just about the greatest understatement of all time!

Bertie's picture was splashed across the front page of every newspaper, with banner headlines suiting the intellectual status of each individual publication. These fell into roughly three groups, represented by the clinically factual but somewhat desiccated *Court Uproar!* style employed by the quality broadsheets to the slightly more multi-dimensional *Macaw Clinches Old Bailey Case* theme favoured by the popular dailies, but the prize in this particular competition went to the gloriously entertaining *Battling Bertie Bags Bungling Burglars!* offered by one of the leading tabloids, thus perpetuating the fine tradition of inventive lexicology for which it was globally admired.

Once the court had reconvened, all the following procedures seemed lacking in excitement. Coberley's inadvisable comment, duly noted by Sally, was repeated, giving Mr Penry-Williams very little room to manoeuvre. His closing speech was not as impressive as his cleaning bill. The jury had seen and heard enough and were prompt in returning their verdict. The decision was unanimous – there were no *12 Angry Men*-style arguments here, no soft-spoken architect to cast doubts! Perhaps they weren't keen to be in the same building as Bertie for a second longer than necessary.

Guilty on all charges, Pritchard and Coberley received sentences of four years each. In addition, Pritchard was fined heavily for contempt since he was deemed to have provoked the witness unnecessarily, thus igniting the unexpected but entertaining chaos that followed. Judge Cruikshank, despite the tremendous interest in the case, retained a solid and pragmatic approach to the entire affair.

'I appreciate some aspects of this case have been quite extraordinary, but when stripped of its more colourful characters there still remains at its core a grubby little crime perpetrated on an innocent women by two men who felt they were justified in their actions merely because they were employed by a government agency. We have laws to circumscribe the actions of such agencies, laws designed to contain abuse to a very necessary minimum. In the vast majority of instances these agencies work tirelessly and without recognition to ensure we live in a safe and stable society – and for that we are all profoundly thankful – but while we readily acknowledge some of their work is potentially hazardous, they still need to operate within these laws. An inability to do so, to me, indicates a slide towards a police state.' He paused and removed his spectacles, a sure sign to those in the court who knew him well that he considered matters had come to a satisfactory conclusion. 'I wish to remind those who feel they can abuse the public for no good reason that the law is above us all, and if that law is broken, no favours will be given to any person. Not in my court. Not now, and not in the future.'

It was noticeable Mr Justice Alistair Cruikshank's meteoric rise to the exalted position of Lord Chief Justice began almost immediately the case was concluded, but to the public he was thereafter always affectionately known as Bertie's Judge.

Simply getting out of the building proved impossible for Celeste and Bertie. A great crushing phalanx of television crews and reporters from across the globe crowded the steps outside, spilling over the pavements and into the street, where passing traffic had to negotiate its way around the seething throng. The police struggled valiantly, attempting to compress the hacks back on to the pavement for their own safety, but these efforts were only marginally successful and a Paraguayan sound recordist was mown down by a motorcycle despatch rider, suffering minor injuries to the buttocks.

This unfortunate incident merely stoked tempers further.

Shoulder-mounted cameras craned, staring lenses thrust forward, with microphone booms waving above like grey socks blowing in a Hebridean gale. Each tussled with his neighbour to get a better shot and a great deal of unprofessional barging eventually led to Sky News punching the BBC on the nose.

The noise and confusion outside greatly disturbed Bertie. He liked to be the centre of attention but this was alarming. Wilf held Celeste back at the door. 'I don't think it's a good idea to leave at the moment,' he said, shielding his eyes against the glare of spotlights and veritable storm of flashing cameras. The frenzy waxed noticeably the moment Celeste and Bertie were glimpsed through the doorway and a great roar of expectation rose from the scrummage.

'They won't go away, will they?' she said, turning her back and holding Bertie close, stroking his head reassuringly. He sat on her arm gripping the leather gauntlet with more than his usual strength. She felt him tremble. 'There, my angel,' she said soothingly. 'Mummy's here. Good Bertie, safe Bertie. I love you, Bertie.'

The crowd suddenly broke through the ineffectual police cordon and surged forward, impacting with a terrible thump against the main doors. Lenses rattled against the glass like the exuberant clack of mating tortoises, ogling inwards with huge, empty eyes. Bertie looked over Celeste's shoulder and hissed at them.

'This is really frightening him, Wilf. We have to do something.'

'Could we put him in a box or something and smuggle him out?' suggested Wilf, then threw his hands up placatingly at Celeste's angry glance. 'Sorry, sorry, real bad idea. Forget I ever said it.'

'He's never been caged in his life and I'm not starting now. What about the back door? Courtrooms always have a back door, don't they? That's how famous people avoid the media.'

'True, but those vultures are everywhere. The entire building's surrounded.'

'Was it worth it all this?' Celeste asked softly, watching the tempestuous fracas through the windows.

'Yes. Absolutely,' replied Wilf firmly. He'd heard such agonising before on many occasions. 'Someone had to stand up to those two thugs.'

'But look what's happened. I can't even go to the shops without being harassed, and what about you? These sort of people strike me as vindictive. They always have to take out their anger on someone and I'm worried it'll be you. I hope this won't mean the end of your career.'

'What career! I had one fifteen years ago but it went on a day trip to Skegness and never came back. No, surprisingly, this won't do me any harm at all – those media vultures out there will ensure I'm handled with kid gloves from now on.' Wilf did not mention his visit to Hugo. She did not need to know what threats he'd employed to secure his own future. 'Besides, my boss has finally realised I've got a bit of talent and has put me forward for promotion at last.'

'Wilf, that's wonderful news. Thank goodness something good has come from all this.'

'For you, too. You're a global celebrity now. A hop, skip and jump and you'll have your own TV show. Milk it, Celeste, milk it while you're hot!'

'Me? On TV? That's a joke.'

'You'll be on television tonight, however much you try to avoid it. God, listen to them out there!'

'Wilf,' she said firmly. 'We have to do something. Bertie is getting very frightened. Those flashguns terrify me, so imagine how he feels. Can't you go out and talk to them, get them to back off so that we can go home?'

'They won't go. They just won't. You could set up camp in here and stay until hell freezes over but that lot will be still waiting outside. You have no idea how tenacious they can be. No idea at all. Sooner or later you'll have to face them, either now or …' His voice tapered off slowly.

'Or what?'

'We might just be able to persuade them to let us through if we promised a press conference, but only if Bertie is there. He's the star – Britain's going macaw mad at the moment!'

Celeste looked dubious. 'Surely that'll be just as stressful.'

'Not if you have it at home. At least there he'll be in a familiar environment.'

She thought for a long while, teeth gnawing at her lower lip, then nodded dubiously. 'Well, OK, but I want you there as well just to make sure matters stay civilised.'

Bertie sat on his perch behind the sofa, watching all the fuss and bother with great interest. The normal tranquillity of the house had been turned upside down since lunch, and now the far end of the salon was filled with wall-to-wall cameras. Hacks sat cross-legged on the parquet and made last-minute adjustments to their equipment. Cables snaked across the floor, through the patio doors, across the lawn and into vans parked in a line down the street beyond the garden wall, their roofs sprouting all manner of antennae and dishes.

Celeste fussed him, always there to keep him calm, and Bertie took comfort in her continual attention. Having witnessed the events in court the previous day, the assembled journalists sincerely hoped her presence would have a soporific effect on the macaw. Wilf sat on the portmanteau beside the bureau looking, to Bertie's eyes, even more faded than usual. Why on earth didn't he wear something a little more colourful? A splash of vibrant yellow wouldn't go amiss. Perhaps then he'd pull. No female in her right mind, it seemed to Bertie, could possibly find grey attractive.

Wilf glanced at his watch. It was almost four, the appointed hour. Celeste had wanted as much time as possible for Bertie to settle back into his domestic routine while the press had asked for it to be no later so they could report back to their editors in plenty of time for their evening deadlines.

Celeste regarded the group of technicians and reporters with wary concern. She now just wanted to get the interview over and done with as soon as possible and return to her quiet life. She was also desperate to see James again. He'd been gallantly discreet in the weeks leading up to the trial and felt it wouldn't be wise to be seen at Greenwich. The press had been keeping a close eye on them both, but now Celeste felt a real need for his company. She'd been surprised by the depth of her feelings.

She had also greatly missed their enjoyable little scenarios and promised something very special indeed for his next visit. An innocent Wilf was sitting on the new clothing and equipment she'd ordered.

'We're ready now, Miss Gordon,' said a man from the BBC, identifiable by his beautiful shiner of a black eye. 'If you would like to sit here on the settee then Bertie will be in shot over your shoulder without having to leave his perch.'

Celeste did as she was asked, feeling exceptionally self-conscious, and sat with undisguised apprehension while carrying out a quick final check on her make-up in a compact mirror. A touch of powder reduced the sheen of her skin, she'd applied minimal eye shadow and her lips were tinted with a colour known to women as 'Exotic Arabian Ruby' and to men as 'red'. She wore a sober black suit and a pale cream blouse with a single beryl brooch at the throat. However, her appearance was, as always, dominated by her hair. Those long, flowing tresses flamed under the lights like waves of molten copper, beautifully vibrant and voluminous. There was no doubt she was an extraordinarily striking woman. 'Is this all right?' she asked. 'I'm a little nervous.'

'Smashing. Perfect. Now, just relax, Miss Gordon. Everyone ready?'

The room was suddenly filled with the muted whisper of cameras. Bertie cocked his head to one side and listened intently.

'Right, here we go. Miss Gordon, how do you feel now that the trial is over?' This was a predictable start, something which made everyone feel comfortable. It was a question taken straight from chapter one of the *Ladybird Guide to Post-Trial Interviews*.

'Very relieved. I've been under a tremendous strain over the last few months and I'm just glad it's now all over.'

'Did you have any doubts as to the outcome?' asked ITN. Routine. Boring. Everyone was still settling down.

'None. I always knew we'd win.'

'But it could have gone the other way?'

'That's true, but the judge was brilliant. He was prepared to give Bertie as much time as he needed to remember.'

'Was Bertie's evidence vital?' There was a distinct rustle of interest. This was what they were after – the Bertie angle. Celeste was pragmatic enough to realise these people wouldn't give her the time of day if it wasn't for him.

'Oh, yes, absolutely vital. He was the only witness to the actual assault apart from me, and I was knocked about a bit and stunned. I can only vaguely remember his assault on those two but I can assure you it was pretty terrifying. Well, you all saw what happened in court yesterday. That was a big chamber. The attack in here was frighteningly more concentrated.' A wave of unease rippled through the reporters. They all seemed suddenly conscious of the fact they were in extremely close proximity to a creature which displayed all the sprightly psychological instabilities of Dr Jekyll and Mr Hyde! 'Then the three of them crashed through those doors and out into the garden.'

'And was that the last you saw of Bertie until he was returned by the police?' This was polite and gentle questioning, very British – they appeared to be anxious indeed to avoid arousing the wrath of the big bird sitting behind the sofa.

'Yes. Bertie was returned by Detective Constable Thompson here.' Celeste smiled at Wilf.

'Hello, Wilf,' said Bertie suddenly. 'Got any nuts?'

'Now then, Bertie, don't be rude,' chided Celeste gently. 'Perhaps later.' The press thought this sudden interchange highly interesting and waited with bated breath for another casual interjection by the macaw, but he appeared disinclined to oblige and turned to cleaning a feather or two. 'Anyway, he was still attacking those two horrible men as they ran away.'

'Better than a Rottweiler, eh, love?' sniggered a dubious looking character who represented that ultimate bastion of serious journalism, *Celeb Goss, Lip Gloss & Weight Loss Magazine*.

'Much better, I would say. I've never known him do anything like it before. It was – well, quite a surprise.'

'Can you get him to sit on the sofa beside you and say something else?' asked a representative of the Israeli State News. She sat sandwiched between two Iranian and Libyan correspondents who had obligingly shuffled up to make room.

'I'll try. Bertie, come here.' Celeste patted the arm. Nothing happened. Bertie refused to move. She glanced back at the cameras and grinned ruefully. 'Sorry. Never work with animals.'

'Can you try again? Please?'

'Well, OK. Bertie, Mummy loves you. Come on, come sit.' Wilf found her tone of voice intoxicatingly persuasive. He would certainly have leapt to her side had the invitation been directed at himself.

Bertie recognised the comforting familiarity of Celeste's voice, leaned forward and with a minimal flutter, hopped onto the back of the sofa. He waddled back and forth for a moment, then moved carefully onto the arm and sidled up to her, staring steadily at her face. His tail feathers were so long they almost brushed the parquet floor beside the settee. Some of the journos looked a trifle uneasy at the proximity of his scimitar talons. He enjoyed the fuss given by Celeste and dutifully stretched out his chin so she could tickle under his bill. He liked that very much and began to purr, which caused a great deal of amusement amongst their crowded guests. 'That's nice,' he said dreamily. Several reporters shook their heads in disbelief; the damned bird was more eloquent than most Premier League footballers.

'Can't he say something else?' asked another American journalist, perhaps more familiar with the concept of trained animals. Disney parrots could take the lead roles in any Rodgers and Hammerstein musical.

'Are you hungry?' asked Celeste.

Bertie perked up. This sounded much more promising. Here was something plain and simple he had no difficulty in understanding. 'Hungry. Yes. I like nuts.'

'Yes, Bertie, I know.' Celeste produced a bag of walnuts. 'What do you say?'

'Thank you.' Bertie was impeccably polite and began to dispose of the nuts in a quick and professional manner, his interest in the proceedings momentarily diverted. He was quite happy to graze while Celeste answered further questions and worked his way through half a dozen shells, then his attention was suddenly drawn to a technician who, while the interview was proceeding and keen to stay out of shot, crawled forward on his belly to place yet another microphone at Celeste's feet.

This movement triggered a strange train of thought in Bertie. He paused, cocked his head to one side and sat quite still. Something struggled up out of the jumbled lumber room that was his memory.

Something about crawling.

And kneeling.

Kneeling! Yes, that was it. The Kneeling Man. He hadn't visited for a while now but Bertie well remembered him. The Kneeling Man was always so polite. The Kneeling Man was fun. His head made an excellent perch. He always brought fruit or some other tasty little snack, but most important of all, The Kneeling Man was the only person in the world who made his mum a very happy woman. Not unnaturally, he made the simple association between the actions of the technician and his friend. He cleared his throat theatrically, as he had seen many times on the television, and was rewarded by the instant attention of the world's media.

'The Kneeling Man,' he announced precisely in received English.

No response. There was a collective puzzlement.

'The Kneeling Man,' he repeated a little louder. What was wrong with these people? Did he have to spell it out for them? 'Hooded, gagged, and strapped in the bondage wardrobe!' A stunned silence filled the room. Were they all deaf? 'James Timbrill,' he said, even louder still, enunciating as clearly as he could. 'The Kneeling Man. Here. Leather. The bondage wardrobe.' He executed a perfect reproduction of a cracking whip and the accompanying yelp of pain. 'Here. With the handcuffs. Many times.'

There was a speechless moment of absolute shock. Frozen faces stared in gaping, slack-jawed disbelief.

'Bertie!' shrieked Celeste. 'Oh, no!' Her ashen face was a mask of anguish. Her eyes bulged. She tried to say something but only a strangled mewl came out. Totally mystified by this entirely unexpected response, Bertie turned his attention back to the walnuts while the room around him erupted …

The PM sat in the privacy of his study, the door firmly shut. He did not want the staff around him to see the wide grin of satisfaction on his normally grave face. They would wonder why he was so happy. They would whisper that he knew something they didn't. This they would not like. They would want to find out the reason for his contentment and he would then find himself fending off a wearisome barrage of polite and not-very-subtle enquiries as to the reason for this unusual good cheer.

That needed to be avoided.

The flat screen monitor on his desk displayed the usual BBC News 24 channel as a reduced window set within a full-sized exterior scene of a quiet Downing Street. An external security camera pointed to the left and he could see the traffic passing back and forth along Whitehall the other side of Mrs T's unscalable gates. He glanced at it occasionally while working his way swiftly through a series of papers covering such diverse subjects as the preparations for a state visit by the President of Mexico to an amendment advocating an increase in the spacing of urban lamp posts to save on running costs.

Ah, the delights of running a country!

The smile broadened. It came easily. He was in high humour. A scheme long planned had finally come to fruition, a scheme of his own making, one so subtle and ingenious even Hugo Chaplain remained entirely unaware of its existence. The scheme had, by necessity, been concocted in his own mind and executed by his own hand. No one else had been involved. No one else knew or guessed or even imagined of such a scheme, and therefore no one else would ever disclose its secrets. It was his and his alone, and it had been entirely and satisfyingly successful.

The scheme had been to rid himself of JSON.

Oh, clever scheme!

It had all started with a carefully orchestrated but outwardly coincidental meeting in the House of Commons. The PM had bumped into Quentin Austerly on his way to the chamber and during their hurried conversation, casually mentioned he thought it odd the MoD was the only major Whitehall ministry not possessing a relaxation and entertainment suite for its senior officials. Perhaps there was room at the back of the building, well out of the way, that might prove a suitable location? Always so embarrassingly eager to please, Austerly acted with predictable energy while also demonstrating his impertinence by claiming the idea was his own. This, the PM knew, would certainly upset Chaplain – the man was paranoid about secrecy – and so Hugo moved to deflect the course of events in his habitually vicious manner. Exit Austerly and Sharples. Alan Denmark, too. Pity. A talented man, but sacrifices needed to be made. This left the stage open for the spectacular rise of James Timbrill – the whole point of the exercise – thus successfully completing the first stage of the PM's plan.

Timbrill's unexpected arrival was critical since he knew the man did not figure in JSON's salacious files. The PM chuckled at the delicious irony of it all. It had actually been Chaplain himself who'd put forward Dickless Jimmy's name without any need of prodding in that direction – and Hugo had no idea that in doing so he'd just sealed his own fate.

This unacceptable lack of information on Timbrill would need to be rectified in short order. Knowing Hugo's casual predisposition to illegal action, the PM gently nudged him into organising the burglary of Gordon's house in a way so natural, so innocuous, even Hugo had not noticed the delicate tickle. Once the burglary had been committed, it had then been the PM's scheme to anonymously tip-off the police. However, Timbrill's unexpected streak of independence in the House had provided the PM with a God-given opportunity. Having taken the gamble of actually stabbing his new minister in front of the entire Commons, he'd not only made it impossible for himself to dismiss James, thus spurring Hugo into action, but at the same time also ensured there was a satisfyingly cold distance between himself and Timbrill. Naturally, James would have been only too keen to take revenge on the men who'd burgled his girlfriend once their identity had been revealed. With Timbrill eviscerating JSON, the PM was totally confident his own involvement was so far removed from events that no suspicion would ever fall on him.

No doubt Hugo would come whining to No. 10, demanding protection of some sort, but the PM's hands would be tied. He would have to let Chaplain go, but in the nicest possible way, of course. Over tea and biscuits. However, it was imperative Hugo did not catch a single whiff of the PM's involvement otherwise, well, there was enough dirty laundry with his own prints on it to ensure his immediate retirement to the Chiltern Hundreds. He knew Chaplain was far too arrogant to ever suspect him of such Machiavellian deviousness since the PM had, quite deliberately, relied increasingly on JSON over the last year until it was inconceivable to its operatives that he was ever capable of orchestrating such a delicate scheme himself. He had, with supreme skill, not only deflected their suspicions but also ensured his own survival when the inevitable fall came, and he needed to make that survival look damned good for the electorate.

That *had* been his scheme. It *had* been a good scheme, necessarily intricate because of the formidable perspicacity of his opponent, but like any carefully engineered plan it was always going to be subject to unexpected events. Fortunately, and for just this one time, those random events intervened to his great advantage and instead of attempting to steer his plan back onto its intended course, he'd just let it run free.

Who could possibly have guessed the burglars, with all their skill and expertise, would have been thwarted by that macaw? How divinely delicious. How extraordinarily *outré*. There was no way Chaplain could ever see past such a totally unexpected encounter. It was so weird, so unlikely, so bizarre, that it consumed Chaplain's attention utterly, diverting that redoubtable intellect elsewhere, blinding it to the subtle hand guiding the scheme. The path may have been different to the one he'd planned, but the same destination had been reached nonetheless – and at no stage had the PM looked bad. JSON was now gone, the small department completely disbanded, and although Chaplain was still on the books, so to speak, he'd been tending the petunias on gardening leave these past few months. Still keen to make it look as if he was reluctant to let go of such a valuable asset, the PM could now string Hugo along until after the next election and then finally cast him adrift – and Chaplain would be forever in his debt. Free at last.

Oh, yes. Clever, clever scheme!

His smug smile broadened and he began to hum a little ditty to himself, a most uncharacteristic pastime and one which would have thoroughly alarmed his prying staff. The trial had been reported in breathless detail, the macaw's exuberant reaction to the defendants ensuring global interest, and the verdict had brought the whole scheme to a satisfying climax. The two unfortunate JSON operatives, whom he knew had served their country – or rather, served him, which amounted to the same thing – with distinction, had been sentenced accordingly. Another sacrifice, but that's the role of foot soldiers.

The macaw had received a huge amount of publicity. What was his name? That was it – Bertie. Strange name, mused the PM, but then his children had once named their pet guinea-pig Gerald. He pom-pommed his way through an Elgar march, then suddenly threw his head back and laughed out loud. Damn, fancy Hugo being a druid! Yes, it was sizing up to be a wonderful day.

His mirth subsided quickly. He was not a man prone to unnecessary laughter, although the sight of Albert Steptoe crimping the edge of a home-made pie with his false teeth once almost induced a coronary. He glanced at the screen again and saw the press conference at Celeste Gordon's house was just starting. He capped his golden pen, thinking briefly, as he always did now, at how effective it was as a weapon of offence, expanded the window to fill the screen and turned up the sound.

'Miss Gordon, how do you feel now that the trial is over?'

As an expert in the art of fielding questions, the premier smiled at this obvious example of an opening gambit. The woman looked uneasy. Members of the public always did when facing the press *en-masse*. The macaw sat behind her and to one side, staring intently. The PM was always mildly surprised at just how big it was – and how beautifully blue! The woman did not relax as the interview progressed, despite the easy handling by the media. Maybe they were scared she'd set the bird on them – by all accounts, his attack in court had been pretty tremendous. She answered questions nervously, as if she couldn't wait for the press to leave. What the macaw thought was, as always, impossible to tell.

The PM stretched and yawned. There was nothing here of real interest. Self-indulgently, his mind began to wander back to the successful conclusion of his scheme. It had all worked out so beautifully. Every member of the cabinet, now eternally in his debt, breathed a huge sigh of relief on learning Hugo had destroyed his files to save his own skin, and Chaplain would for ever keep his mouth shut to prevent the police moving towards a prosecution over the botched burglary.

Yes, it was all going rather swimmingly. The next general election suddenly looked a much rosier prospect. He had risen above all these sordid dealings, his support holding firm. James, as the innocent victim, had seen his popularity sky-rocket. The PM planned to exploit this mercilessly. His party would bask in the positive publicity and this should reflect well at the polls. Naturally, James would then be quietly sidelined once the premier had been returned to power. Sadly, the man was just too inconveniently burdened with a sense of justice and fair play, but by then the Government would be good for another five years. Indeed, everything was looking grand. Now all the PM wanted was a nice gentle run up to the election. No further nasty surprises. He just needed to keep things ticking along, to avoid any further scandals which could still easily tip his struggling administration over the edge, and this course of benign inactivity should be enough to get him re-elected.

'Are you hungry?' asked Celeste.

'Hungry. Yes. I like nuts,' replied the macaw in that perfectly understandable but oddly cackling, throaty sort-of-way.

'Yes, Bertie, I know. What do you say?'

'Thank you, Mummy.' Impeccably polite, though. The PM reached for his pen again and unscrewed the cap, preparing to return to his work. Bertie stared down at something just out of shot, then looked directly at the cameras and cleared his throat in an amusingly human way.

'The Kneeling Man!' he spoke with perfect diction. The premier frowned. What the hell was he banging on about now?

'The Kneeling Man.' This was repeated with greater emphasis. 'Hooded, gagged, and strapped in the bondage wardrobe!'

The PM's eyes widened in dawning horror.

'James Timbrill. The Kneeling Man.'

The pen dropped from paralysed fingers.

'Here. Leather. The bondage wardrobe.' There was an immaculately performed imitation of a cracking whip and attendant squeak of pain. 'Here. With the handcuffs. Many times.'

The PM went icy inside. He tried to say something but only a stuttering croak came out.

'Bertie!' screamed Celeste Gordon. 'Oh, no!' She covered her mouth with both hands, features contorted with choking dismay, then the conference descended into a shambolic uproar matched only by the swelling shouts coming from the other side of the study door.

Chapter Sixteen

The Prime Minister sat at the Cabinet Room table and pushed a paper-clip around the polished surface with one finger, chin cupped in palm in an attitude of abject despondency. There was absolute silence but for the muted ticking of the clock on the mantle behind him. His staff were instructed to deny all access and to hold back the storm of calls, allowing him a short time to collect his thoughts. In front of him lay the morning's newspapers. He sighed heavily, cast an eye over the headlines again and winced with pain.

'What a cock-up,' he said quietly. James's exotic peccadilloes screamed out at him in dismaying detail. The broadsheets unleashed their criticism in severe and august tones whereas the tabloids excelled themselves with headlines which, he had to admit, were really rather amusing.

Photographs of James, Celeste, and Bertie stared up at him, the images continuing to dominate the inner pages, one after another. Like radioactive contamination, thought the PM morosely, and just as deadly. He dribbled the paper-clip around the table for another minute, then aimed carefully and flicked it across the room and into a pot plant.

That turned out to be the highlight of his day.

The door opened and Hugo Chaplain shuffled in, head down, shoulders slumped, his normally plump features grey and drawn. The PM hadn't seen him in weeks and noted the obvious deterioration in Chaplain's condition. He appeared to be under some considerable stress, which gave the premier a truly pleasant feeling inside. Chaplain collapsed in a seat opposite without waiting for permission.

'Well?'

Hugo cowered. He attempted to say something, but thought better of it and simply shook his head.

'Shall I tell you about my day so far?' said the PM in a conversational tone, sitting back and lacing his fingers behind his neck. 'Shall I tell you what has happened already this morning, bearing in mind,' he glanced over his shoulder at the clock behind, 'it's barely half past nine?' Hugo seemed to deflate slowly like a leaky football so the PM got up and moved around the table, leaning forward and murmuring into Chaplain's ear. 'Well, my dear Hugo, shall I?'

'Prime Minister, this is not particularly constructive considering –'

'Be quiet, Hugo! Be very quiet.' The venom in that whispering voice made Chaplain's bowel trip unpleasantly. His mouth closed with an almost audible snap. 'On the bright side I merely have to contend with the press gleefully reporting yesterday's news conference in all its disgusting details, and once the implications sank in, a united howl for my blood,' he slapped a hand on the scattering of newspapers and their scornful headlines. Hugo winced at *Pervert's Polly Porks Pathetic PM!* No reader, not even one possessing a generous amount of sawdust between the ears, could fail to get the message. 'Moving on, the constituencies are on the point of rebellion and my party is in complete turmoil. That's the good news. That's actually what's been buoying me up so far today. Now, let's skip to the bad news. Apart from an avalanche of demands for an explanation from the House, the Lords, and even the blasted EU, I am now facing a vote of confidence scheduled for this afternoon.

'A vote of confidence!' he roared savagely in Hugo's ear, spittle flying from his lips, his face a frightening shade of purple. Normally quiescent veins pulsed in dendroids of crimson outrage. 'One which I am not entirely convinced I can win.' There were no flies on Viv Bell – capitalising on the government's fresh agony, he'd added to its discomfiture by arguing successfully it was no longer morally competent and had been granted an emergency vote of confidence for later that afternoon.

'You do have a majority, Prime Minister,' offered Hugo meekly.

'Of five! A majority of five – including the Speaker who, as you may recall, is indebted to us most obligingly after we covered up that fracas with the wetsuit and the depilated penguin! Now then, Hugo, I want you to listen very carefully while I explain some simple mathematics to you. Of those five, one is lying comatose in intensive care having fractured his skull falling off a skateboard. I fully appreciate we have to question the wisdom of a forty-seven-year-old actually getting on a skateboard, but there we go, he did, gravity lent a helping hand and now my majority is cut to four. Want to hear what's happened to them?' The PM gave Chaplain no choice in the matter. 'The first is in Lerwick, cut off by a vicious Atlantic storm – no one in, no one out – and the second is so far up-country in the gas fields of Eastern Siberia he's eating mammoth steaks for lunch. You don't have to be Einstein to deduce half of four is two,' he ground out with controlled venom. 'Two! No, don't look out of the window – look at my fingers, Hugo. How many am I holding up? Two! The two that, I've just learnt, took off from Los Angeles last night and are due to land in Beijing within the hour. Well, bugger me with a blunt buttered baguette, majority gone!'

'I don't need to remind you, Prime Minister, that if the vote is tied you are afforded the benefit of the doubt.'

'Really? Thank you for pointing that out, Hugo. It had actually slipped my mind.' The PM's sarcasm was vitriolic. 'Are you really so naïve as to believe I can continue to command authority if a vote of confidence is tied? You are assuming, of course, that all my troops can be persuaded to the cause. The whips are being brutal, but there remains one who cannot be whipped – well, not by us, apparently, one who as a result of this debacle now cannot be relied upon to toe the line. I don't really have to tell you who that person is, do I, Hugo. You already know who I'm talking about, don't you, Hugo.

'Timbrill,' whispered Hugo, eyes widened with dismay.

'Bingo! The one I had cause to stab in the House – just in

time to save your skin, if I recall correctly. The one who, of all my beloved cabinet, should have figured most prominently in your files but who, through your catastrophically inexcusable ineptness, totally slipped through the net. Now Timbrill has been outed to the world's media as some kind of jolly, leather-sniffing pervert by that blasted parrot and guess what – he's about to become the hero of the hour. Can you explain that to me?'

'A hero? But how?'

'Because Timbrill's planning to cheerfully admit to his sordid predilections. And do you know what – all my instincts tell me the public are going to love him! He's going to emerge from this shambles as a paragon of honesty. Some kind of kinky knight in shining leather armour with a striped arse and sackfuls of goodwill. You mark my words, even as I face political annihilation, Timbrill will be universally lauded for being the only minister in living memory who has the courage to stand up and tell the absolute truth.

'Don't you see, Hugo, contrary to the strictest Westminster code, he's now prepared to answer any question truthfully and that cannot, under any circumstances, be allowed!'

Hugo's eyes wandered aimlessly around the room as if his mind had lost the capacity to focus. 'Has he indicated how he will vote?'

'Not yet. He's still in Gloucester and will make his decision once he's listened to his constituents. Listened to his constituents!' ranted the PM, red-faced and shaking his fists in snarling fury. 'Whenever has a politician ever listened to his constituents? Apparently, they like him down there in the sticks. He's promised to listen to their views and will vote in accordance with their wishes. He's calling it true democracy, the seditious little bastard. Bloody Gloucester – I'll not have those slack-jawed, turnip-munching yokels deciding whether my Government stands or falls!'

'Then we still have time,' blurted Hugo, suddenly animated. 'Arrange an accident. Kidnap him and tie him up – at least he'd like that. Offer him –'

'We? *We*, Hugo? Don't you think you're making an
240

assumption here?'

'I don't understand, Prime Minister.'

'Then let me explain. You're fired, Hugo. JSON no longer exists and so I've no need of your services any more. I've only been keeping you on these last few months through a sense of gratitude for services rendered. You'll get a full pension, of course – so long as you keep your mouth shut!' There was no bonhomie there, no cosy Assam with custard creams. 'Your security clearances have been withdrawn. Your files, or at least those surviving your last purge, will be shredded. If anyone snoops, there'll be nothing left. Call it the final act of a grateful employer.'

'Grateful!' gasped Hugo, obviously struggling.

'Yes. I'm doing this to keep you out of prison. You've been a very loyal and valuable person to me, but I have to ensure no evidence remains that might inconveniently surface at any enquiry. Plausible deniability, Hugo, plausible deniability.' The PM slumped back in his seat. What he'd planned for so long to be a moment of supreme victory had, in fact, actually turned out to be utterly dispiriting. Sacking Hugo should have left him elated – it certainly would have before that parrot uttered its devastating news – but now there was no pleasure in it; the damned bird had even spoiled his much-anticipated moment of triumph. He did not look at Hugo as he turned his pen over and over, tapping each end lightly on the table. Hugo stood and loitered for a moment, as if waiting for a last-minute reprieve, but none came. The PM spoke only once after that, but it wasn't really what Hugo wanted to hear.

'Close the door behind you on the way out, there's a good chap.'

They tracked James down to his home in Prior's Norton just a few miles north of Gloucester. The black-and-white thatched cottage snuggled next to the ancient Norman church and was surrounded by its own grounds. At the front, across a hedge-lined lane, were fine views eastwards over Cheltenham and the beech-fringed hills of the Cotswolds beyond, while at the rear the land dropped away west over the fertile Severn Vale to the rumbustious peaks of the Malverns.

It was a lovely location and James found nothing more healing for body and soul than to bumble about cutting the grass with his sit-on mower and harvesting the fruit every autumn, distributing bags bulging with apples, plums and damsons to his friends in Parliament. He tidied up as best he could but Westminster called and in his absence the cottage was cared for by Mrs Glynis Badham, wisdom-endowed, frizzy-haired housekeeper extraordinaire, and Gavin the gardener, soft-spoken, amiable, and callous-handed, who helped maintain the garden while running the farm next door with impressive inefficiency. Both were locally born, both had rarely ventured beyond the county boundaries, both regarded Cirencester as a bit too exciting, let alone London, and both were as honest, sane, grounded, and utterly normal as was possible.

The village had always been a haven of peace and tranquillity, but now all that had changed. The media circus had arrived at some unearthly hour in the morning, their vans clogging the single-track lane past his home. Intricate telescopic masts poked up above the hedges and trees, bristling with antennae. Squat, saucer-like radio dishes pointed at far-away satellites. It looked like GCHQ was having a yard sale. The multi-talented Mrs Badham brewed tea and provided chocolate chip cookies, this masterful strategy putting the reporters in good humour.

James stood on his doorstep and surveyed the encircling ring of cameras. 'Gentlemen, I'm going to make a statement,' he said, 'after which I will answer any questions.' In that trivial way which occasionally comes upon one about to say something really important, he noticed the feet of the camera tripods were digging holes in his lawn.

'I'd like to make something very clear with regard to the events of the last few days. I, too, saw that extraordinary news report from Miss Gordon's house yesterday. Like yourselves, I was completely dumbfounded by Bertie's unexpected allegations, and so, in front of you all, I wish to categorically state —'

James peered at the ranks of hacks and cameras and saw the

242

look of cynical expectation on their faces. They knew what was coming; another futile denial by yet another sleazy politician, one so keen to hang on to his pathetic career he'd go against the word of Bertie, who, after the dramas of the trial, now stood in the public eye as a champion of truth and justice. Perhaps he'd claim Bertie was lying, that he was confusing James with someone else, or that the bird was simply mad.

James couldn't do that.

'Yes, I wish to state as emphatically as I can that everything you've heard from Bertie is, without exception – the complete truth!'

There was yet another moment of shock. The previous few days had been a purple patch for shocks. There'd been a bit of dearth until Bertie had got stuck in, then they'd all come along together, one after the other. Like buses! Pencils skidded to a halt once more, jaws dropped – again. There was a collective gasp of breath and, for a few seconds, nobody said anything.

James continued. 'There are some things you need to know about Bertie. I've known him for a number of years and I can tell you he is quite simply extraordinary. He possesses dignity and intelligence, he loves his mother, and is willing to spill blood to protect her from harm. To me, Bertie epitomises everything we humans admire. He is faithful, courageous, loving and honourable, possesses no guile or deceit, and he never lies, so when he revealed the nature of my – erm, interests, I can assure you he was telling the absolute truth and I'm very relieved it's now no longer a secret.

'Some of you look astonished and all of you look sceptical, but both Bertie and I share a common quality. Neither of us lies, so you arc all now in the unique position of facing an honest politician who will answer any question truthfully and without prevarication!'

'Well that makes a refreshing change,' exclaimed Reuters with evident disbelief, obviously also speaking for his colleagues. 'How will you be voting in the House this afternoon?'

'I will be consulting my constituents and my decision will reflect their wishes. These are the people I represent and they will no longer be ignored. I'm holding a meeting in Gloucester within the hour to counsel opinion.'

'Are you under pressure from No. 10?'

'Yes. With such a small majority every vote is of paramount importance. Some of our own MPs are unable to attend, reducing our majority further. It will be extremely close. Extremely. Every MP, whether in Government or Opposition, will be subject to intense pressure, and those MPs who remain uncertain can certainly benefit from the situation.'

'Have you been offered a deal?' asked Channel 4 immediately.

'Yes.'

'What's the deal?' There was no subtlety to the questioning.

'I've been offered the post of Home Secretary,' replied James with honest simplicity. He was breaking a major political taboo here – in all probability the current incumbent had no idea his job had been offered to someone else, but James just wasn't interested, even though the post was one of the highest in the land.

'Will you take it?'

'No. To accept means an obligation to support the Government in the vote. That may be contrary to the wishes of my constituents. Although this will be a three-line whip, I will vote in accordance with the will of the people of Gloucester. If they feel this Government is not worth supporting then so be it.'

'Mr Timbrill, the Prime Minister is on the phone again,' called Mrs Badham from the kitchen window. 'He wants you to stop talking to the press immediately.' There was no subtlety to Glynis. She was a Pledge and duster woman through and through. 'I can see you're busy so I'll tell him you'll call back later.'

'Thank you, Mrs B,' replied James. The hacks grinned. Not often did a conversation of such importance take place between a cleaner and a prime minister. On the whole, it appeared Mrs Badham had displayed a masterful upper hand.

An hour later, James stood on a bench in Kings Square and looked around sadly. The heart of Gloucester had been a dismal place for many years, a gum-spotted expanse of windswept disappointment surrounded by unloved buildings and drenched in grubby mediocrity. The place just cried out for more trees, for grass and flowers, a place for kids to play, shoppers to meet, tourists to sit and inebriates to lie down after their lunchtime excesses. However, rumours of redevelopment were now rife. Things were about to change. James sincerely hoped the plans included lots of trees.

A sizeable crowd was gathering. Word had got around. People stood in knots and groups, some holding shopping bags, others with hands in pockets, grinning. Small children pointed, jumping up and down in excitement beside their parents. At the back, a gang of hooded teenagers circled the indistinct fringes of the crowd on their mountain bikes like mechanised urban vultures. More people drifted into the square, attracted by the sight of camera crews and their equipment.

Flanked only by Mrs Badham, who'd asked for a lift into town to do some shopping at Iceland, James lifted up the megaphone. 'Hello, everyone,' he said, somewhat startled by his amplified voice. 'Glad to see you all. My name is –'

'Percy the Pervert!' yelled one of the hoodies mischievously. Everyone laughed, including James.

'Yes, well, I'm James Timbrill, one of the two MPs representing your city.'

'Where's the other one?' called a man. The citizens of Gloucester were noted for their heckling. They liked to get stuck in straight away. Audience participation.

'He's in London busily ignoring the wishes of his constituents,' said James cheerfully. Gloucester was in the curious position of having half the city inclined to the left, the other half to the right. 'As you may be aware, a vote of confidence is to take place this afternoon in the House of Commons and before that vote I would like to know how you, the people I represent, feel about the situation. This vote is of vital importance to the Government. If it is lost, the Prime Minister will be forced to dissolve Parliament and call a general election.'

'No bloody loss there,' quipped an elderly man, sipping

coffee from a Styrofoam cup.

James continued. 'As Secretary of State for Defence, I would normally vote with the Government. It would be seen as an unforgivable betrayal not to do so, but events over the last few months have eroded my faith in the honesty of this administration.'

'How's the leg?' This shout came from the middle of the considerable crowd now ranged across the square. James reckoned there were several thousand people listening, all regarding him with no small degree of curiosity. A distant policeman surveyed the crowd and radioed for back-up just in case things got lively, despite the well-known fact that the people of Gloucester were spectacularly apathetic in their rioting zeal. They preferred instead to express their displeasure with a 'Tch!' and slightly aggressive arching of an eyebrow, which placed them right up there at the radical cutting edge of British political extremism.

James could sense there was no hostility here, just a growing interest. An assumption he was about to make a party political broadcast was not being fulfilled. Here was something much more intriguing. Always up for a nose, passers-by paused in their passing, swelling the sea of faces.

'No, I haven't forgotten I was assaulted by the PM. I have no real love for this present administration and its dubious methods. Like yourselves, I believe the burglary at Miss Gordon's was sanctioned by someone high up in Whitehall, so I'm left with a dilemma. The Government whips have exerted colossal pressure on me in a way I have, frankly, found most unpleasant. Offers have been made and bargains proposed, but in all this there has been no regard whatsoever for you, the people whom I have tried to represent with honesty and integrity for the last seven years.

'So, I'm here as your MP to ask a simple question. What would *you* like me to do? We live in a democracy so I'm giving you the opportunity to have your say. I will listen and I will debate, and if you want me to continue supporting this present administration then, as your elected representative, I will do so. However, should you feel the time has come for a change then by all means let's have a change. I can offer you this opportunity because I intend to stand down at the next election. Let's face it, I wouldn't find it entirely unsurprising if you'd prefer not have Percy the Pervert as your MP,' he concluded dryly. Laughter rippled through the gathering.

'I admire your honesty and don't even mind having a pervert as my MP, just as long as he's a competent pervert!' observed a lady in a blue bobble hat. There were a gratifying number of nods to this sage observation.

'Well I do mind,' snapped another woman nearby. 'You're nothing but a disgrace.'

'Madam,' said James calmly, 'what's a disgrace is that politics has become unaccountable to the people. Yes, there are certain colourful things I like to do in the privacy of my own home. You may find these things odd and amusing, even distasteful, and fortunately you live in country where you're fully entitled to your opinion, but those things are – or were – private, they're not illegal and they certainly haven't effected my judgement at Westminster. I've been honest enough to acknowledge my proclivities. They are no longer private and I know that from this day forward I'll be forever subject to ridicule, but I certainly don't consider myself to be a disgrace.'

'So are you going to stay or not?' came a distant call.

'No, I'm not planning to remain in office. The question here is not whether you want me as your MP, but whether you think this Government should continue or not.'

'Hang on a minute. If we decide it's time for a change, then you'll go ahead and vote yourself out of a job?'

'I suppose you can look at it that way.'

'That's a bit daft, isn't it?' said a distinguished-looking gentleman. 'You're a local lad. Lots of people know you, so who will we have to represent us?'

'The local party chairman and his members will select a new candidate,' answered James. 'I am confident they'll do a good job.'

'Yeah, an out-of-towner with a funny accent and sustificut in something pointless!' objected the gentleman. This brought another collective smile. For some reason, genuine Gloucester
247

people were genetically incapable of pronouncing the word 'certificate' correctly. Even James himself had occasionally lapsed in the Palace of Westminster, eliciting sniggers of condescending derision from those around him.

'Yeah,' he countered instantly, 'and I'll bet he'll come here on the buzz and won't know what daps are, either!' There was a widespread guffaw from the crowd and James knew he'd scored a big point reminding them he was a local. A buzz is a large vehicle with seats. If you want to catch a buzz, you wait at the buzz stop. Dap is another idiosyncratic term unique to the area – as far as the people of Gloucester are concerned, a pump is used to inflate tyres, a Plimsoll is a diagram painted on the side of a ship, and an espadrille is something French and therefore to be regarded with deep suspicion. A dap is a canvas shoe. They come in two colours. Black or white.

James sensed a momentum building. There was now a whiff of hostility in the crowd – but it wasn't directed at him. The distant policeman looked increasingly nervous. A few people started shouting, drowning each other out. James felt a tug on his jacket and looked down at Mrs Badham. 'I think you've got your answer, Mr Timbrill, so I'll be off to the shops now,' she said calmly, putting on her gloves. 'I'll be over on Tuesday as usual. The guest bedroom is already aired and made up. Miss Gordon and Bertie will be staying, of course.' She turned without saying goodbye and walked away, threaded a path through the crowd.

James looked out over the throng. The policeman was waving at him furiously and making desperate cutting actions across his throat in an attempt to get James to finish. He didn't seem at all happy. Positively animated, in fact. People were now shouting from all quarters of the square, shaking their fists to make their point – and James felt a little warming glow of pleasure at their hearty response. He smiled. To think, all this passion the result of a careless remark by a macaw!

But it wasn't just Bertie's revelations that had got the crowd fired up. Unknown to anyone, the two nuclear power stations located down the Severn estuary contributed to this uncharacteristically radical behaviour. Their natural West

248

Country stubbornness had been subtly stirred by exposure to radiation, that charmless by-product of fission which showed an annoyingly independent streak when it came to matters of containment. Any leak – and over three decades of operation it's inconceivable that even the tiniest smidgen of contamination hadn't made a bolt for freedom – had been wafted upstream by the prevailing south-westerlies and deposited over the city, this feathery shower of radioactivity gently dosing up its inhabitants, encouraging their obstreperousness while also clearly affecting that part of the brain which controls the pronunciation of the word 'certificate'.

So, at a time most inconvenient for the Prime Minister, the good people of Gloucester decided their moment had finally arrived. Fed up with a raft of unfair tax hikes, buoyed by the success of the egg campaign, and spurred on by a curious mixture of irritation and irradiation, they demanded change, a few because of a deeper feeling of unease, but most just for the sheer hell of it. At long last a useful outlet had been found for all that quiet, frustrated anger so often felt by the British public, and in a giddying moment of collective democratic effervescence, James was left in no doubt as to their decision.

No doubt at all.

James returned home after the meeting had broken up, finding the lane now clear of trucks. He saw Celeste's car in the drive. She'd motored down from London with Bertie to escape the suffocating attention of the media. The cottage offered sanctuary, sitting in its own gardens and providing privacy from outside intrusion. She'd obviously found the spare key in its cunningly concealed location under the doormat and, on hearing the sound of his car, met him at the front door. She drew him in and embraced him. Behind her, Bertie's happy purring filled the old building.

'Mistress,' he sighed. 'I'm so glad you're here. I now have an extraordinarily difficult decision to make.'

'I know. Mrs Badham rang from a call box in town.' A mobile phone remained an object of profound suspicion for Glynis. It wasn't that she found technology particularly difficult to handle – her knowledge of vacuum cleaners was legendary – she simply didn't understand how messages could possibly be transmitted without a wire. 'She already knows your decision.'

'That's one smart woman.'

'I could help.'

'How?'

'I'm happy to place you in a position where you'd be unable to return to London for the vote. This would remove any sense of responsibility from you. Personally, I'd have no difficulty sleeping tonight knowing I'd had a hand in ending this Government, especially since Wilf remains convinced Downing Street sanctioned the burglary.'

'You have no idea how wonderful that sounds but I think I'll pass. There's a need inside me which can only be satisfied by a personal appearance at the House. An important part of that need is to see the look on the PM's face at division time.'

'So you'll be voting against your own party.' Celeste considered this to be one of the most courageous things she'd ever seen. It was clear James was terribly torn; on the one side by his loyalty to his Westminster colleagues, on the other by his deep sense of honesty and fair play. This being politics, the two, naturally, were irredeemably incompatible.

'That's what my constituents have just asked me to do. In surprisingly strong terms, as well. I don't know what got into them. They seemed to be spurred on by something quite unnatural – and that's another strange thing,' he added thoughtfully.

'Yes?' prompted Celeste.

'They weren't at all concerned about Bertie's revelation. They actually didn't care in the slightest what exotic path my personal life has taken. What's more important to them is my honesty and, although I never thought I'd say this – competence!'

'This low opinion of yourself is totally unjustified. You're a smart, clever, scrupled, genuine, extremely capable, and inventive man. These are not qualities that can be hidden. I can see them, Mrs B and the excitable folk of Gloucester can see them. Even Gav's cows can see them, one of whom, by the way, is munching her way through your peonies as we speak.'

'Rather than being allowed to retire, I've been urged to stand as an Independent MP. Actually, "urged" is an understatement. I've been *ordered* to stand. They need me. How can I refuse?'

'Then don't. Follow your heart, James, and everything will work out just fine. I promise.' Celeste hugged him again, resting her head on his shoulder. He suddenly became aware of her urgent need for comfort. This was more than just a hug; there was a heavenly intimacy in her touch not experienced before. They stood together in a timeless moment of complete bliss. 'And I do love you so much,' she added simply. 'I think I always have, right from the moment I caught you thieving Patti's pastries!'

Overwhelmed, James closed his eyes and buried his face in Celeste's burnished copper hair, his heart tripping and skipping in a joyous burst of euphoria.

'I love you,' added another voice. 'Yes, I do.' Bertie scampered into the room, claws clicking on the old wooden floor, his long tail feathers swishing from side to side across the oak boards as he waddled along, He looked up, head cocked to one side, his bright eyes watching them embrace.

'I love you too, my divine, glorious Mistress. Poor Patti, she had no idea her matchmaking efforts would ever have such dramatic consequences.'

'Mistress *and* lover,' corrected Celeste. 'Be gentle – I'm still a virgin!'

'I'm not,' said Bertie brightly.

'Can you cope, my gorgeous leather man? When you take me on, you take Bertie as well.'

'It'll be my honour.' James gazed with adoration into Celeste's sparkling green eyes and knew he would never leave her side again. His political problems, the conflicts of interest he faced, the fact that he was about to make a hugely far-reaching decision of international significance, and even the exposure of his wayward sexual inclinations, all of these meant nothing because now they would always be together and his life was complete. 'I love you so very much, my darling Celeste,' he murmured.

251

'Then why aren't you kissing me?' she asked.

'But you've never allowed me above the knees.'

'Oh, James, you have my full permission to roam wherever you want!' She melted into his arms, her arms wrapped around his neck, body pressed close. Their kiss was intimate and gloriously passionate.

For the first time in her life, Celeste simply let go. She lost control and it felt wonderful. She just couldn't help herself. God, this man could kiss! Why hadn't she done this before? Bertie bobbed up and down as he did whenever he was in a bonny mood. It was as plain as the bill on his face his mum had at last found herself a mate. He'd known all along they'd spend the rest of their lives together – so why on earth did these pink monkeys devote so much time in avoiding the inevitable?

Celeste eventually broke their embrace, a little breathless and flushed. She gripped his shoulders with both hands and stared into his eyes. 'Now, go and do the right thing,' she ordered firmly, then smiled with what could only be described as a look of coquettish lasciviousness. 'And I'll be suitably dressed waiting for your return, so you'd better damn well hurry.'

James grabbed his car keys and bolted for the door, but turned at the sound of Bertie's voice calling after him. 'Oh yes, yes, yes,' the macaw trilled happily, 'Now we're cooking!'

And Finally ...

The old lady carefully manoeuvred her tray through the kitchen door and padded slowly into her sitting room. It was good to be home, to be surrounded by the familiarity and easy lived-in comfort of her own cottage, even after a blissful three-month visit to her nephew and his very acceptable wife out in Turkey. It had been so nice to switch off, ignore the papers and their endless messages of woe and despair, enjoy a spot of top-notch sunshine, and eye up the local young men – the Turks were a devastatingly handsome race, no doubt about it; black-haired, olive-skinned, and impeccably mannered. As if that wasn't ample enough reason for her visit, her nephew's traditional mountain village house now enjoyed a lovely pool which she'd used every day to help keep her ravaged joints supple. Sadly, she was already stiffening up even though she'd barely been back home a few hours, and armoured herself against the cold evening with a long cotton night gown, thermal bedsocks, ancient furred slippers that resembled squashed raccoons, and a fleeced dressing gown wrapped tight as a winding-sheet around her frail body.

Despite the warm clothes she still felt that psychological chill which comes with advancing age and placing the tray containing her solitary evening dinner on a table beside her chair, bent to the hearth and switched the fire to its highest setting. She lowered herself stiffly, her aching limbs wracked with arthritis. 'Bastard wind!' she muttered for the umpteenth time, cursing the cause of her pain. Every joint hurt, the legacy of years spent enduring frigid winter gales. That same wind now whined softly as it sought to insinuate its way into the cottage, but thick drapes pulled across the windows kept it at bay. She arranged a fluffy beige blanket over her legs and snuggled. The wing-back chair was old and faded but had moulded comfortably to the contours of her body from years of use. More importantly, it was positioned as close to the fire as was possible without igniting spontaneously.

She transferred the tray onto her knees, inhaled the delicious aromas rising from the overfilled plate and sighed happily. Home-made steak and kidney pie with roasties and a mountain of fresh veg. Perfect!

She stabbed the remote at the TV. 'Good, just in time for the news. I wonder what that pillock of a Prime Minister has been doing while I've been away,' she muttered to no one in particular, tucking into a generous slice of pie.

A drama unfolded before her eyes, a drama that arrested the fork halfway to her gaping mouth. A kidney slid off the inert tines and fell with a plop into the waiting lagoon of gravy below, splashing brown on to her dressing gown – but she didn't notice.

The fire, now cranked up to a nuclear maximum, began to scorch the blanket draped over her feet – but she didn't notice.

The wind moaned suddenly, rising and swelling to rattle the windows in a renewed effort to penetrate her defences – but she didn't notice.

Her inflamed joints, the cause of continual pain from the moment she woke to the moment she closed her eyes at night, were hurting even more than usual – but still she didn't notice.

Mouth sagging in shock, she stared utterly transfixed at the screen, at an ex-Prime Minister leaving Buckingham Palace having asked the monarch to dissolve Parliament, at a blue parrot in someone's lounge, at an unseemly scuffle of news crews, at a jostled reporter yelling excitedly into his microphone – and at a distraught, wide-eyed, copper-haired woman.

'I'll be goddamned,' she whispered. A forgotten image of long ago suddenly returned, an image of a very young girl with a bright open face and dancing orange pig-tails. 'Well, I'll be goddamned to hell – it's Skippy Gordon!' She began to

chuckle. The chuckle swelled into a witch's cackle, then a
hooting laugh, and the laugh waxed uncontrollably, gathering
force until she found herself wracked and red-faced, tears
streaming down her cheeks and shoulders shaking convulsively.

'That's my girl!' gasped Miss Rose Jelf.

THE END

Actually, no. Not even close to the end. Bertie's adventures
have only just begun …

Just One Damned Thing After Another

'History is just one damned thing after another'
– Arnold Toynbee

A madcap new slant on history that seems to be everyone's cup of tea …

Behind the seemingly innocuous façade of St Mary's, a different kind of historical research is taking place. They don't do 'time-travel' – they 'investigate major historical events in contemporary time'. Maintaining the appearance of harmless eccentrics is not always within their power – especially given their propensity for causing loud explosions when things get too quiet.

Meet the disaster-magnets of St Mary's Institute of Historical Research as they ricochet around History. Their aim is to observe and document – to try to find the answers to many of History's unanswered questions … and not to die in the process.

But one wrong move and History will fight back – to the death. And, as they soon discover, it's not just History they're fighting.

Follow the catastrophe curve from eleventh-century London to World War I, and from the Cretaceous Period to the destruction of the Great Library at Alexandria.

For wherever Historians go, chaos is sure to follow in their wake

The Nothing Girl

Jodi Taylor brings all her comic writing skills to this heart-warming tale of self-discovery.

Known as "The Nothing Girl" because of her severe stutter and chronically low self-confidence, Jenny Dove is only just prevented from ending it all by the sudden appearance of Thomas, a mystical golden horse only she can see. Under his guidance, Jenny unexpectedly acquires a husband – the charming and chaotic Russell Checkland – and for her, nothing will ever be the same again.

With over-protective relatives on one hand and the world's most erratic spouse on the other, Jenny needs to become Someone. And fast!

Fans of Jodi Taylor's best-selling Chronicles of St Mary's series will adore the quirky humour in this new, contemporary novel.

Things We Couldn't Explain

Things We Couldn't Explain is a comic story of young love, thwarted desire and the slippery nature of faith. It's ideal for readers who have enjoyed The Fault in Our Stars and The Rosie Project.

Some things just can't be explained. It's the summer of '79 and the small town of Jericho, Ohio is awash with mysteries. Anne-Marie is beautiful, blind, virginal – and pregnant. Ethan is the boy next door who would do anything to win her heart.
 in the sunset, the town is besieged by zealots, tourists and profiteers. Can love survive amidst the madness?
 A comic tale of young love, thwarted desire and the slippery nature of faith...
Author Information: Betsy Tobin is the acclaimed author of four novels: Bone House, short-listed for the Commonwealth Prize and winner of a Herodotus Prize in America, The Bounce, Ice Land, and Crimson China, a BBC Radio 4 Book-At-Bedtime and shortlisted for Epic Romantic Novel of the Year. Her books have been published throughout Europe and North America and two have been optioned for feature film. Betsy also writes for stage and radio, and is a past winner of the London Writers' Competition for her short story, Joyride. Born and raised in the American Midwest, she now lives in London and Wales with her husband and four children, and teaches writing with Arvon and First Story.

Other titles you may enjoy

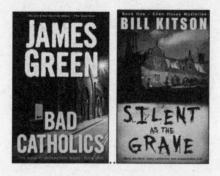

For more information about **Mike A. Vickers**

and other **Accent Press** titles

please visit

www.accentpress.co.uk

For news on Accent Press authors and upcoming titles
please visit

http://accenthub.com/